# Waiting in the Crescent City

Désirée's Story - Part Two

D. Riesau-Moreno

Casa Moreno Publishing

Waiting in the Crescent City

Désirée's Story ~ Part Two



Print version ISBN: 979-8-9916800-1-1



This book contains material that may be considered offensive, controversial, or triggering to some readers. This includes, but is not limited to, themes of violence, discrimination, sexual content, and strong language. The historical and cultural backdrop of the story may contain elements that conflict with present-day values or perspectives.

Reader discretion is advised. If you are sensitive to such topics, you may wish to consider this before proceeding.

Published by

CASA MORENO PUBLISHING

Original Cover art and design by Trent & Annalise Shadburne – Shadburne Creative

*Waiting In the Crescent City*

Désirée's Story ~ Part Two

a novel by
D. Riesau-Moreno

# *Books by D. Riesau-Moreno*

***Désirée's Story – The Series***

A Child of War ~ Part One

Waiting in the Crescent City ~ Part Two

Hiding as Just Désirée ~ Part Three

Ending Nightmares ~ Part Four

Like Ashes in the Wind ~ Part Five coming soon

# *Dedication*

for Desi
and lost girls everywhere

# *Contents*

# Chapter 1

## *Start at the beginning*

It was hot. The air felt thick and sticky. I could feel the weight of it as I breathed, feel it clinging to my skin like a steamy wet blanket. Everything was strange: the smells, the air, the landscape, the noises, the people, the language, everything. All of it might have been tolerable and easier to deal with, but as soon as I arrived, Bill left me there alone. Well, not completely alone. He delivered me to his mother at his family home in New Orleans, but then he left, and once again, I had to figure out who I needed to be, only this time in a new country.

We arrived late Wednesday evening, but Bill left early the following morning, which wasn't nearly enough time for me to have any sense of comfort in this new place. Begging him not to go didn't make any difference. The war in Europe had only just ended, and he still had work to do.

"*S'il te plaît, ne me laisse pas seul ici*. Bill please, *ne me quitte pas*," I cried over and over.

"You're not alone, Désirée. Mama will take care of you now. You'll be safe here with her and Laila. You'll go to school, make friends, and have the life you should have," he said for the millionth time, so sure of what I needed.

"We talked about this. I need to get back to Paris, but I'll be home as soon as I can. *Attends-moi, Chère.*" He didn't come back for nearly three months.

I was thirteen years old, had just fled my country, could barely speak English, and Bill left me among 'almost' strangers in a place as foreign to me as the Sun is to the Earth, and just as hot. I was miserable, angry, and unbelievably hot.

"Miss Dezrae. You get yourself up out of that bed, child, or Miss Bea's gonna come up here and drag you out. She sure will," Miss Laila announced after I'd been lollygagging for too long, according to her and Bill's mother. I wasn't sure what lollygagging meant, but it was clear from her crossed arms and the worried look on her dark face that they wouldn't let me mope around in my room, feeling sorry for myself for much longer.

"*J'ai trop chaud et je suis trop triste,*" I whined, rolling back into a ball beneath the sheet, with the ceiling fan humming above my head and not offering any relief.

"Cain't do nothin about the heat, sept maybe open up these doors and let in the breeze," she said, pulling open the tall glass-paned doors leading out onto the covered gallery, then she came back to stand over the bed, her hands on her hips and her head shaking, concern etching the corners of her eyes.

"That sadness you carryin', child, you put that away. You gots a whole life ahead of you, now get on up outa that bed and get it started. Miss Bea is waitin' on you downstairs," she said, gently encouraging my compliance.

My English studies didn't include Southern dialects, so it took a minute to translate everything she said, but I knew I couldn't put it off any longer.

I had to accept this new place, this new life, and figure out who I needed to be. If Bill had stayed, he could have explained things to me and guided me past the uneasiness I was feeling, but he left me to figure it out on my own. I was so mad at him for leaving.

"*Bien. Je me lève*," I said, not even wanting to attempt an English reply as I threw aside the sheet and headed outside to cool off in the morning breeze.

The second-floor gallery wrapped around the east and south sides of the house, overlooking a large garden. Everything was lush green and in full bloom, with a variety of plants and flowers I had never seen before. The lawn was mown in precise lines, bordered by meticulously groomed flower beds, and mature trees majestically guarded the corners of the property. It reminded me of the palace gardens in Paris I used to walk through, but that was in a different life, and the memory instantly stabbed my heart.

*Has it only been five days since I was in Paris?* It felt like forever ago, and a deep sadness tugged harder on my heart.

*Stop that, Désirée. Don't think about them anymore. You need to figure out what they expect of you here. You need to learn the rules and the language. Merde!*

*"En cas de doute, commencez par le début,"* (When in doubt, start at the beginning.) *Maman's* sweet voice reassured my mind. I hadn't heard her voice in a very long time, and the sound of it calmed me in a way nothing else could.

So, I walked back inside to start my new life in New Orleans, at the beginning, with a cool shower, because it was hot in America.

"Good morning, Désirée," Bill's mother said as I came downstairs for the first time since he left. "I hope you're feeling better today." She looked me over for signs of impending hysteria.

Beatrice Marchand was an elegant woman in her late fifties, smartly dressed in a lightweight navy-blue tailored suit trimmed in white. Her shoulder-length brunette hair was gently held back with tortoise-shell combs, one of which captured a single streak of silver shooting up from her widow's peak. Sharp, steely blue eyes highlighted her flawless skin and perfectly understated makeup. She looked ready for the day.

"*Bonjour, Madame. Je vais bien.* I am fine. Zank you," I replied, slowly translating French into my best English. I had to start sometime.

"*Il fait chaud ici...* Is hot here. *Fait-il toujours aussi chaud?* Is all time hot?" I asked, hoping I got the translation right, and praying the answer would be no.

"Oh sugar, it gets a lot hotter than this in the summer. You'll get used to it," she said, though I didn't think that would be possible once I understood the translation.

"Come, sit with me, and have some breakfast. Everything is always better after a good meal, don't you think?" It was clear from the start that she'd be speaking to me in English, even though she could speak perfect French. I'd have to pay attention to keep up.

"*Oui Madame.* My mozer zay zis. *Ma mère dirait ça.*" I said after I understood the gist of what she'd said.

"Most people call me Miss Bea or Mrs. Marchand, but you may call me Mama Bea. The correct phrase is, my mother *would* say that."

She waited for me to translate, and this became the way I began learning to speak English. She would say something and wait for me to figure it out. I would respond as best I could, then she would correct my pronunciation and grammar.

"*D'accord,* Mama Bea. Zank you. I can help for breakfast?" I asked, wanting to do something useful.

"*May I* help *with* breakfast?" she corrected. "No need, child. Eulaila will bring it in. Let's you and I get to know one another, shall we?"

She sat at the head of the large dining table set for two. Taking the seat next to her, I waited for the interrogation to begin. I knew she would have questions, because adults always did, so I braced myself for them.

"*Je suis curieux,*" she began in French, clearly wanting to speak without the translation delays. "Why did you choose to come here? Beau told me you had a choice to stay in France or come to the States. Why did you leave? I know about the troubles you've had and understand fear must have played a large part in your decision, but was there another reason?" Her eyes searched mine for the answer.

The directness of her question seemed fueled by her mother's intuition, but my instinct told me I should match her frankness with my own if I was to have any chance of securing her support in this new life. I would need to trust her, and I knew Bill trusted her above all others, so I let my guard down.

"Too many bad things happened. I was a danger to the people caring for me. That won't change for a long time, if ever. The French don't forget their injuries. Bill said I could stay in France, but if I did, I would still have to hide. It just felt like I didn't belong there anymore." I took a breath to collect my thoughts and searched her face for clues to her reaction, but I couldn't find any, so I continued.

"When I first met Bill, I was pretending to be Marie Rondeau, but he saw *me*, not the pretend girl, but the real Désirée that no one knew. Bill didn't care about the bad things; he only saw me, and I saw him. We trusted each other from the beginning." My throat tightened as the memory of that night flooded back, and I had to swallow hard to take a breath.

"When I had to choose, I thought about everything: what I was giving up and what I'd already lost. I knew it all happened for one reason."

A sigh escaped my lips as I recalled the past five days and everything that led me here. I tried to imagine where I would be if I made the other choice or if one thing had been different along the way. Coming to America with Bill was the right choice, and I needed her to understand that.

"And what is that reason, Désirée?"

I took a deep breath and when I looked into her eyes, I saw Bill reflected there: the man she raised, the son she loved, and I knew she wanted the truth.

"That Bill and I are supposed to be part of each other's lives," I said without looking away. My future was unclear, but deep in my heart, I knew that was true.

Mama Bea sat there considering my explanation, watching me while she sipped on the coffee Miss Laila had brought in for her while I'd been talking.

Uncomfortable under her gaze, I went to pour myself a cup of coffee from the coffeepot on the sideboard, then added a spoonful of sugar and a little cream, just the way I liked it. Mama Bea's surprised look seemed to say she was unaccustomed to seeing a child my age drink coffee in the morning. I savored it anyway. I liked coffee, and I hadn't thought of myself as a child for a long time.

Miss Laila pushed her way through the swinging door carrying a tray filled with plates of food and small glasses of juice, carefully placing them down in front of us. Each plate held two fried eggs, strips of crisp bacon, a spoonful of something grainy and white with a dab of butter melting on top, and a tall, round biscuit. It seemed like a lot of food for so early in the day. A bit of fruit and yogurt would have satisfied me, but I thought perhaps all Americans ate this way, so I started eating.

"That's right, child. You eat on up now. We gots to get some meat on those skinny bones of yours. Ain't that right, Miss Bea? This child needs some good Louisiana cookin' to fill her out good and proper," Miss Laila said as she swept through the swinging door. A moment later, she stuck her head back through the door. "Miss Bea. Jacob says he be ready for you and Miss Dezrae as soon as you finish up here."

"Thank you, Eulaila. Tell Jacob we'll be ready to leave right after breakfast," Mama Bea said.

We ate in silence for a few minutes, each savoring the dish in front of us. I tried the grainy white blob and found it to be tasteless, but for the butter on top. I could imagine it as a base for a meaty sauce or seasoned with fresh herbs to improve the flavor, but it wasn't something I liked, so I pushed it aside. Perfectly cooked eggs and strips of deliciously crisp bacon delighted my taste buds, but the biscuit was the most surprising. It was like biting into a warm, fluffy cloud that melted inside my mouth in drifts of flaky goodness. It was marvelous, and I wanted to learn how to make them.

"Don't you like the grits, Désirée?" Mama Bea asked when she saw me push it away from the last bite of egg I was attempting to snag on my fork.

"Grits. Zis is name?" I asked, pointing to the now cooling white mass.

"*Is* this *the* name, is the proper way to ask that question. Yes. We call them grits. Don't you like them?"

I didn't want to hurt anyone's feelings, but food was something I felt I knew something about, and the now almost solid white blob on the plate in front of me felt like a waste of space. Fruit or potatoes would have been a better option.

"They have no flavor on their own, so I don't see the point of having them on the plate," I answered truthfully, in French, so she understood me.

Mama Bea smiled when she heard my reply. "When you can say that properly in English, I will instruct Eulaila to leave them off your plate."

I didn't want her to think I was being ungrateful, so I gave her a positive review of the meal, offered in my best English. "I love za bread. *Je veux apprendre à les faire.* I want learn... I want *to* learn *to* make zem."

She shook her head, smiling at me. I hoped that didn't mean I'd said something wrong. I was pretty sure I said it correctly.

"Why you call his name Beau?" I asked, hoping to understand her relationship with Bill.

She smiled, and it seemed like she was recalling a sweet memory. "We christened him William Beaulaurier Marchand. Everyone called him Beau until he was about five years old. One day, Beau marched into breakfast and announced that from then on, we were to call him Bill Marchand, just like his father. I never did. He will always be my Beau. I already had a Bill."

She watched me for a while, and when she spoke again, it was in French.

"You are quite a surprise, Désirée. I imagined you so different. I knew you were young, but not quite so young. In your letters, you sounded older, and now that we've met, I understand why that was true. You've lived a life far beyond your years already." The expression in her eyes said she was trying to understand something, but I wasn't sure what it was.

"I wonder, Désirée, do you know why Beau wanted to bring you here?"

I didn't, but I wanted to. Why me? I was just a girl he met on a mission during the war. Why was I important enough for him to pull strings to get me out of France? There were a lot of whys in this situation, but not a lot of answers. Bill was gone.

"I don't know, but I think it's the same reason. We are supposed to be in each other's lives. Bill said we are not done, and he asked me to wait for him. But I thought he would stay with me, at least for a while." I dropped my head to hide the sadness I was feeling.

"Sweet Jesus," she said in English, rolling her eyes to the ceiling and leaning back in her chair. After huffing through her nose a few times, she looked at me. "If I had a dime for every time my Bill asked me to wait for him, I'd own the entire city of New Orleans and all the land around it. He was always going off to do some important something or other and asking me to wait for him. I always did... He was worth waiting for."

Most of what she said went over my head, but from the dreamy look in her eyes, it was clear she was remembering something good; her face glowed with the memory.

"Leave the dishes, child. Eulaila will take care of this. You run on upstairs and brush your teeth and hair, then get back down here. You and I have things to do today. Go on now." She shooed me out of the room with a wave of her hand.

As I was walking up the stairs, I heard her say, "Lord have mercy, we've got a bumpy road ahead."

# Chapter 2

## *A new home*

My introduction to New Orleans was a lot like my introduction to Paris had been, guided by the skillful hand of a woman who loved the city she was showing off. Mama Bea was born and raised in New Orleans, and she knew it like the back of her hand: all the history, all the stories not taught in the history books, and she willingly imparted her knowledge to me.

Beatrice Marchand was a teacher, first as a high school English teacher and currently as an English professor at Loyola University. She sat on the Board of Directors for Marchand Industries and several charitable organizations and private schools, one of which she took me to on that first outing.

Academy of the Sacred Heart was a Catholic girls' school only a few blocks down the road from the house, and our first stop was a meeting with the headmistress.

"Sister Mary Agnes, so good of you to see us on such short notice. I want to introduce Miss Désirée Gautier, who has recently arrived in our fair city. We would like a moment of your time to discuss enrolling Désirée into

Sacred Heart for the fall term. Perhaps you can assist us," Mama Bea said, sweeping into the nun's office as if expected. Apparently, her position on the school's Board of Trustees encouraged the headmistress to welcome us into her inner sanctum.

"Mrs. Marchand, what a delightful surprise. Welcome, please sit down. May I send for refreshments?" Sister Mary Agnes asked as Mama Bea and I settled in the two armchairs facing the nun's substantial desk in the darkly paneled room. She wore a full-length habit with a short black veil, and seemed pleased to welcome us, but my nerves were on edge.

"No, thank you, Sister. We won't take up too much of your time," Mama Bea replied.

"Of course, Mrs. Marchand. Well, perhaps we should start with the records from her previous school. Where did you go to school, my dear?" the nun asked me.

"I should explain a bit about Désirée, Sister," Mama Bea said. "She has only recently arrived in New Orleans from Montreal, where she was living with her grandmother, a long-time friend of mine. Désirée's father was Mrs. Gautier's only child, and her mother was an American from upstate New York where Désirée was born. When her parents went to Europe with the Canadian Forces, they left Désirée in Montreal with Mrs. Gautier. Then, following their tragic wartime deaths, Mrs. Gautier reached out to me, informing me of her own failing health and her anxiety about her granddaughter's future. She asked that I assume responsibility for Désirée's care and education should her health fail. Tragically, Mrs. Gautier passed away in April, leaving poor Désirée with no living relatives. Of course, I immediately sent for her to come live with me here in New Orleans. I'm sure you understand."

I listened carefully, trying to follow along, and soon realized she was lying to the nun. There always had to be a grain of truth in every lie; I was from somewhere else, and my family was dead, but I hadn't arrived from Montreal, and she didn't mention Bill at all.

"Oh... well, of course," the nun said, her expression sympathetic but more curious than before.

"Unfortunately, we haven't any official records to offer. Désirée's education has been less than conventional. Under Mrs. Gautier's close supervision, private tutors instructed her in the usual disciplines, though her classes were primarily conducted in French. Nevertheless, I'm sure you will find her well versed in the courses normally offered at the seventh-grade level," Mama Bea said, looking as confident as she sounded.

Frustrated and struggling to follow the conversation, I heard her say no records, tutors, well versed, but I didn't understand everything and vowed I would learn English as quickly as possible. I had done it before with German.

"Ah, I understand, Mrs. Marchand," Sister Mary Agnes said, then she turned to me. "Do you speak any English, my dear?"

"I know... a little English. I am learning," I said slowly, looking up. I knew the questions were about to begin, so I sat straighter in my chair, preparing to listen carefully and answer as best I could.

"Wonderful. Tell me about your studies. What subjects did you work on?"

"I study... studied mazmatics, geography, history of Europe, Rome, and Greece, art and music, and languages," I explained, translating each subject by name from French into English, and unsure if what I studied during my time with Katarina would be enough. I remembered all of it, being cursed with an excellent memory, but most of what I studied was in German, not in French.

"How old are you, Miss Désirée?" she asked.

"Zirteen."

"What languages did you study?"

That was a tricky question. Nervous about revealing too much, I looked to Mama Bea for guidance. Her smile and tilting her head seemed to say it was up to me to reveal the depth of my language skills—or not if I didn't want to.

"I studied za French, *bien sûr*. Spanish, some Portuguese, English, and German. Zat all." I wasn't sure if knowing German would be a bad thing, but I didn't want to start with a lie.

Sister Mary Agnes stared at me for a long time, apparently trying to decide who I was and where I fit in with the Marchand family. I wasn't sure of that myself. It would have been so much easier if Bill had been there, but he wasn't.

She pushed a button on a rectangular box sitting on her desk and it must have made a sound in the outer office because a second or two later, a voice came through the box. "Yes, Headmistress?" the voice asked.

"Please ask Evelyn Duret to come to my office immediately. I believe she is in Sister Natalie's class. I have a task for her. Thank you, Sister," she instructed the voice, then she addressed Mama Bea.

"I've sent for one of our eighth-grade girls who will take Désirée on a quick tour of the school while you and I finish up here. Miss Désirée, it has been a pleasure meeting you, and I look forward to seeing you again. Come with me, dear, and Evelyn will show you around."

She led me out of her office and into the waiting company of a pretty girl dressed in a neat school uniform: a dark plaid skirt, a white short-sleeved blouse, white socks, and saddle shoes.

"Evelyn, I apologize for taking you from class, but I require your assistance. Let me introduce Miss Désirée Gautier, who will join us at Sacred Heart next term. Please take Désirée on a tour of the school. Don't disturb the classes in session, but show her around the school, the library, the gymnasium, and the athletic field. Mrs. Marchand and I will meet you on the front steps in about twenty minutes. Thank you, dear." She dismissed us with a wave of her hand then returned to her office to work out the details of my enrollment with Mama Bea.

"Hi, Désirée. Nice to meet you. I'm Evelyn, and *you* have just saved me from being bored to tears listening to Sister Natalie drone on and on about cell structure. I hate science. Don't you?"

I wasn't exactly sure what she was asking, something about science, but she seemed friendly enough, so I nodded my head in agreement.

I followed her through the hallways, intently listening—she talked a lot and very fast—while trying to keep track of the places she was showing me: the main offices, the library, and lots of classrooms filled with girls of all ages. Sacred Heart was many times larger than La Maison, and I felt like I might get lost among all those girls.

I thought that might be a good thing as I followed Evelyn into a large, empty room.

".... and this is the gymnasium where we have our indoor athletic classes and assemblies. Where did you go to school before? Are you from around here? You don't talk much, do you?"

Evelyn was asking questions. Where school? Where from? Don't talk? I shook the translations into my brain and attempted to answer her.

"I not from here. No school before, only teachers. My English is no... not good, *encore*, yet." I said, the sound of my voice echoing in the vast room.

"Do you speak French!? *Parlez-vous français*?" she asked, seeming to be excited by the possibility.

"*Oui*. But I must learn talk... learn to... speak za English. *Mais je dois apprendre à parler anglais,*" I said, hoping she understood.

"How exciting! I'm taking a French class next year. It will be wonderful to have someone to practice with. Follow me, Désirée, and I'll show you the cafeteria, then we need to meet Headmistress. Who did she say you came with?" she asked, giving me a strange look.

Again, my brain was slow finding the translation, and I could feel myself getting more frustrated.

*I must get better at this, and soon.*

She said something about the headmistress, but after that, she'd asked a question.

"*Quoi*?" I asked, hoping she understood the word.

"I asked who brought you here. Did you come with your mother?" She spoke slower this time.

"No. Not my mozur. Madame... Mrs. Marchand she bring me here."

"Hmm. Marchand. I know that name, but I can't remember where I heard it. It'll come to me later. Things like that always do."

Evelyn chattered away as she led me back through the school to the front of the building, where Mama Bea waited by the car with the Sister Mary Agnes.

"*Merci*, Evelyn. I like your school. Zank you for za tour." I said, speaking slowly to make sure I had the correct words, and then I offered her my hand to shake. In Paris, we would kiss cheeks at such moments, but this wasn't Paris.

"*De rien*, Désirée. It was my pleasure to meet you. I hope we can meet again soon." Evelyn replied, taking my hand and leaning forward to kiss cheeks with me. I recognized the gesture as her attempt to do something she thought of as French, but it didn't matter; it was familiar, and I felt accepted by it.

"Thank you, Evelyn, for welcoming Désirée this morning. I'm sure she'd enjoy the company this summer if you'd like to come by for a visit. It's Marchand House, down on St. Charles by the university. Have your mother call me, and we'll set something up." Mama Bea said, shaking the girl's hand.

"Sister Mary Agnes, thank you so much for your help today. I will be in touch. Come, Désirée, we have a few other stops to make."

Mr. Jefferies pulled the car away from the school and drove down the long driveway, then through the gate, heading north onto St. Charles Ave.

"Well, we certainly have our work cut out for us, Désirée," Mama Bea said, leaning back in her seat. "This isn't how I planned to spend the summer, but we'll make it fun. It's been a long time since I've taught someone so young." She looked satisfied with how the meeting had gone.

"*Je ne comprends pas,*" I said, not understanding what she meant.

"You must take a test; the seventh-grade final examination. If you pass the test, you will enter the eighth-grade next term." Her eyebrows arched up as she spoke, steely blue eyes studying me.

"You know zis test?"

"I am familiar with it, but fortunately for us, Sister Mary Agnes gave me a sample of the test to help you prepare. We shall begin working on this tomorrow." She handed me a folder full of sheets of paper.

I flipped through the pages, trying to decipher the questions, but they were all in English. Each subject had multiple pages, some questions were multiple-choice and others you had to write your answer in the space provided. English, mathematics, history, geography, and science were all being tested.

My ability to read and write in English would be the biggest challenge, but I knew I could do it. I'd done it before under far more stressful circumstances.

"Put that away now, darling. We're going shopping for some summer clothes for you, and then we'll take a quick tour of New Orleans so you can see a bit of our city," she said, patting my legs bouncing next to her.

I set aside the folder and stilled my jittery legs. It was exhausting translating conversations in my head all the time, only understanding the basics of what people said, but that just fueled my determination to learn English as quickly as possible.

"I must learn za English fast... quick, for za test. Yes? You zink is possible?"

She gave me a long, hard look, like she was assessing what she believed to be my strengths and weaknesses. Whatever she saw in me at that moment allowed her to relax, confident in her assessment. She took my hand in hers, squeezing gently.

"I have been a teacher for a very long time, Désirée, and have seen hundreds of students pass through my doors. Some are there to pass the time, uninterested in learning more than the basics, just enough to get them through life. There are others, however, who have a fire in their eyes, a curiosity that pushes them to learn and ask questions. I believe you are in the second category, a girl who will challenge herself to succeed despite the difficulties. But... it is not up to me. You are the one who'll need to decide how this will go. Either way, you will be in school next term. It's up to you whether you enter the eighth grade or the seventh. Do you understand?"

I leaned back in the seat, trying to translate everything she said, and knowing I missed a lot, but it was clear from her tone and the look in her eyes that she was challenging me as others had before. There was no doubt in my mind that I would accept her challenge and do my best. There had never been any other option for me.

"Yes, madame. *Je comprends*. Pass test; go to grade eight. Not pass; go to seven. How many... *combien*... class for school? *Combien de temps à l'obtention du diplôme?*" I asked, suddenly realizing I might have a long road ahead.

"You will attend school through the twelfth grade," she said in the same challenging tone.

I blew out my breath in a heavy sigh, finally grasping the magnitude of the task ahead. It would take five years if I passed the test, six if I didn't. I would be at least eighteen by then. It felt like a long time to wait to get my life started. Just because I had to leave France, I hadn't given up my dream of becoming a professional chef, and was determined as ever to achieve my dream, but I knew the first thing I had to do was master the language. *Merde!*

"Drive up to Canal, Jacob," Mama Bea told Mr. Jefferies. "I want to go to Godchaux's to shop for Désirée, then we'll go up to the market for the groceries."

"Yes, Miss Bea. You need me to do anything while you're shopping with Miss Dezrae?" Mr. Jefferies asked over his shoulder.

"Yes. Thank you, Jacob. Go down to Woolworth's and buy three, no, four student journals and two boxes of pencils. Is there anything you would like, Désirée?" she asked.

I needed to orient myself in the flat landscape. There was a river somewhere, but I hadn't seen it yet. "*Je voudrais...* I want... would like to have map of za city."

She gave me a funny look. "Jacob, Miss Désirée would like a map of New Orleans, and get a big red pen while you're there," she said, arching her eyebrow at me.

The car turned onto a broad boulevard, almost as large as the *Champs-Élysées* but not nearly so beautiful. Streetcars, painted green and red, were rolling up and down the middle of the street, with people jumping on and off at the corners. It was a wild and noisy city with lots of people everywhere, rushing around like a hive of bees. The buildings were modern, less than one hundred years old by the look of them, young compared to most of Paris, but I knew New Orleans had been a city since the early 1700s and wondered where the older part was located.

We stopped in front of a tall building with seven floors of windows towering above the entrance. Mr. Jefferies pulled the car up to the curb, then got out to open the door for us.

"I'll be here when you're ready, Miss Bea. Have fun shopping, Miss Dezrae," he said as Mama Bea led me into the vast department store.

# Chapter 3

## *Culture Shock*

Mama Bea and I spent the next couple of hours shopping for everything she thought I needed. I didn't really need anything, but she insisted on buying me a whole new wardrobe, from underclothes to party dresses.

By the end of her shopping spree, I felt overwhelmed, not only by her generosity, but by the sheer volume and variety of things displayed for sale in that enormous store. Not even during my time with Katarina in Paris, shopping at the chic salons she frequented, had I seen so much to choose from.

"Zis too many zings. I not need all zis. *C'est trop, madame,*" I said, uncomfortable with her generosity and how much it reminded me of my time with Katarina.

"It's nothing at all, darling. You brought little enough with you. Allow me to indulge my whim. I haven't shopped in ages, and I've never had a daughter to fuss over before. Besides, Beau asked me to get you a few things while he's gone," she said with a generous smile. Then she spoke to the woman who'd been helping us.

"Have all this sent to the house, Gladys. Charge it all to my account. Thanks so much for your help today." She signed the bill, handing it to the salesclerk.

"Of course, Mrs. Marchand. I'll wrap them up and have them delivered this afternoon. It's been a pleasure to serve you and Miss Désirée. Please come again soon."

Everyone was so polite, and I wondered if it was like that everywhere in America.

"*Merci beaucoup, madame*. Zank you, Mama Bea."

"You are more than welcome, Désirée. Now, let's get downstairs and see if we can find you a hat to keep the summer sun off that fair skin of yours."

I followed her to the elevator, and when the doors opened, we stepped in to join a smartly dressed young woman who was bending over to adjust the seam of her stockings. She lifted her head in amazement when she saw who joined her in the elevator.

"Why, hello, Miss Bea. What a surprise to see you! I didn't know you shopped at Godchaux's. Have you heard from Bill? I haven't heard a word from him in months, and I am so worried." Her sad smile and troubled expression didn't quite reach her eyes.

She was blonde, pretty and looked to be in her early twenties. From what I could understand, she was asking about Bill and said something about being worried. I wondered what her relationship was with Bill.

*Are they friends or more than friends?*

Thinking about that made my stomach do a few back flips.

"Good afternoon, Charlotte." Mama Bea said, with a crisp tone to her voice. "Nice to see you again. Beau is fine, still in Europe. I'm sure he'll write as soon as he can. I must apologize for hurrying off. We have several other stops to make today. Come, Désirée," she said as the elevator doors opened onto the first floor.

"Of course, Miss Bea, but who's this girl you have with you? I don't believe we've met before." Charlotte turned to me as the three of us stepped out of the elevator.

"Charlotte, this is Miss Désirée Gautier, who has recently come to New Orleans to live with me. Désirée, this is Miss Charlotte Bentley, a *friend* of Beau's. Say hello, dear," Mama Bea said with an arched eyebrow.

"Hello," I said, not really wanting to. There was something about Charlotte that made me anxious, but I wasn't sure what it was.

"Well, aren't you a sweet little thing? Where did you come from? Never mind, Bill will tell me when he gets home. Miss Bea, when you write to Bill, tell him I am very disappointed he hasn't written to me as often as he promised, but I do miss him terribly," Charlotte said, as if Mama Bea would, of course, deliver her message.

"I will tell him, Charlotte. Good day."

Mama Bea guided me down the aisle towards a counter filled with hats perched on stands.

"Here, try this on," she said, abruptly placing a wide-brimmed straw hat onto my head.

"Somezing wrong, Mama Bea?" I sensed her tension after the encounter with Charlotte and wondered what upset her.

"No, dear, nothing more than usual," she said, her expression somewhat pensive. "I think this one will do nicely," Mama Bea told the woman at the counter, pointing at the hat she placed on my head. "Please put the bill on the Marchand account. Thank you, dear." She signed the bill then took my arm. "Come, Désirée."

She marched us out of the department store onto Canal St., where Mr. Jefferies was waiting for us at the curb.

"Let's go to the market, Jacob. I feel a beignet moment coming on." Mama Bea said when we got into the car. She was always saying funny things like that.

"*C'est familier ici.* Zis... part... *c'est comme la France.* Yes?" I said as we drove into the French Quarter, the oldest part of the city. It felt like being transported back to France, but in different era, remnants of the past everywhere I looked.

The streets were narrow, with tightly packed brick buildings, though none as tall as those in Paris. It felt like the streets of Châlons with many of the buildings boasting beautiful iron balconies jutting out from the facades and painted shutters adorning every opening. It was an exciting place, not only for its familiarity but also for the sounds and aromas coming from the open doorways we passed. Lively music drifted out of the buildings, and the smells of cooking food were everywhere I turned.

"Parts of France, yes, but there's more of a Spanish influence in the Quarter. Many of the old French buildings burned in a couple of devastating fires in the 1700s. The Spanish rebuilt most of what you see here in the Quarter, especially around Jackson Square, where we're headed." Mama Bea explained.

Distracted by the sights, I didn't understand everything she said, then Mr. Jefferies parked the car at the end of a narrow street, and we all got out.

"We'll meet you in the market, Jacob, after we indulge ourselves at Café du Monde. Do you have the list?" Mama Bea asked.

"Yes'm. Laila wrote it all out for me. Got it all right here," he said, patting his coat pocket.

"Good. We'll meet you there when we're done. Thank you, Jacob."

"You want... some drink... sir?" I asked. It was hot, and he'd been waiting for Mama Bea and me all day. He gave me a funny look when I asked, almost like the question surprised him.

"No, Miss Dezrae. I's fine. Thank you for asking. You go on and enjoy yourself with Miss Bea. I'll see you later," he said, his dark face lighting up with a big, toothy grin.

I followed Mama Bea down the street to a café at the end of a long building with a big striped awning off the end. There were lots of tables and chairs sitting out front, like at the sidewalk cafés in Paris. Mama Bea led us to an empty table, and when the waitress came over, she ordered beignets, chocolate milk, and a *café au lait*.

There was no menu on the table, and I couldn't find one posted anywhere. I must have had a question mark on my face because Mama Bea was smiling at me.

"That's all they serve here, darling, beignets, coffee, milk, and fresh orange juice. Nothing else. They've been doing it the same way since 1862, twenty-four hours a day, seven days a week. The only day they close is Christmas day." She spoke slowly, so I could translate, and I thought I understood most of what she said.

"Always zis menu? *Seulement quatre choses?*" It amazed me that a café could stay open for so long, only serving four items.

"It's been the same forever. No need to change a good thing."

I understood what she meant as soon as I took that first bite of the hot beignet covered in powdered sugar. I had to blow air into my mouth to cool it, and then that sweet, doughy goodness filled my senses, transporting me even farther back to France. A sip of chocolate milk through a paper straw brought me back to New Orleans with a smile on my face.

"You look as if you enjoyed that," Mama Bea said, smiling at me across the table. "When I was a girl, a little younger than you, my mother and I would come to the market every Saturday morning to do the shopping. She and I would stop here at the Café du Monde to share some beignets and chocolate milk. Mama never did like coffee. Let's finish up here and go find Jacob. We have another stop to make today."

By the end of the day, my brain was reeling with all the translating I had done, and with everything I'd seen and experienced.

My first glimpse of the French Market took my breath away; long rows of vendors selling every kind of produce and seafood and meat in quantities not seen for years in the markets of France. I saw one vendor take heads of lettuce from his stall and toss them to the ground, apparently considering them unsellable. It was shocking. In France, people would fight over those heads of lettuce, desperate for anything nourishing.

There was so much of everything everywhere I looked. There were no lines to wait in for things you might not get when you got to the front; everything was laid out in abundance to pick and choose from. Americans appeared untouched by what Europe had just endured, living their lives apart from the brutality of war.

Stunned by it all, I couldn't help but feel sad and guilty for having landed in good fortune. I had done nothing to deserve it. It was my countrymen who had suffered. Many hadn't survived. And there I was, once again the lucky one, living in a country of vast abundance among privileged people. It felt the same as it had with Katarina, the thing that set me apart from my countrymen forever, all the wealth and privilege.

After supper that night, I thanked Mama Bea for everything and retreated to my room to sort out my feelings. I put everything that she purchased away in the drawers and closet, so I didn't have to look at them, so they wouldn't remind me of how guilty I felt.

The cool air on the gallery beckoned me, and I was sitting outside in the dark when Mama Bea came into my room.

"Désirée? I came to see if you needed anything, honey." She must have sensed my distress because she sat down next to me on the lounge chair, with concern in her eyes.

The moment I looked at her, I burst into tears; my exhaustion finally taking over. I couldn't have held them back even if I tried.

"*C'est trop, Madame. C'est trop*" was all I could manage, all control of my feelings pushed beyond my limit.

She gathered me into her arms, and I let her hold me without protest, so complete was my misery.

"Too much of what, darling?" she asked as she gently stroked my back.

"*Trop de tout.* Everyzing. *C'est trop comme avant...* wiz Katarina. Is too much, Madame. *Je ne mérite pas ça*. Not deserve, not want all zis," I cried, burying my face into her dressing gown.

"Oh, sweet girl, only God knows what we deserve, and He's not offering us any explanations. The best we can do is be grateful for what we're given and share what we have. I know this is difficult for you, darling, but there is nothing you need to feel bad about. Everything is as it should be. You said it yourself this morning; you are where you're supposed to be. Come now, sweetheart, let's get you into bed. We have a busy day ahead of us tomorrow." She guided me back into the bedroom and straightened the covers over me after I'd climbed into the comfortable bed.

She gently ran her hand down my cheek. "Goodnight, Désirée. Sweet dreams."

After she turned out the light and left the door ajar, I heard her outside in the hallway talking with Miss Laila.

“Is Miss Dezrae alright, Miss Bea?”

“She’s fine, Eulaila, or she soon will be. Désirée is a lot stronger than she realizes, but she’s had a bit of culture shock today, and it may take a while for her to become accustomed to our ways. We’re all going to have things to get used to from now on.”

“That’s for sure. It’s gonna be nice havin a young person round the house again. Been a long time, Miss Bea.”

“It has, and it’s promising to be an interesting summer. Has Jacob locked up?”

“Yes’m. Locked up good and tight. He's waitin’ on me downstairs. I just wanted to make sure you and Miss Dezrae were doing alright for we went to bed. You need anything?”

“No, Eulaila, thank you. Tell Jacob goodnight for me. I’ll see you both in the morning.”

“Night, Miss Bea.”

I curled up into a ball beneath the unproductive ceiling fan, buried my face into the softness of the pillow, and silently spilled out my sadness and my loneliness. I had left everyone I cared for behind except Bill, and he had left me. Unstoppable tears soaked my pillow that night.

# Chapter 4

## *Nightmares and other lessons*

"*Pas plus! Arrêtez! Je ne sais pas! Je ne sais pas!*"

I woke before the scream escaped my throat. Throwing off the covers and jumping from the bed, I landed halfway across the room before I realized I wasn't in the dungeon, there were no monsters lurking in the corners.

It took a few minutes for the shaking to stop and my breathing to slow down. That same nightmare had plagued me many times over the past fifteen months, and I learned if I didn't wake myself up in time, it got a lot worse.

Unwilling to tempt the nightmares again, I threw the old woman's shawl around my shoulders and stepped out onto the gallery to sit and listen to the night sounds, hoping to settle my mind. It was well past midnight, everyone and everything having found their rest except me.

The air was more refreshing than earlier. A soft breeze chilled my skin with tiny prickles as it whispered through the old oaks guarding the property. I pulled the shawl tighter, hoping for whatever comfort it would offer.

The nightmares always left me restless, the instinct to flee deeply ingrained in the dream. Except it wasn't a dream, it was a memory, one I wished I could forget, along with a few others.

There was no peaceful place to settle, so I wandered back inside, searching for comfort but still suspicious of any lingering ghosts in my room.

Inside, the house was quiet and mostly dark. The only illumination was the soft glow of the streetlights filtering in through the upper floor windows. White walls reflected what light there was, sparkling on the polished wood railing encircling the stairwell, defining the path around it. My bare feet tread silently on the wood floor as I made my way around the balustrade, quietly stepping past Mama Bea's bedroom door, the sound of her soft snores confirming her slumber.

Bill's room was next to Mama Bea's, and even though I knew he wasn't there, I wanted to be where he'd been, where I could feel his presence in the things he'd touched and used. Bill was the only person connecting me to this strange country, and his absence left me feeling lonelier than I had ever felt before.

His bedroom took up half the front of the house, and Mama Bea's room took up the other half. The furnishings were warm polished wood, masculine in their simplicity: a sizeable four-poster bed, a tall dresser, a desk, and a leather chair flanked by bookshelves filled with mementos of a life lived in that room. Two club chairs, with a small table between them, sat by the gallery doors, a chessboard on the table, waiting for the resident to return. Bill was gone, but the scent of him lingered in the air, musky with a hint of spice. He had been there only a few days before, but he hadn't stayed long.

I needed to feel close to someone familiar, someone who knew me, so I crawled up onto his bed, covering myself with the folded quilt laying at the foot, then curled up like a cooked shrimp. There were no more tears because the nightmare had frightened them from me. Only a profound sadness, a feeling of loss, and emptiness remained.

*I didn't think it would hurt this much, Bisabuela;* I told the old Spanish woman in my mind.

*Would you have chosen differently had you known?* I imagined her asking.

*No,* was my answer, as hard as it was to admit. I had made my choice and knew I would have to live with that decision, but I wished it didn't hurt so much.

The voice of Bisabuela repeated her last words to me before I left France. *'You're young, niña, just beginning your life. Take the good memories with you and leave the rest, then go make new ones. Trust in yourself, niña, always listen to your heart.'*

With a deep sigh, I relaxed into the comfort of Bill's bed, resting my head where his had been, and finally finding the rest I needed as I fell into a dreamless sleep.

I learned long ago to always be aware of my surroundings, to always be on guard, and I woke when she came in, knowing she would probably come looking for me. The door opened slowly, then the shushing sound of her slippers on the wood floor gave away her presence in the room.

"I thought I might find you in here. Did you have a nightmare?" Mama Bea asked when she saw my eyes were open.

"I have... had... wrong... bad dream."

"I had a bad dream," she gently corrected.

"I had a bad dream," I repeated. "Zis place... room, feel good for me. help... helped to sleep."

"Oh darling, I know what you mean. I come in here sometimes myself when I need a little comfort." She wandered around the room with a sad look on her face, running her hand over the books on the shelf, picking up things at random, examining them carefully and then putting them down somewhere else, as if remembering when they arrived in the room and where they belonged.

"Do you want to talk about your dream?"

"No, Madame." That was the last thing I wanted to do. "Do... does he live here?" I asked, needing some reassurance that Bill would return.

Tenderness filled her eyes as she sat down on the bed next to me, gently brushing my hair off my face and tucking it behind my ear.

"He does, sometimes. This is his home and always will be. Beau has been a grown man for a while, Désirée. He just hasn't settled anywhere else. The war has kept him busy and away a lot more than I would have liked, but I suspect he'll be home soon."

I understood most of what she said. Her reassurance of Bill's return was all I could hope for. But there were still questions I needed answers to, things that would help me understand what they expected from me and how I should behave.

"Mama Bea? Is me... hiding now... still?"

"Am I still hiding, is the correct question. No, darling, you have nothing to fear any longer."

"Why you lie to za nun about me?" It troubled me she had lied. I didn't want to talk about my past to anyone, knew I should never speak of it, but I felt there was some other reason she lied, and I needed to understand why.

Her forehead wrinkled as she pinched the bridge of her nose between her fingers. She gave me a look full of worry, seeming to measure her response, or maybe gauge my reaction to what she would say.

"I must know, Madame," I said in French. From the way she was acting, it must be something important. I wasn't a child and didn't want her to treat me like one. The danger I posed for anyone who helped me hadn't suddenly disappeared, and I needed to understand where the threat might come from.

She blew out a soft breath before answering in my language. “It’s nothing you need to worry about, darling. Beau and I will take care of it. It involves how he brought you into this country. Beau cut some corners and will need to correct them. So, for now, it would be better if everyone believes you were born here in the States. I explained to Sister Mary Agnes that you were born in New York, and during the war you lived in Montreal with your grandmother until she died. It’s a simple enough story explaining your background and upbringing. Most people will believe what they’re told.”

“Bill is in trouble because of me,” I said, recalling my hasty escape from France. Frightened that someone would identify and arrest me, I did exactly as he instructed throughout the entire trip. I stayed in the background, quiet and as invisible as possible, and Bill stayed by my side the whole way.

“Don’t worry about Beau,” she said, gently stroking my cheek. “He knows how to handle himself and what to do. All you need to think about is learning our language and settling in here. This is your home now, Désirée. If you’re ever troubled again, sweetheart, you can always come to me.”

Nothing had changed. I would always be hiding something; my past, my inescapable guilt, and right then, I knew I would need to be extraordinarily careful, not only for my safety, but for Bill’s, too. The weight of my sadness increased tenfold.

“*Je comprends, Madame*. I understand.” *Some things never change.*

After breakfast, Mr. Jefferies brought in the things he purchased at Woolworth's the day before.

"Here they are, Miss Bea, and the map Miss Dezrae ask for," he said, placing the items at the end of the dining table next to her.

"Ah, yes. The map. Let's open it up, Jacob, so Désirée can get an idea of what New Orleans looks like from a bird's-eye view."

Mr. Jefferies unfolded the street map of Greater New Orleans, spreading it across the end of the dining table and smoothing it flat with his large, dark hands. It showed the streets of New Orleans all lined up in straight lines, going roughly north, south, east, and west. There weren't many curved streets and hardly any hubs with multiple streets converging, like they did in Paris. Each city block was a square, and significant places were easily identifiable, like the enormous park by the river, which had been our last stop the day before.

"Here you go, Miss Dezrae. You want me to show you where the house is on the map?" he asked.

"No, *merci*. I find," I said, stopping him before he could point out the location.

I studied the map for a moment, at first amazed at how familiar it looked. The way the Mississippi River wound around the bulk of the city reminded me of the Seine winding its way through Paris.

When I saw the river up close from the shore of Audubon Park took my breath away. I thought it would be like the Seine, flowing through the city with walkable bridges and neighborhoods on both sides. But it wasn't anything like the Seine; it was enormous. All that muddy brown water had a power flowing fiercely beneath the seemingly calm surface. I could feel it beneath my feet as I stood on the shore. It was another example of how different America was.

I found the park on the map, pointing to it with my finger. "We go to zis park... um... yesterday. Yes?" I said, looking up at Mama Bea and Mr. Jefferies for confirmation.

They both nodded, so I continued retracing our steps from the park to the house on St. Charles Ave, counting the blocks and turns we made the day before.

"Here is za house," I stated confidently, pointing to a square on the map. They confirmed my guess with two sets of raised eyebrows and nodding heads. Mr. Jefferies marked the location with a red circle.

Then I moved my finger from the house to the school. That was easy because the school was only a few blocks away on the same street. Then my finger moved up St. Charles, going east and then northeast, all the way to Canal Street, the most prominent street on the map.

I pointed to where I thought the department store was located, and Mr. Jefferies moved my finger over one block. He marked the school with another circle and then the department store with an x.

I continued from the department store on Canal, tracing my finger up one of the tiny streets that went northeast through the French Quarter; nine blocks up, right turn, then three blocks to the market and Café du Monde on Decatur. Mr. Jefferies marked that location with two x's. From there, I retraced the route back to the house, then sat back in my chair, confident I remembered our way.

Mama Bea and Mr. Jefferies stood together across the table from me, looking at the map and then at me with surprised expressions, like I had three heads or something equally unexpected. Mama Bea shook her head, chuckling through her nose.

"Do me a favor, Jacob. Take that red pen and draw a line along Carrolton Avenue from the river up to Claiborne, then from Claiborne up to Canal, then east down to the river," Mama Bea instructed, giving me a hawk-like stare.

Mr. Jefferies smiled his toothy grin at me. "Sure, Miss Bea. Be happy to." He took the red pen and made the lines as directed, snickering under his breath the entire time. When he finished, he stood back, still smiling like he knew something I didn't yet know, but soon would.

"Thank you, Jacob," Mama Bea said, then she threw her gaze back to me.

"You seem to have a keen sense of direction, Désirée. It's something the professors at the university would call spatial awareness, an understanding of where you are at all times."

I struggled to translate what she said but knew it must have something to do with the map.

"I like know... where I... are, am," I said, frustrated I couldn't say it correctly.

"I like to know where I am, is the correct way to say that."

"I like to know where I am," I repeated, attempting to mimic her intonation, which earned me another smile.

"As you can see, Désirée, New Orleans is a large city, perhaps not as large as Paris, but still quite large. There are areas of this city that are unsavory and inappropriate for a girl your age to venture into unaccompanied. The red line Jacob drew on your map is the boundary of those areas. You are never to go outside this boundary, under any circumstance, without a responsible adult with you. Is that clear?" She spoke slowly, pointing to the area above the red line on the map for emphasis.

I could tell she was serious, and after I understood the basics, I wanted to protest. She was banning me from the French Quarter, at least without an adult with me. That was disappointing. So far, that area of the city was the most interesting and tantalizing. I wanted to explore it more, but I knew better than to complain. Besides, there was a lot more of the city to explore below the red line.

"Yes, Madame. *Je comprends*. I understand."

"Good. Put the map away and let's get down to teaching you proper English. Who taught you to speak English, Désirée? How did you learn it?" she asked, picking up the student journals and pencils from the table and heading to her study at the front of the house.

"Katarina, she teach me some words, but I learn wiz book," I said, following behind her.

"Book? What book?" she asked as she put the journals down on her desk and took the seat behind it.

"*Dictionnaire*... dictionary. English, French dictionary. Bill give me. I read words and remember," I explained, pointing to my head.

"You memorized the English, French dictionary? The entire thing?" she asked with a look of disbelief.

"Oui. I remember words I read," I said with a shrug.

"Do you remember everything you read?" Her eyes narrowed and lines formed across her forehead.

"Most all, important zings, I remember. When speak... I zink words, French/English, English/French zen speak, say za words. *Mais*, I not speak right... za correct way," I said, lamenting my ignorance.

"Remarkable." Mama Bea shook her head as if she still didn't believe me. "Nevertheless, we will start at the beginning, with the letters of the alphabet and their sounds."

For the several days, all I did was study English. beginning with the ABC song, which I sang constantly, making everyone smile all the time.

Eventually, I learned English the same way I learned German: first secretly with a dictionary, and then listening, reading, writing, and repeating. Soon, the student journals filled with my neatly printed words flowing across the pages, with lots of red corrections added by Mama Bea.

The biggest struggle was trying to think in English. If I could do that, then speaking would be easier. The words were all there in my head, floating around with their French translations, all the big words and little words waiting to come together in a coherent sentence. But those big and little words fit together differently in French than they did in English, and the rules for combining them remained stubbornly elusive. Mama Bea was a diligent teacher, and I was a determined student, so between the two of us, we drummed those elusive rules into my brain.

One blustery afternoon, I was reading the book Mama Bea sent to me before I came to America. It was the English version of a book I read many times sitting on my Papa's lap: *The Three Musketeers* by the French author Alexandre Dumas. I knew the story well and could visualize the pages written in French, so when I began reading the English version, I didn't have to think about the translation. I read the words out loud, listening to how they sounded, absorbing the way they fit together to paint the pictures of the story. By the time I finished the book, English no longer felt as foreign to me, as confusing as it had been.

There were times when it felt like I'd be struggling forever to speak properly, to understand even the simplest of conversations without constantly tripping over the translations, missing the nuances. Then, one day, as I listened to the morning radio broadcast, all those English words came together in perfect order, making perfect sense, and the French translations faded into the background. It was like a jigsaw puzzle finally completed, revealing its hidden picture in vivid detail. I could think in English.

I didn't immediately start speaking like an American girl. My French accent remained distinct, and I still struggled with the th's, but I made a point of mimicking the way Mama Bea spoke as much as I could.

"Good morning, Mama Bea. Did you sleep well? It looks like it will be a beautiful day, don't you zink?" I asked, walking into breakfast, the words falling easily from my lips, like they were there all the time. I felt like I had conquered an enormous obstacle.

Mama Bea glanced at me over her coffee cup, one eyebrow slightly raised. "Good morning, Désirée. Ready to get started this morning?" she said, as if everything was exactly how it should be.

# Chapter 5

## *Who are you?*

### June 1945

*How do people live in this heat?* I asked myself, not for the last time.

It was too hot to be just about anywhere and only slightly better in the shade of the big magnolia tree standing majestically in the garden. I found a bit of comfort inside the gazebo, the old, well cared for structure encircling me with its certainty. Maybe it was because I knew Bill had been there, probably many times as he was growing up. I imagined him sitting on the same cushioned bench, maybe even reading the same book I was reading. It felt good there; it felt like Bill was there with me.

"But zare, as he was alighting from his horse at za gate of za Jolly Miller, wizout anyone—host, waiter, or hostler—coming to hold his stirrup or take his horse, D'Artagnan spied, zrough an open window on za ground floor, a gentleman, well-made and of good carriage..."

I liked reading aloud, listening to the words, imagining the pictures they drew. Then a voice came through the hedge behind me.

"Who you talking to?" the voice asked.

"Who is zare?" I nervously asked the voice.

"It's me, back here," a boy's voice replied. "I heard you talking, but no one was answering, so I was wondering who you were talking to."

I looked behind me, through the lattice of the gazebo, searching for the owner of the voice. He was standing on the other side of the short hedge that separated the two properties. He looked older than me, but not by much, and had dark hair that fell across his forehead into a pair of blue eyes, which were staring at me through the lattice.

"I was reading, not talking to anyone."

"What's your name?"

"Désirée."

"That's a pretty name, Désirée. I'm Robert Easton. All my friends call me Bobby. Pleased to meet you. Welcome to the neighborhood... Désirée," he said, his eyes brightening when he said my name a second time.

"Zank you, Bobby. You live in zis house? I see you before in za garden," I said, curious about him. I had seen him from the gallery outside my room and watched as he'd toss a small ball high in the air, then catch it in a glove he wore on his left hand.

"So, you've been watching me, too. I've seen you a few times, up on the gallery," he confessed.

"You watch me? Why?" It made me nervous being observed without knowing it, though I'd been doing that to him.

"You're new around here, and anything new is worth looking at," he said, peering at me intently. "Are you only here for the summer?"

"No. I live here wiz Mrs. Marchand. I come to live wiz her."

"Where did you come from? Where's your family?"

I hated starting new relationships with a lie, but I had no choice but to use the story Mama Bea had invented to explain my background and presence in her home.

"Montreal. My family is dead." I thought such a blatant statement would leave any listener with nothing to say, which was exactly how I wanted it. The fewer details given, the better.

"I'm sorry for your loss, Désirée. Truly I am. I lost my brother last year at the D-Day landing on Omaha Beach." His voice became quiet, as if the memory instantly brought back painful feelings.

I knew how that felt and knew exactly where and when that horrible but glorious event took place. It was heartbreaking to see the sadness in his eyes, knowing his brother's sacrifice had helped to free my country from the bondage of Nazi Germany.

"I am sorry about your brozur. It is hard to lose family."

"Miss Dezrae? There's a telephone call for you," Mr. Jefferies called out from the porch.

"I come, Mr. Jefferies. *Enchanté*, Bobby. I must go now." I said, hurrying away.

"Be sure to tell Miss Bea you met Bobby Easton. She knows me."

"Hurry, child. Miss Bea's waitin' on you." Miss Laila shooed me through the house and into the study, where Mama Bea was sitting behind her desk, talking on the telephone.

"Come here, Désirée. Someone wants to speak with you," Mama Bea said, handing me the telephone receiver.

I nervously lifted the receiver to my ear, unsure whose voice I would hear.

"*Allô?*"

"Hello, Chère. How are you?" Bill asked, speaking in French.

A sigh of relief escaped my lips when I heard his voice, then I remembered I was still mad at him for leaving.

"I'm hot. You didn't tell me it was hot here."

"I'm sorry, Chère. I forgot about that part. Are you doing alright?"

"Yes, I'm fine. I'm learning English so I can take a test for school."

"Mama told me. She says you're learning quickly. Have you met anyone since you've been there?"

"I met a girl at the school and a boy who lives next door. His name is Bobby. And I met Charlotte Bentley. Is she your girlfriend?" I asked, wondering if he would tell me.

"You did?"

"Yes. She said she's very mad at you for not writing to her as often as you promised, and that she misses you." I wondered if he would answer the question now.

"Did she? I suppose I will have a lot to make up for when I get home. Are *you* still angry at me for leaving?"

"Maybe, but I will think of something for you to do to make it up to me."

He laughed. "I'm sure you will, Chère. I'm sure you will. Where did you meet that boy?" he asked, his tone changing to one of amused suspicion.

I waited a few seconds before answering him. "He talked to me through the bushes by the gazebo."

"You shouldn't be talking with boys alone, Chère. It's not safe for a young girl like you." He sounded like a protective father.

I rolled my eyes and sighed. "Why? He was nice, and he told me to tell Mama Bea that I met him."

"Well, that's good, and you do that, but believe me when I say the boys in the States aren't the same as the boys you've known. Things are different there," he warned. When I didn't respond, he changed the subject.

"I'll be home soon, Chère. We can talk about it then. We'll have some time to go do a few things together before school starts. Would you like that?"

"Yes. But when will you be home, Bill? Everything is strange here. I don't know how I'm supposed to be."

I don't know why I thought he could fix everything, but at that moment, I did, and I needed him, needed his strength and support to help me understand everything.

"Just be yourself, Désirée. All you need to worry about is passing that test, and from what Mama says, you'll be fine."

"Will you come soon?"

"I'll be there soon, a few more weeks. Wait for me, Chère."

Every time he said those words, it signaled the end of our conversations, and my heart sank again.

"*D'accord. Au revoir*, Bill." I said, handing the receiver back to Mama Bea, who had been standing outside the study door. She put it to her ear, watching me as she finished the call.

"Beau? ... Yes, I'll tell her. You stay safe, son, and we'll be here when you get home... I love you too. See you soon. Goodbye." She placed the receiver gently down onto the cradle, then looked over at me, her eyes slightly moist with a touch of sadness showing through.

"It's never enough. Is it?" she asked.

"No, it is not enough."

It wasn't all study that first summer as I waited for Bill's return. Well, it was mostly studying, but there were other things to occupy my mind. There was a lot to learn about America, and once I could communicate, things got a lot easier, and then a lot harder.

Every Wednesday afternoon was Mama Bea's Bridge Club when, according to Miss Laila, the ladies of New Orleans society would gather at one of their homes, then sit around card tables eating tea sandwiches and drinking sweet tea while they played cards and gossiped.

I had been there for a month when it was Mama Bea's turn to host the Bridge Club. She was busy in her study while Mr. Jefferies shifted the furniture in the living room and set up the card tables and chairs. I wandered around, trying to stay out of the way, but wanted to be helpful, so I headed to my preferred location, the kitchen.

Miss Laila was preparing the hors d'oeuvres for the Bridge Club, and it looked like she could use some help. Her normal relaxed demeanor was unusually nervous.

"May I help Miss Laila? I want to help you." I watched her nervous strokes of the knife, spreading the long, thin slices of bread with a pimento cream cheese mixture.

"Sure, Miss Dezrae. That be fine if you want to. Go wash your hands, then you can help me with these sandwiches," Miss Laila said, wiping her hands on her apron, then mopping her dark forehead with a hankie she pulled from her apron pocket.

"Seems hotter than usual today. Don't you think?" she asked.

"For me, it is all time hotter zen usual," I replied with a shrug.

"I suppose it is for you, but you'll get used to it. Guess it just be my nerves today. Havin' to fuss over those society ladies always makes me nervous," Miss Laila confessed with a crooked smile.

I watched her work for a moment, her large, dark hands moving through her tasks with renewed confidence. Her skin was the color of freshly brewed coffee, silky looking, her hands big and strong, almost like a man's hands. She was a big woman, not overweight, but large in stature and full in her figure. The light blue uniform she wore hugged her body, accentuating her curves but covering her modestly, the hem falling below her knees and the sleeves covering her arms to the elbow. She rarely looked unkempt, wearing her hair neatly styled with a small white cap atop her head, matching the white collar and cuffs of her uniform.

The way she moved around that kitchen reminded me of the sous-chefs in the kitchen at the George V in Paris, sliding from one task to the next without skipping a beat while keeping her eye on what she had gently simmering on the stove.

Before I came to America, I had never met people like Miss Laila and Mr. Jefferies and wanted to know more about them. It felt like they belonged in that house, like they were permanent and essential parts of the Marchand family. Yet sometimes they behaved in ways which made me think they felt unwanted, or perhaps undervalued, though never by Mama Bea.

Now that I could understand what people were saying, I noticed this shift in mood with Miss Laila and Mr. Jefferies whenever visitors would come to the house. Some of those people would say or do something rude or dismissive to them, as if they had no feelings. Things like that confused me about Americans.

Miss Laila and I worked side by side, putting together everything she planned to serve the Bridge Club ladies. There were three different tea sandwiches: pimiento cream cheese, ham and cheese, and curried egg salad, each cut into triangles, squares, and circles. I arranged them artfully on a platter garnished with sprigs of parsley.

Earlier that morning, Miss Laila had peeled, cleaned, and boiled four dozen large shrimps and had them chilling in the refrigerator. We curled the cooked shrimp around the edge of four beautiful footed China dishes with their tails hanging down, then filled the dishes with a delicious tangy tomato sauce.

Small China bowls filled with a variety of nuts; spicy pecans, honeyed walnuts, and candied almonds sat conveniently on each card table in the living room. There were small butter cookies in the shape of hearts and diamonds, spades and clubs, frosted with red, white, and blue icing. I arranged them on a tiered serving piece, along with small mint candies sprinkled among them.

It looked like a lot of food for such a small gathering. Only twelve ladies were attending, and once again, I thought this was another example of the abundance held so lightly in America.

"Miss Laila? Why so much food? Not so many are coming for so much food. No?" I asked, wanting to understand the thinking behind such a display.

Miss Laila let out a belly laugh when she heard the question. "That's cuz Miss Bea wants to make sure the ladies have plenty to nibble on while they's playin' cards. Most of them tipple a bit in their tea," she said with a conspiratorial wink. "Miss Bea don't want them gettin' too tipsy, so she always makes sure there's plenty to eat. You can help me set all these trays out on the table before the ladies come. I'll bring out the drink pitchers."

We arranged the trays of hors d'oeuvres on the damask-covered dining table. Stacks of small plates of fine china, silver flatware, and matching damask napkins, neatly folded into triangles, sat on one end of the table. The centerpiece was a tall urn filled with cascading fern fronds and a variety of flowers in shades of red, white, and blue.

The following Wednesday was America's Independence Day, and the Bridge Club ladies would not be meeting the following week because of family obligations. This gathering would be the Bridge Club's 4th of July celebration, which explained the patriotic theme of the décor.

Looking at the table laden with all the savory and sweet dishes, I decided it needed one more item, something Julian Laurent would call a palate cleanser. I found everything I needed in Miss Lailas' well-stocked kitchen and quickly chopped up watermelon, peaches, red grapes, and blueberries into a bowl, drizzled a mixture of lemon juice, a bit of honey and finely chopped mint over the top, then tossed it gently together, letting the dressing and juices from the fruit mix well. Miss Laila seemed pleased with the dish after she tasted it.

"Never thought of mixin' dressin' on fruit before. Sure do add somethin new, don't it? You go on upstairs and get yourself ready, Miss Dezrae" she said, shooing me out of her kitchen. "Miss Bea wants you to meet the ladies today. Go on now. Let me take care of the rest."

I wasn't sure why I needed to dress up any more than usual. A simple blouse with cropped pants and slip-on loafers seemed fine to me. This had become my uniform since arriving, being the most comfortable clothes Mama Bea had purchased for me. It was too hot to dress up in anything but the lightest of garments. I didn't think I'd ever get used to how hot it was, nearly all the time.

But I made the effort for Mama Bea's sake. She liked it when I wore the dresses she bought, so I opted for the lightest floral sundress in the closet. It was a pretty dress with a semi-fitted bodice gently flaring to a knee-length hem and sporting flouncy short sleeves. I slipped on my Mary Jane shoes to complete the outfit.

Since coming to New Orleans, I rarely gave myself more than a quick glance in the mirror to ensure my tidiness, but that afternoon, the girl looking back at me captured my attention, and I couldn't look away.

At least my hair was blonde again. Mama Bea had taken me to the beauty parlor to reclaim my natural color the minute she saw the quarter-inch strip of blonde hair exposing my previous disguise. The new color almost matched my natural color perfectly, and the hairdresser cut short bangs across my forehead, conveniently covering my scar.

I almost looked like me, but not quite the Désirée I remembered from long ago. This version of me was older, taller, with a supple body and limbs turned a warm tan color from days spent outside. The bright blue eyes staring back at me reminded me of the girl in Picasso's mirror. The same spark was there and the same expression of uncertainty.

"Who are you?" I asked the girl in the mirror. "Which one are you?"

*I'm just Désirée, no one special.* At least, I hoped I could be.

A knock on my bedroom door pulled my attention away from the mirror.

"Désirée, honey, are you ready?" Mama Bea asked, opening the door and peeking in.

"Yes, ma'am. I am ready," I said, turning around to show her I had dressed up for the occasion.

"You look lovely, darling." A smile lit her face.

"Do I look like Désirée Gautier?"

Her eyes flashed open, concern instantly filling them. I regretted asking. I hadn't meant to upset her.

She took my hands in hers, smiled and said, "You look like Désirée, a beautiful young lady in a pretty summer dress, ready to go to a party. Gautier is only a name, darling, one of many you've had, as I understand it. That name does not define you, sweetheart, nor do any of the others. Désirée is who you are and always have been. Be you, darling. That will always be enough."

The doorbell rang, signaling the Bridge Club ladies had arrived. Mama Bea gave me a look I'd seen before on Katarina, eyebrows arching high, like she was about to take the stage. Then she reached for my hand.

"Come on, sweetheart. Let's go rescue Jacob and greet our guests."

# Chapter 6

## *Bridge Club surprises*

That afternoon, Mama Bea had arranged a surprise for me. Not only would it be the first daytime party she'd hosted since I'd been there, but it would also be my introduction to her New Orleans society friends. The real surprise was that she'd invited Mrs. Elanor Duret, Evelyn's mother, to join the Bridge Club that afternoon, and Mama Bea asked her to bring Evelyn along so we could get to know one another.

"Mrs. Duret, so glad you could join us this afternoon. May I call you Elanor? We're rather informal here, so please call me Beatrice," Mama Bea said as she greeted the new arrivals.

"Of course, Mrs. Marchand, I mean Beatrice. Thank you so much for inviting us to your home. It's as lovely as I imagined. I believe you've met my daughter, Evelyn," Mrs. Duret said as Evelyn stepped up to her mother's side with a big smile on her face.

Mama Bea shook Evelyn's hand. "Hello again, Evelyn. I'm pleased you came. Désirée, darling, come and greet our guests. They seem to all be arriving at once," Mama Bea said as six more ladies walked up to the door.

A flurry of activity ensued as all the ladies greeted each other and complimented Mama Bea on the beauty of her home, which I knew was mainly due to the efforts of Miss Laila and Mr. Jefferies. Mama Bea introduced me, Evelyn, and Mrs. Duret to the rest of the Bridge Club, who all warmly welcomed Mrs. Duret. But some seemed more pleased that Mama Bea finally had a companion to live with her—as if Miss Laila and Mr. Jefferies didn't count.

"I'm so happy you've found someone to share this big house with you, Bea. I can't imagine how hard it's been since... well, I know you've been lonely, so I'm happy for you," Mrs. Helene Wilkinson said, her eyes lingering on me with questions behind them.

"Thank you, Hellie," Mama Bea replied. I could tell the woman's remark had opened a wound, Mama Bea's eyes becoming distant, her mouth tightening, but she shook it off quickly.

"Ladies, we have refreshments if you're interested. Please help yourselves while I get these two young people settled where they can get better acquainted."

Mama Bea guided her guests to the dining room where they all oo'd and aww'd over the table, then began filling their plates with samples of everything offered.

"Jacob will see to your drinks, ladies. I'll be back in a moment, and we'll see if I've invited an expert into our bridge game." Mama Bea said, gently stroking Elanor Duret's back.

We followed Mama Bea through the swinging door into the kitchen, Evelyn wide-eyed and cooing at everything she saw, apparently dazzled by the house. It was a beautiful house; large open spaces, high ceilings, elegant, understated furnishings and décor, tasteful without being opulent. I could understand her fascination with it.

Once inside the kitchen, Mama Bea leaned hard against the countertop, taking in a deep breath, then releasing it with a sigh.

"Eulaila, please put together a tray of refreshments for these young ladies. After the Bridge Club fills their plates will be fine," Mama Bea said with a conspiratorial wink.

"Sure, Miss Bea. Gots some set aside right here, in case we needed more," Miss Laila said, reaching for a serving tray and two plates from the cupboard.

"The gazebo has always been a favorite place for young people to gather, Désirée. Why don't you and Evelyn go outside and get to know one another? Eulaila will bring out the tray," Mama Bea said. "These card games usually last a couple of hours, unless your mother is a better player than she's admitting to, Evelyn. In which case, who knows how long this will last?" she teased with a raised eyebrow. Then she left to join her guests.

I led Evelyn outside to the gazebo where we settled ourselves into the comfortable cushioned bench built into the inside walls. Miss Laila brought out the tray, setting it on the small table in the center of the structure.

"If you need anythin', Miss Dezrae, come get me," she said, giving me a nod before leaving.

Evelyn leaned back against the gazebo wall. "You are so lucky. I'd give almost anything to live in a house like this."

"Yes, it is a beautiful house."

"Well, you've got to tell me everything. You know, you have saved me from utter boredom twice now. Mother was beside herself with joy when Mrs. Marchand called to invite her to the Bridge Club. Mother's been dying to join this group for ages, and when Mrs. Marchand asked her to bring *me* along, well, it was all I could do to keep her from leaving me home. She told me if I embarrassed her, I would regret it forever, whatever that means. Of course, I would never do such a thing. Where are you from, by the way?"

Evelyn was chatty, like my friend Camille in Paris had been, full of questions and wanting to know, but liking the sound of her own voice best. She was a pretty girl, with hazel eyes and soft features, not yet sharpened by emerging adulthood.

"I was born in New York but live... lived in Montreal. My family is dead. Mrs. Marchand is now my family." I thought I had better get that part out of the way so she wouldn't ask a lot of questions I wouldn't answer. The statement usually made people change the topic, but Evelyn was curious for more information.

"Oh, you poor thing. How did they die? Were they in the war?"

"I not like talking about it. Is too hard. *Trop triste*," I added, trying to put her off this line of questioning and hoping the French would distract her.

"Who are you talking to now?" a boy's voice came through the bushes behind the gazebo.

Evelyn's eyes flew open, her hand covered her mouth as she stifled a giggle. "Who's that?" she whispered.

I shrugged, grinning at her, then answered the boy's question. "I talk wiz my new friend, Evelyn."

"Oh. Well, did you tell Miss Bea you met me?" he asked.

"Yes," I said, trying to stifle my own giggles.

"Oh. Well, what did she say?"

I clamped my lips closed and shook my head, trying to compose myself so my response would achieve the effect I wanted. After clearing my throat, I answered.

"She say, Mr. Robert Easton should remember his manners and come to za front door for a proper introduction, as any souzern gentleman would," I said in my best imitation of Mama Bea's voice.

Bobby burst out laughing. "She did, huh? Well, I'll be right over."

Once we heard him move away, Evelyn and I started laughing so hard we nearly fell off the bench.

"Who is he?" she wanted to know. "What does he look like? How old is he?" Evelyn was a stream of questions to which I had no answers.

"*Je ne sais pas*. I do not know. Perhaps we will learn about him togezur."

A few minutes later, Mama Bea and Mr. Jefferies marched Bobby Easton across the yard toward us.

"You see? Here he come wiz Mrs. Marchand."

"Ladies, forgive the interruption. May I present Mr. Robert Easton, Jr., our neighbor, who is eager to make your acquaintance," Mama Bea said, arching her eyebrow in Bobby's direction. "Robert, may I present our guest, Miss Evelyn Duret? And I believe you've already spoken with my ward, Miss Désirée Gautier. Now that you are all properly introduced, I'll leave you to get to know one another. Robert, I expect you will remember you're a gentleman in the company of young ladies," she said, giving him a look that spoke volumes of what she might do if he forgot the directive.

"Yes, ma'am. On my honor, I will remember," he promised, blue eyes lighting up and sparkling with mischief.

"Good. Jacob, if you would, please bring more refreshments for these young people and perhaps something to occupy their minds. That Chinese Checkers board from up in Beau's room would do nicely. Enjoy yourselves, children," Mama Bea instructed. Then she went back to her card game with Mr. Jefferies following behind.

"Well, this is nice," Bobby said, taking a seat on the bench across from me and grinning from ear to ear. "What ya two been talking about?"

"Are you Dr. Robert Easton's son?" Evelyn asked, peering at him.

"The very same. My friends all call me Bobby. Robert is my father's name."

"Well, what a coincidence. Your father has been our family doctor for years. Perhaps he's mentioned the Duret family? My father is Jonathan Duret, the banker." Evelyn was excited about this connection between them, but from the roll of Bobby's eyes, it appeared he had heard this reference to his father countless times before.

"Father never talks about his patients, which is fine by me. I don't have much interest in medicine anyway."

"Really? I thought all doctor's sons became doctors." Evelyn batted her eyes at him.

"What you like to do, Bobby, ozur zen baseball?" I asked, attempting to change the direction of the conversation.

"Oh, I like baseball, but mostly, I like to build things. I've got a shop in my garage where I tinker around with a few things."

"What do you make?" I asked.

"Are you going to be an architect? Father says that's an excellent profession. He says there's going to be a building boom as soon as the war is over," Evelyn said, still batting her eyes in Bobby's direction. I wondered if she had gotten something in her eye, as much blinking as she was doing.

Bobby shook his head. "No, not an architect, an engineer. I want to build rockets that will fly to the moon and back. Maybe even to Venus or Mars. I build small models in my workshop and test them out by the river." He looked from me, then to Evelyn, then back to me again, apparently nervous about our reactions to what he revealed about himself.

I wasn't sure what rockets were, but from the sparkle behind his eyes when he spoke, Bobby's passion for them was clear.

Evelyn laughed nervously. "Oh, that's just science fiction. Everybody knows Flash Gordon is just pretend, and all that space stuff could never really happen. Goodness, we've only been flying in airplanes since the Wright brothers."

"Might be science fiction now, but it won't always be if I have anything to do with it. Someday, we'll be able to go far enough out there to turn around and see the entire Earth, its vast blue oceans and drifting continents spinning in the vacuum of space." His eyes brightened with the possibilities his vision offered.

I fell a little in love with Bobby Easton at that moment. There was something about him that gave me a comfortable feeling, reminded me of Alex. Bobby wasn't what I would call handsome; his nose was slightly crooked, and his mouth was wide and full-lipped, but he had a boyish charm and captivating blue eyes, like deep pools of still water.

"What have you been doing since you got here, Désirée? Besides reading," he asked.

I shrugged, sighing a bit at the boring nature of my activities. "Nozing, but I study za English, and now za ozur zings for za test I must take for school."

The questions on their faces said they needed more explanation. "I must take za grade seven test, so I will go to grade eight."

"Well, that's easy. I can help you study for it, Désirée. I didn't do that well on the science or math parts, though, so I won't be much help there," Evelyn offered.

"Science and math are my best subjects. I aced that part of the seventh-grade final. Didn't do as well in history, though. I couldn't seem to keep all those dates straight in my head," Bobby said.

It was still hard keeping up with conversations that went by swiftly, but I understood their offers of help. "Zank you, it is very kind. I must zink of somezing to do for you."

"Well, I already have an idea about that," Evelyn said. "I can help you with history and geography and literature, then you can help me prepare for my French class next term." She picked up a tea sandwich from the tray and leaned back against the wall of the gazebo with a big smile on her face, like she had just solved her biggest problem.

"Of course, I will help you wiz za French," I told her. "And for you, Bobby? What can I do?"

"Oh, I don't need nothing. What do you like to do, Désirée?"

"For me, what make me happy is za cooking. I like to cook delicious zings. I will make you somezing for helping me wiz za science. Do *you* like to cook, Evelyn?" I asked, imagining how fun it would be to have a friend who liked to cook as much as I did.

"Oh, good gracious, no. I don't think I could boil an egg, even if I had to. Our girl, Judith, takes care of all the cooking in our house. Mother barely ever goes into the kitchen except to tell Judith what she wants her to make for supper. When I'm married, I'm going to live in one of these big Uptown houses and have my own servants to do for me. Mother says if I marry the right man, I won't have to lift a finger." Evelyn liked to talk, and she had a lot of funny ideas about things. Bobby just sat back, rolling his eyes.

The three of us spent the rest of the afternoon in the gazebo, talking about movies and movie stars, music and popular songs on the radio, and baseball, about which Bobby was a wealth of information. By the end of the day, the three of us had formed an alliance, the goal being to help me pass the seventh-grade final exam. Evelyn agreed to come over to help me study American history and geography, and to practice French, and Bobby said he would work with me every day until the test to make sure I passed the science and math parts.

It felt good having friends again. I missed my friends in Paris and wondered if they ever thought about me, or if Marie Rondeau had already faded from their memories.

It would have been a stellar day except for something Evelyn said after Bobby went home. She'd been going on and on about the society columns and magazine articles she read, especially the ones that talked about Charlotte Bentley.

"Charlotte's name is always in the newspaper, talking about her going to lots of parties and charity galas. Everyone says she's the most beautiful young woman in New Orleans, from one of the wealthiest families. And I heard a rumor about her," Evelyn said, stopping to look at me to decide if she should share her ill-gotten information or not.

"Have you met Mrs. Marchand's son, Bill Marchand?" she asked.

I didn't want to lie to her, but I couldn't tell the absolute truth either, so I said, "I have spoken to him on za telephone." It was the truth, just not the whole truth.

"Well, from what Mother says, Bill Marchand is the most eligible bachelor in all of New Orleans, maybe even the entire South. You're so lucky to be living here with them. Anyway, I heard that he and Charlotte Bentley are secretly engaged, but they're waiting for the war to be over to announce it in the newspapers... Is it true?" she asked, clearly hoping I would confirm her information.

"*Je ne sais pas.* I not hear zis, but I am new here and do not know all zings."

My brain reeled trying to process that information. *Could it be true?* I couldn't think of one reason Bill would keep something like that from me, but he avoided answering my question about Charlotte when we talked, so I couldn't help but think he was hiding it.

Doubt started creeping into my mind.

# Chapter 7

## *Homecoming disasters*

On Monday, August 6, I was in my bedroom pouring over one of the many cookbooks I borrowed from the library. I was searching for a new recipe, something complicated, so I wouldn't have to think about how angry and confused I was about everything.

Cooking always helped me push away my feelings, allowing me to focus on the steps of the recipe, the dance of ingredients leading to some new flavor or texture. And I needed a distraction.

A few days earlier, I took the stupid test, but that wasn't the problem. What upset me was what I learned after taking the test. Bill and Mama Bea planned to lock me up in a boarding school, where I would have to live behind brick walls for nearly nine months out of the year.

After the test, Sister Mary Agnes took me on a tour to see my new accommodations. It was all I could do to keep from running out of that building, screaming my head off. I never said a word to her, but I had a few things to say to Bill when he got home.

I felt like such a fool. I thought Sacred Heart was like La Maison, a home for orphan girls and a school for all girls. I wasn't an orphan anymore; Bill and Mama Bea were my family now, and the school was only a few blocks away. It made no sense why they would want to lock me away in there.

Then, to make things even worse, when I came down to breakfast that morning, the news was blaring on the kitchen radio, talking about the atomic bomb the Americans dropped on Japan. The reports said the force of the bomb was 2000 times greater than the biggest bomb ever created. They never spoke of the casualties, but they reported "an impenetrable cloud of dust and smoke cloaked Hiroshima after the bomb hit, and an accurate assessment of the damage was not yet available."

I could only imagine the devastation unleashed on the unsuspecting population of that city, tens of thousands undoubtedly lay buried beneath the rubble. I'd seen what regular bombs could do. On my way out of France, we flew over lots of French towns destroyed by the bombs the Allies and Germans dropped on each other and the French people. It was heartbreaking to think about.

Neither Mama Bea nor Miss Laila could get me to talk about what was bothering me. I just stayed up in my room most of the day, waiting for Bill to get home. He called on Friday to let us know he'd be home by Monday afternoon, so I left my bedroom door open, wanting to hear when he came in.

By late afternoon, I settled on a recipe for Torte Milanese, which is basically a big pastry filled with soft scrambled eggs and roasted peppers, spinach, ham, and cheese. Step by step, I visualized how I would prepare the dish. It was a complicated enough recipe to keep my mind off everything else for a while.

When I finally heard Bill's voice coming from the entryway downstairs, all thoughts of anger and frustration evaporated. It felt like I could breathe again, like the waiting had held me suspended in time until the moment I heard him, and the world started spinning once more.

I ran to the stairs, wanting to throw myself into his arms, but I stopped short at the top and stood perfectly still. When I looked down, Charlotte Bentley was draped around Bill's arm, holding on tight like she was afraid he'd run away.

"Thanks, Jacob. It's good to be home. You remember Miss Bentley and Carson, of course," Bill said, greeting Mr. Jefferies with a warm shake of his free hand.

Then Mama Bea came out of her study, pulling Bill out of Charlotte's grasp and into her own embrace, holding him close and rubbing his back. "Beau. It is so good to have you home, son."

He must have whispered something in her ear because when they stepped out of the embrace, she lifted her head toward the top of the stairs, and he turned to look up. Our eyes met for a brief second, and it was pure recognition; he saw me, and I saw him. Then I fled to my room with renewed frustration, closing the door behind me.

I wasn't supposed to know him. As far as anyone outside that house knew, Bill Marchand and Désirée Gautier had never met in person. Not trusting my ability to pretend in front of Charlotte Bentley, I threw myself onto the overstuffed chair in the corner of my room and back into the torte recipe, hoping to calm myself down.

That had not been the way I imagined our reunion would go.

A few minutes later, Bill knocked softly on my door and then peeked his head in like he was unsure of his welcome. "Hello, Chère. Aren't you happy to see me?" he timidly asked, speaking French as we always did.

“I’m not supposed to know you. Remember?” I said, sounding petulant.

“Right. I’m sorry about this, Chère. I didn’t expect to run into the Bentleys at the airport, and I couldn’t refuse their ride into town.” He looked sorry, his eyes pleading for forgiveness, his brow furrowed.

“I’ve missed you, Désirée. I can see we have a lot of catching up to do. Won’t you come down and let me introduce you? I want you to meet Carson, my oldest friend.” He reached out his hand to me, his eyes encouraging me to take it, to come to him.

I uncurled myself from the chair, set the cookbook aside, and willingly stepped into Bill’s open arms. With my eyes closed, I rested my cheek against his chest, feeling the beat of his heart sync in rhythm with mine. I felt whole at that moment, complete in the comfort of his embrace.

“Come with me, Chère. Let’s go down and meet the Bentleys. You and I can talk later. I promise,” he said, stroking my cheek with a tender touch.

Reluctantly, I pulled on my Gautier mask and allowed Bill to lead me downstairs to face Charlotte Bentley.

“Here they are,” Mama Bea said as Bill led me into the living room.

Charlotte and a man who looked to be Bill’s age were sitting together on the couch across from Mama Bea, sipping on something Mr. Jefferies had undoubtedly served them. They both looked up when we entered, Charlotte barely giving me a second glance and riveting her attention on Bill. The man, however, couldn’t seem to take his eyes off me as he rose from his seat to greet me.

“Charlotte, I believe you were mistaken. This couldn’t be the little girl you described to me. This is a beautiful young lady, not a child at all. It's a pleasure to meet you, Miss Désirée. I'm Carson Bentley, an old friend of Bill's. Welcome to New Orleans," he said in an overly friendly manner, his hazel brown eyes looking down at me intently as he lifted my hand to his lips in a courtly greeting.

"Watch yourself, Carson," Bill chided his friend. "She's only thirteen years old. Still a child, by all standards of decency."

"You know me, Bill. I'm nothing if not a gentleman," Carson said, dismissing the warning.

Bill guided me to the settee beside Mama Bea, who gave the Bentleys a brief history of who I was and why I was there. It was a tragic story of friendship, family loss, and a rescued orphan. Mama Bea was quite good at spinning a tale when she had to. I sat there quietly, like the grateful child they expected me to be. I never said a word, but I listened and observed the interaction between Bill and the Bentleys.

Occasionally, I caught Bill glancing at me with questions behind his eyes, like he wanted to get inside my head to hear what I was thinking. But I kept Désirée Gautier firmly planted on that settee, never letting the turmoil inside me leak to the surface.

They talked about the war, politics, and the atomic bomb, which they all agreed was a necessary but tragic event if it meant the end of the war with Japan. Then their talk turned to business and something about contracts, which didn't interest me in the least. I stopped paying attention until I heard Carson suggest Bill go out to supper with them. They were meeting friends at the Carousel Bar, and Carson was bent on getting Bill to go with them for a welcome home celebration.

Before Bill could decline the invitation, Mama Bea spoke up. "Go on, Beau. Go out and have your welcome home with your friends. We'll have plenty of time to catch up tomorrow."

Bill looked at her and then at me. I rolled my eyes and looked away as if it didn't matter.

"Are you sure, Mama?" he asked.

"Of course, she's sure, Bill. You've been away for so long I can't think of letting you out of my sight for a moment. Besides, you need to catch up with everyone. It'll be so much fun having all of us together again." This from Charlotte, who couldn't seem to keep her hands to herself, touching Bill's arm and leaning into him as close as she dared.

Mama Bea nodded with a wry smile as the Bentleys and Bill rose to leave.

"Charlotte, Carson, so nice of you to bring my son home to me. I'm sure we'll see each other again soon," Mama Bea said as she rose to walk them to the door.

"My pleasure, Miss Bea. I rarely get to do a favor for Bill Marchand. Miss Désirée, it has been my distinct pleasure to make your acquaintance. I hope we can get to know each other better," Carson said, taking my hand once again.

Charlotte looked down her nose at me. "Yes, it has been nice seeing you again, Désirée. I'm sure you and I are going to be good friends. I've always wanted a little sister," she said, hanging onto Bill's arm and smirking like she'd made a joke or something.

*That's not likely,* I thought, but I offered her a sweet smile anyway, to keep up appearances.

Bill gave Mama Bea a kiss on the cheek as they reached the front door. "Don't wait up, Mama. I'll see you in the morning." Then he looked back at me, still sitting in the living room. He came over to stand in front of me, his expression clearly conflicted. With a release of breath, he bent down to kiss my cheek.

"We'll talk tomorrow, Chère. I promise." Then he followed Charlotte and Carson Bentley out the door.

Bill was gone... again.

My heart sank to the floor. His leaving with Charlotte confirmed all my fears. I was a complication needing a solution, and boarding school was the answer. Bill would go on with his life and I would have to get used to it, but right then, I didn't think I ever would.

"Come on, darling. Let's go see what Eulaila has made us for supper. I've got a foul taste in my mouth that I need to get rid of," Mama Bea said, her own inner struggle clearly written on her face.

# Chapter 8

## *Taking a stand*

A sleepless night left my mind tormented with doubts about why I had even come to America. I felt stupid and naïve for thinking I was important to him, that he wanted me in his life as much as I wanted to be there.

*Why would he?*

"Beau had a life before he met you, Désirée," Mama Bea said when she tucked me into bed the night before. "My advice, for what it's worth, is to trust him and be patient. Find your place here, darling. This is your home now."

Well, if that was true, and they both had said it, then I was going to make them keep their word. But right then, I wasn't sure how I would accomplish that.

They were talking in the dining room when I went downstairs the following morning. Halfway down, I stopped to listen, eavesdropping being the one available option for finding out information they might not share openly with me. It was an old habit.

"She's had a few dreadful nights. Nightmares, I think. I usually find her curled up on your bed the next morning. For the past few days, she's been unusually quiet. Ever since she took the test at Sacred Heart, I can't seem to get her to talk about what's bothering her. She's been waiting for you to get home, Beau. It didn't help that you came in with Charlotte Bentley draped on your arm," Mama Bea said, a disapproving tone to her voice.

"It was unavoidable, Mother. Should I go up and get her?" Bill asked.

"No, I'm sure she'll be walking in here any minute now."

That was clearly my cue to make my entrance, though I didn't know how she knew I was there. *She must have psychic powers or something.*

"Good morning, Désirée," Mama Bea said with a knowing look in her eye the second I walked into the dining room.

"Good morning, Mama Bea. Good morning, Bill," I said, reaching for the coffeepot to pour myself a cup before sitting down to face them.

*Breathe Désirée. You can do this.* I'd been working on my argument all morning, but my hands were shaking, and I was having a hard time not spilling the coffee while under Bill's sharp gaze.

"Morning, Chère. Did you sleep well?" he asked.

I shrugged in response, rolling my eyes to the ceiling.

He sat back in his chair, staring at me, rubbing his chin like he was trying to figure out what he was looking at.

"Alright. Let's have it, Chère. What's bothering you? Mama and Laila tell me you've not said a word to them since you took that test." His eyes held concern, but the twitch at the corners of his mouth showed amusement. I didn't think any of it was funny.

I sipped my coffee, looking at them over the rim of the cup. They were waiting for my answer, and I knew they wouldn't wait for long, so I put the cup down and spoke my mind.

"Why you want to send me away? You say zis is my home. You boz say zis, but it is not true. You want to send me away from here, to live in zat school. Why you not tell me zis?"

They both looked at me like I had lost my mind. Bill's forehead wrinkled up like he was trying to figure out what I said, or maybe why I said it.

"We're not sending you away, Chère. We're only sending you to school." He clearly thought that was a reasonable explanation, but I didn't.

"Why must I live in za school? You say zis is my home, zen I live here, not at za school."

"It's a boarding school, darling. That's how it works. You stay there for the school year, and come home on holidays. I thought you understood this. Sacred Heart is the best school in New Orleans." Mama Bea was gentle but firm in her explanation.

"No!" I stomped my foot under the table for emphasis. "I will not go zare. It is not za only school. Bobby Easton, he go to za Isidore Newman school. I will go zare and live here in my home, like you say to me."

I felt fierce at that moment, but a little scared too. My heart was beating hard in my chest, rushing blood through every part of me. It was rare for me to speak my mind to adults, having trained myself to always guard my thoughts. But a power coursed through me I wasn't willing to let go of.

Bill leaned forward, his elbows resting on the table, hands clasped in front of him, and he stared at me for a while, shaking his head. Then he laughed.

"Did you just stomp your foot at me, Chère?"

With feigned shame, I had the grace to lower my eyes.

"I don't believe I've ever seen this side of you before," he said, still laughing.

"You say I must be myself. V*oilà! C'est moi,"* I said, throwing my hands in the air.

"Beau. You can't possibly be considering this," Mama Bea said.

"Well, Mama, I can't fault her logic. We both told her this was her home, and so it is. I guess we'll have to make other school arrangements. From what I understand, Désirée, it will disappoint Sister Mary Agnes to hear you won't be attending Sacred Heart next term." He had a funny look on his face, like he had a secret or something.

"Why would she care?" I asked them both. Bill's arched eyebrows offered no clarity whatsoever.

Mama Bea looked at me with her arms crossed and her head shaking like she didn't quite know what to do with me. "Sister Mary Agnes called first thing this morning, Désirée, to give me the news about your test. Apparently, they gave you the wrong test. The test you took was the ninth-grade entrance examination, and Sister Mary Agnes was very pleased to report you passed with a score of 91.5%. Quite a remarkable feat for a thirteen-year-old."

"What does zis mean? Must I take za correct test?" This turn of events confused me.

"No, Chère. What it means is you're a lot smarter than people expected. You'll go to the ninth grade in any school you choose," Bill said, a big smile lighting his face.

"Oh, zis is good. I will go to school wiz Bobby, and I live here." Pleased and relieved at how this first problem turned out, I knew the other one was going to be trickier.

"What am I going to tell people when they ask why I'm not sending her to Sacred Heart?" Mama Bea asked, her eyes rolling up to the ceiling.

"Well, Mama, you can tell them you have a willful girl on your hands and a son who wants to indulge her."

Mama Bea relented with a sigh, agreeing to call the Isidore Newman school as soon as she broke the news to Sister Mary Agnes. Their talk turned to business during the rest of the meal, so I waited until I could speak with Bill alone.

When we finished eating, I helped Miss Laila clear the table while Mama Bea retreated to her study to settle the details of my education. Bill remained seated, drinking coffee and smoking a cigarette while he read the morning paper. When I came back in to put things away in the sideboard, he reached out and took my hand.

"I can tell you're holding onto something else, Chère. You're biting the inside of your lip, which is a sure sign your brain is working overtime. Let's go out on the porch to sit and talk for a while. It's been far too long since you and I had a good long conversation. Would that be alright with you?" he asked, always giving me the option to refuse.

"Okay, Bill." It was what I longed for, but I was nervous about what to say.

Still holding my hand, he stood up to lead me out onto the front porch, where a warm breeze gently blew through the old oaks shading the front of the house. We sat together on the big porch swing, Bill on one end, me on the other, with my bare feet tucked under me. I leaned back against the pillows, easing into the motion of the swing as Bill extended his long legs out across the floorboards, rocking back and forth with his heels.

"Will you tell me what's bothering you?" he asked, now speaking in French. When I didn't answer with more than a shrug, he tried a different tactic. "Then tell me about Bobby. What's he like? He was just a kid the last time I saw him."

"Bobby is nice," I said. "He's funny and smart. He likes baseball, and he builds things in his workshop."

"What sort of things?"

"Models of boats and airplanes. But mostly, he builds small rockets that he tests by the river. He wants to be an engineer and build spaceships that will go to the moon." I liked Bobby. He had been the best part of the past two months, making my transition into my new life a lot easier than it might have been otherwise.

"It sounds like you've made a good friend, Chère. I'd like to get to know him. Would that be alright with you?"

I wondered why he was being so cautious with me, but then realized I was doing the same with him. It had been almost nine months since we spent time together. The terrifying three-day journey from Paris to New Orleans didn't count.

"Of course, Bill."

I needed to cut through the tension building between us, so I took a chance to broach the touchy subject. "Tell me about Charlotte Bentley."

"Ah, there's the girl I remember. Is that what's bothering you, Chère?"

"Are you going to tell me about her?" I persisted, nudging the side of his leg with my foot.

"Yes, Désirée. I'll tell you anything you want to know," he said, capturing my foot in his hand. His touch wasn't forceful, but he held my foot almost like a question, as if he'd instantly release me should I even think of pulling away from him, which I never would.

"Tell me," I said, wiggling my toes.

He placed my foot on his thigh, resting his hand over it, lightly running his fingers down the side, back and forth in a gentle caress. Then he told me about Charlotte, how he'd known her since he and Carson were in grade school. He never paid much attention to her, being a few years older, until one time he came home from college for the holidays and ran into her at a party.

"We'd go out whenever I was home. It was easy, and Charlotte was fun to be with. Then Pops died, and when the war started, I went into the military. We've only seen each other a few times since then."

"My friend Evelyn told me she heard a rumor that you and Charlotte are secretly engaged and will get married when the war is over. Is that true?" Surprised that I asked it out loud, my stomach flipped nervously as I waited for his answer.

Bill took a full breath, then let it out with a low humming sound from deep in his chest, his closed eyes sheltering his thoughts. When he opened them, all I could see was the same wide-open honesty I'd known with him from the beginning.

"No, Désirée. That is a rumor, nothing more. I'm not ready to marry anyone right now," he said, gently rubbing my foot, then he gave it a gentle squeeze.

"But the truth of the matter is, the Bentleys and Marchands have known each other for a long time. My father and Carson's father had business dealings over the years and there was talk of a family/business merger between Charlotte and me, mostly coming from the Bentleys' side of things. When Pops died, and the war started, everything changed for me."

"I think she's in love with you." I wondered if he would tell me how he felt about her.

"Charlotte is in love with the idea of me, who she thinks I am. She doesn't know who I really am."

"Are you going to tell her?"

"Who I am? No, Chère." He shook his head with a deep sigh. "Charlotte isn't the kind of woman who'd understand something like that. I'll tell her I'm not ready for marriage and she'll get bored waiting. Carson won't be happy. He's been pushing hard for Charlotte and me to get together since his father died. I'll have to make it up to him somehow." He rocked his heels harder, pushing the swing back and forth, then slowed the motion down to a gentle glide.

"Have I eased your curious mind, Chère?" he asked, steel-blue eyes capturing mine.

"Hmm, for now," I said, unwilling to look away.

"I seem to recall I promised you I'd make up for all this when I got home. Have you thought of anything you'd like to do?"

"Yes."

"Alright, let's have it."

"First, I want to go to supper at Antoine's, and I want to visit their kitchen while we're there." I hadn't been inside a big restaurant kitchen in over a year and a half. Mama Mia's tiny kitchen didn't count.

"Antoine's, is it? Well, I think I can arrange something. You're going to have to get a new dress. You can't very well go to supper in cropped pants, a summer top, and bare feet." He smiled, squeezing my foot again and tickling the bottom. I made a half-hearted attempt to pull away, but he held firm. "Anything else?"

"I would like a garden of my own. A kitchen garden like I had at home." Saying it out loud felt childish, but I longed for a place where I could grow things again and get my hands in the dirt.

"A garden, huh? Well, you have this entire property; you can have as big a garden as you want. Have you thought about where you want it? What you want to grow?"

"Yes. I have a plan, but I was waiting to ask your permission."

"You don't need my permission for something like this, Chère. I told you this would be your home, and I meant it. Will you let me help you make it? Can it be our garden? I don't know much about growing things, but I've got a strong back, and I know how to shovel dirt." He looked at me and smiled, still giving me a choice: include him or not.

There was no doubt in my mind I'd always want him close.

"Oh yes. It will be our garden, Bill. I will grow herbs and garlic and chives. And I will cook for you with all the things I grow. Yes, I like this plan." For the first time since I'd arrived, I felt truly happy.

"I like it too, Chère." He leaned his head back against the swing, his eyes closed, face relaxed, just breathing in and out with the motion of the swing.

"This is nice, being here with you. There's no place on Earth I'd rather be than right here on this swing," he said, his warm hand still holding my foot.

Sitting on that swing with him was the only place I wanted to be. I could have stayed there forever.

# Chapter 9

## *Paying respects*

"How about you and I go visit with your friend Bobby after breakfast?" Bill suggested the following morning. "I'd like to pay my respects to his mother while we're there."

"Jane has taken John's loss very hard, Beau," Mama Bea explained. "Most of the time, she sits waiting for his return. She hasn't accepted his death."

I'd been around Mrs. Easton a few times but avoided her whenever possible. She always seemed to be agitated whenever we talked. "Where is John? Why isn't he here with you?" she would ask me, her voice rising with frustration. My accent seemed to disturb her, apparently reminding her of John, who'd gone to France and not returned. I usually stayed out of her sight. Being around her made me sad because she always seemed to forget about Bobby, her other son who was right in front of her.

"For some, it's too hard to accept, Mama. The war denied them the last goodbye," Bill said, staring out the window, a faraway look in his eyes that spoke of lost friends.

"I know you'll be gentle with her, son," Mama Bea said. "By the way, we're going to need a birth certificate for the school. Sister Mary Agnes has agreed to send Désirée's test results to the Isidore Newman registrar, though I'll need to send Sacred Heart a hefty donation. Are you sure we're doing the right thing, Beau?"

My heart stopped beating for a few seconds when I thought of them changing their minds about the school.

Bill's expression was so intense, I thought he might change his mind, but then he let out a long, slow sigh. "No, Mama. I wouldn't say that exactly, but I don't think we can change Désirée's mind about this. We'll figure out a way to make it work. I'll take care of the birth certificate."

I wish I could have read his mind at that moment. A variety of emotions played across his face, from worry to amusement. Even though I saw doubt in his eyes, it didn't appear he would change his mind.

"Zank you, Bill, about za school."

"It's going to be different for you, Chère. You've never gone to a school like that, and I'm worried about how you'll get on with people. It's still a new country for you, and things are different here."

"I know how to make friends. You do not need to worry."

He raised his eyebrows till I thought they'd disappear into his hairline, then he looked down his nose at me. "You seem to forget, Désirée, you're younger than the kids you'll be going to school with, including Bobby Easton. That fact alone gives me cause for concern."

I shrugged, probably even rolled my eyes at him. "I am younger, but my experience is much older. Zis is true, no?"

He closed his eyes and shook his head. "That's what I'm worried about, Chère. Those kids don't know what they're in for. Go get your shoes on while I pull the car out."

"We do not need to drive, Bill. We can go zrough za gate," I explained, thinking the gate between the properties would be the fastest route to Bobby's house.

“I want to put some miles on my car. It’s been sitting idle for too long. Mama, I thought I’d take Désirée up to the lake house to see if everything is alright up there. Have you been up there this summer?” he asked, rising from his chair.

“Haven’t had time, son,” Mama Bea replied, lifting her eyes from the newspaper. “Maybe we can go up for a few days if the weather holds out.”

“That sounds good. We’ll be home in time to get ready for supper. I made reservations for the three of us tonight at the Blue Room. Get your shoes, Désirée. I’ll meet you outside.”

When I went outside, Bill was sitting behind the steering wheel of his car he'd pulled out of the garage. The top was down, and the engine was idling with a low hum. He ran his hands around the steering wheel, stroking it like he was reacquainting himself with an old love. The car’s sleek black body sat close to the ground, and it had beige leather seats and a polished wood dashboard. Bill looked as if he had found his favorite toy.

“What do you think, Chère? Do you like her?” A boyish grin lit his face.

“It is beautiful, but I know nozing about cars. Is it very fast? I remember you say you are a fast car guy.” I loved the way I could playfully tease him about almost anything.

His boyish grin turned devilish. “It is fast, and I am. Hop in, and we’ll go.”

We didn’t have far to go, and just moments later, Bill and I were standing at Bobby Easton’s front door, waiting for someone to answer the doorbell.

“Bobby will be at za park playing baseball wiz his friends,” I said.

“We’ll go there after I pay my respects to his mother,” he said as the door swung open.

Millie Prince, who was the Easton's maid and Miss Laila's daughter, answered the door with a smile that reached from ear to ear when she saw who was calling.

"Why, Mr. William, I didn't expect to see you till this weekend. Mama told me you were back in town for a while. You're looking good, sir. It's good to have you home again. Come in. Mrs. Easton is in the sitting room."

"How are you doing, Millie? How's Bennie?" Bill asked, beaming a smile back at her.

"Oh, he's fine, Mr. William. Still working on the docks with Marcus, as usual. Hello, Miss Désirée," Millie greeted me as an afterthought, but with her usual smile. We'd seen each other nearly every day since Bobby and I became friends.

Millie led us into the sitting room where Mrs. Easton was in her rocking chair, gazing out the garden window, her lap full of forgotten needlework.

"Miss Jane. You have a visitor today, ma'am. Mr. William is here to see you," Millie said, gently patting Mrs. Easton's hand to bring her out of her daydream.

Slowly raising her head, Mrs. Easton stared blankly at Millie for a moment, then her eyes fluttered open when she saw Bill standing in front of her.

"Hello, Mrs. Easton. Do you remember me? I'm Bill Marchand, Miss Bea's son," Bill said.

Her eyes lit up. I'm not sure if it was Bill himself or his Army uniform, but a smile bloomed across her face when she looked up at him. She lifted her hand for him to take.

"Of course, I remember. Bea speaks of you often. It's so nice of you to visit me," she said, fixing her eyes on him, her forehead wrinkling up. It seemed to me she was trying to reconcile his presence in her home.

"Have you brought me news of my son, John? I haven't heard a word in months. Is he alright? Can you tell me when he's coming home?" She looked hopefully into Bill's eyes, her own pleading for answers.

I knew it didn't matter who explained things to her. She'd been told about John's death countless times, but she was unwilling to accept the truth. It was heartbreaking to witness.

Bill answered her in a soft, reassuring voice, giving her hand a gentle squeeze.

"I have no recent information about John, ma'am, but I can tell you he is resting peacefully with his friends and fellow soldiers on the coast of France. He was a good man, a good soldier. You can be proud, ma'am."

"That is so kind of you to say, Major. I *am* proud of my son. John has been the light of my life since the day he was born. I long for the day he comes home to me." She looked up at Bill with pleading eyes and squeezed his hand. "Would you do me a kindness? Would you tell John that his mother misses him and loves him very much?"

Bill patted her hand, then placed it back on her lap. "I will surely do that, ma'am, the next time I see him. Thank you for letting us visit with you today, Mrs. Easton. It was nice seeing you again. Désirée and I are going to go find your other son, Bobby, so I can pay my respects to him, too."

Only then did Mrs. Easton realize I was there. I'd been standing just outside the room, not wanting to upset her while Bill was visiting. She stared at me like she couldn't quite place who I was, then Millie stepped in.

"This is Miss Désirée, ma'am. You remember her, Miss Jane. She's Mr. Bobby's friend, who lives with Miss Bea," Millie explained, not for the first time.

"Oh, yes... I don't know where Robert Jr. is right now. I suppose he'll be home soon," Mrs. Easton said with a confused look on her face. Then she drifted back into her daydream, her eyes losing focus on anything but what was in her mind.

"Don't pay her no never mind, Mr. William," Millie said as she walked us to the door. "She'll be fine. I'm taking real good care of her. Mr. Bobby is down at the park with his friends."

"I know you're doing right by her, Millie. Thank you. Give my best to Bennie. We'll see you both this weekend," Bill said.

When we got back in the car, Bill sat there for a minute, just breathing heavily and shaking his head. "Let's go find the forgotten son, Chère."

Bill drove to the park, then circled around by the river to the baseball field. He parked under a line of trees edging the field where some boys were throwing a ball back and forth. When we pulled into the parking space, the boys all stopped to stare.

"Is that your friend Bobby over there?" Bill asked.

"Yes, zat is Bobby and his friends." I got out and waved to Bobby, who ran over with the other boys.

"Hey, Désirée. I didn't think I'd see you today. You must be Major Marchand, sir. Millie told me you were home." He was looking up at Bill, his eyes sparkling with excitement and admiration.

"Major Bill Marchand, at your service, son. You can call me Bill, though. It looks like you boys are getting ready to play a game. Got enough players?"

Bobby's eyes lit up even brighter. "We were supposed to play another team, but they didn't show, so we're gonna play Home Run Baseball. Do you know it?"

Bobby's friends were walking around Bill's car, admiring every detail from front to back. Jimmy Wilcox whistled loud and long, running his hand over the curved fender. "Man, this is a nice car. Don't think I've ever seen one like this before. What is it?" he asked.

Bill grinned, clearly proud of his favorite toy. "You probably haven't. There aren't many in the States. This is a '37 Jaguar SS 100 3½ Liter Roadster, one of the last ones made. She's sweet, isn't she?"

"Yes sir, she surely is," Jimmy replied, whistling again.

"Well, if one of you boys has an extra glove, I'd be happy to play a few innings with you. I used to play a little ball... back in the day," Bill offered.

"Sure, that'd be great, Major, I mean Bill. I've got an extra glove." This came from Eddie Berg, who was clearly more impressed with Bill than with the car.

I noticed most boys were in awe of any military man, officers especially, and Bill looked impressive in his summer uniform.

Bill removed his jacket and laid it across the seatback, then tossed his hat onto the seat.

"Is it alright with you if I play a few innings with the boys, Chère?"

"*Bien sûr*. I will watch." I settled on the grass under the trees, admiring them as they took the field, Bill standing nearly a head taller than the rest.

In Home Run baseball, each player takes a turn at bat, getting three pitches to make a hit good enough to get around the bases for a home run. The rest of the players cover the outfield and bases, pitch or catch behind home plate. Bill took the third base position while Bobby pitched to Jimmy, who was the first to bat.

Bobby's first two pitches became strikes, but the third was a ground ball running between second and third base. Bill ran up, scooping the ball into his glove, then threw it quickly to the first baseman, getting it there two steps before Jimmy's foot hit the bag. Jimmy was out. Then everybody shifted their positions except Bobby, who they all preferred as the pitcher. Bill went behind home plate to be the catcher, and Sam, who'd been the catcher, was up to bat.

Bill squatted behind the plate, out of range of Sam's swing, waiting for the pitch with his glove raised in front of him. Bobby set up his pitch and then let loose the ball, sending it whizzing toward Bill's glove. Smack! The ball hit the glove the instant Sam swung the bat and missed.

"Keep your eye on the ball, Sam," Bill reminded him.

Two more pitches, another strike and the last ending in a foul ball caught by Jimmy. Sam was out. Then it was Bill's turn to bat.

He grabbed the bat, running his hand down the length of it, then took a handful of dirt, rubbing his hands together before gripping hard to the base of the bat. After taking a couple of practice swings, he stepped up to the plate with the bat resting casually across his right shoulder. He stood straight as a tree, then looked over his left shoulder at Bobby, who'd been waiting on the mound, the ball clutched tightly in his glove. Bill leaned over the plate, crouching down a bit, then raised the bat from his shoulder.

Bobby let loose with his first pitch and when it crossed the plate, Bill stepped back, letting it pass without taking a swing. Strike one. Then he stepped back to the plate. The next pitch became strike two, a foul ball off the third baseline. The last pitch flew hard and fast, a low outside curveball, but Bill was ready for it. He hit a bouncing line drive down the first-base line, too quick for Sam to snag as it went by. Bill dropped the bat and ran like the devil himself was after him. He was rounding third when Bobby got the ball and threw it to Eddie at home plate, blocking Bill's victory. Bill slowed his pace as he got to Eddie, who tagged him out with the ball as he passed.

"You got me fair and square," Bill said, giving Eddie a pat on the back as he went by.

A car pulled up a few minutes later. It was Evelyn's older brother, Randall, with Evelyn and a friend of hers. When they got out, they all stood around Bill's car admiring it, but then Evelyn saw me sitting under the trees and came over.

"Oh, hi, Désirée. I'm glad you're here today. This is my friend, Rose. She goes to Sacred Heart, too. Rose, this is Désirée, the girl I told you about, the one who speaks French."

"Nice to meet you, Désirée," Rose said shyly. She had a sweet face, heart-shaped, with full rosy lips.

"*Enchanté*, Rose."

"Doesn't she have the cutest accent you ever heard?" Evelyn asked as they sat down next to me.

"Ahh. I must speak better so I will not be so different," I said. Then I realized I had to tell her about school and wasn't sure how she would take the news.

"Evie, I must tell you somezing," I began, but then Randall came up to us.

"God, that's a beautiful car. Whose is it?" he asked.

"It belong to Major Marchand. He is playing baseball wiz Bobby." I pointed to Bill as Randall grabbed his glove and ran down to join them.

Evelyn scanned the field. "Oh, my God. Is that really him? You have to tell me everything. Is he as handsome as they say? Is he nice? Has he said anything about... you know what?"

"Yes, it is him," I said with a shrug. I knew Evelyn wanted answers to all her questions, but I tried to keep it as simple as I could.

"He is very kind, but he is only here a few days. I have heard nozing. Evie, I must tell you somezing else."

"Oh, I forgot. How did you do on the test? You took it last Friday, right? Have you found out what grade you're going into?"

"Yes. I will go to grade nine."

"What!?"

"Yes. Zay give to me za test for grade nine. I pass."

"That's great! You and I will be in the same grade now. Maybe they'll even let us room together. That would be spectacular. Don't you think?"

"I am sorry Evie, but I will not go to za Sacred Heart school. I will go to a different school."

She looked totally confused; her face all wrinkled up and frowning. "What do you mean you're not going to Sacred Heart? You said you passed the test."

"Yes, but I do not want to live in za school. I want to live in my new home, wiz Mrs. Marchand, not at za school. Zat would be too hard for me. *Désolée*. I am sorry, Evie."

Evelyn huffed out a breath, pushing out her lower lip in a big pout, her eyes squinting at me. "Well, I can't say I'm not disappointed because I am. I was looking forward to introducing you to all the girls at school. And I can't say I'm not jealous because I'm that too. No one wants to go to boarding school, but most of us don't have a choice in the matter. My parents would never let me decide something like that. I've said it before, and I'll say it again: you are so lucky, Désirée. What school are you going to?"

"I will go to za Newman school wiz Bobby. It is close to Sacred Heart."

"*And* you get to go to school with boys. You are the luckiest girl I know."

"Zank you for your help wiz my test, Evie. Maybe when za school start we can talk on za telephone to practice your French? Is zis possible?" I hoped we could stay connected once school started.

"Well, that's a good idea. We do get to make phone calls, and I'm sure Sister Mary Agnes will let me call once or twice a week if it's for French study." Then she saw Bill and Bobby walking up and quickly whispered, "You just have to introduce me to him... please."

"*Bien sûr, mon amie,*" I replied, knowing the French would appease her.

"Hi, Evelyn. Hi, Rose," Bobby said, dropping his glove and wiping his hands down his pant legs. Bill shook down his own pant legs and rolled down his sleeves as they walked up.

"Bill, zis is Evelyn and Rose. My friends, I present Major Bill Marchand," I said, then I sat back to watch the expressions dance across both girls' faces. It wasn't hard to understand their reaction to him. I was just as captivated. Bill was a handsome man and genuinely charming, especially in the eyes of a young girl like Evelyn, who sat there, suddenly speechless.

"Ladies, it's nice meeting you both. And Miss Evelyn, thank you for helping Désirée prepare for that test. It was very kind," he said, beaming a big smile at her, which I'm sure made her heart flutter. It always did mine.

"If you'll excuse us, ladies, Désirée and I have a road trip to complete before supper. It was a pleasure meeting you," Bill said as he helped me to my feet. "May I have a word with you, Bobby?"

"Yes sir, Major," Bobby said, following us to the car.

"Bobby, you're gonna have to start calling me Bill unless you want me to call you Mr. Easton, and that won't do at all if we're gonna be friends," Bill said, reaching for his jacket and hat.

"Okay... Bill."

"Alright, then. Bobby, it appears our girl here has exceeded expectations on that test you helped her with. Why don't you tell him, Désirée?" he said, looking at me with an arched brow.

I rolled my eyes at Bill, then smiled at Bobby. "I pass za test and now will go to grade nine, at za Isidore Newman school."

"What? You're not going to Sacred Heart? Did you say ninth grade?" Bobby asked, his face a picture of amazement. I shrugged my response.

"That's right, Bobby. The nuns gave her the ninth-grade entrance exam by mistake, and she passed with a high mark. Désirée has decided she doesn't want to go to boarding school, so we're enrolling her in Isidore Newman. She'll be going to school with you."

Bobby stared at me, shaking his head like he couldn't quite believe his ears.

"Dang. I knew you were smart," Bobby said, his eyes wide with curiosity. "I never met anyone who could read a book as fast as you and then remember what they read the way you can. Wow! We're starting high school together, Désirée. That'll be great!"

"I'm glad to hear that, Bobby. Maybe I can come by your place tomorrow and see your workshop. We can talk more about this then. Thanks for letting me step into your game. It was fun. I'd like to do it again sometime," Bill said, reaching out to shake Bobby's hand.

"Sure, Bill. Any time. I'll be in my workshop after breakfast tomorrow if you want to come by. See you then. Good to meet you. Bye, Désirée," Bobby said, stepping away from the car.

Bill got in and started the engine, letting it settle into a steady hum.

"Goodbye, Bobby," I said, then I called out to Evelyn. "*Au revoir*, Evie. *Merci beaucoup.*" She just sat there staring at Bill and me, envy written all over her face.

"We'll see you tomorrow, Bobby," Bill said as he pulled the car away, raising his hand in farewell.

# Chapter 10

## *An ordinary girl to watch over*

We stopped at a filling station on the eastern outskirts of New Orleans to refresh ourselves and fill the car up with gasoline. Bill bought a couple of bottles of soda pop and a bag of nuts for us to snack on. After he'd paid the attendant, he reached into the glove box to pull out a silk scarf, handing it to me.

"Put this on, Chère, otherwise your hair will get blown around once we get on the highway," he said with a devilish grin.

The woman's scarf wasn't something I could imagine Bill wearing, and I couldn't help but wonder who it belonged to.

*Are you giving me Charlotte's scarf to wear?* I was curious but thought it better not to ask.

I wrapped it around my head to protect my hair from the ravages of the wind and held on tight as Bill pulled out onto the highway, gaining speed as he went.

We headed east, then northeast across the Bayou Sauvage and the eastern end of Lake Pontchartrain, then into the town of Slidell, where Bill took a sharp left heading northwest. The landscape was as flat as a crepe, with few distinguishing features other than the endless shrubby-looking trees growing next to the highway.

As he drove through the countryside, I couldn't help but think about the home I'd left behind. I missed the rolling hills, the vineyards, and the tall green forests of France. I missed my farm, my family, the simple life I should have had.

"You're biting your lip, Chère. Something's bothering you. What's the problem?" Bill asked as he turned south onto a quieter road, slowing his speed.

"I don't know. It's so different here, but it's the same in some ways, and that makes it harder," I said, reverting to my native language.

"What do you mean?"

"The way you and Mama Bea live. You're rich and can do whatever you want. It was the same with Katarina. I did not starve like the rest of France, because Katarina gave me everything. But what she gave me made me different, separated me from the French. I'm afraid the same thing will happen here. Evelyn says I'm the luckiest girl she knows."

"Why do you think she said that?" he asked, turning onto a street running along the north side of the lake.

"Because I live with you and Mama Bea, and because you're letting me decide about the school."

"I doubt Evelyn's lifestyle differs much from yours. She comes from a wealthy family herself, but she is right about the school. There aren't many parents who would allow their thirteen-year-old daughters to decide what school they go to."

Bill turned down a long driveway next to a beautiful white house sitting atop a base of stone pillars. A broad staircase led up to the covered porch encircling the house. Shutters covered all the windows against the weather. It looked as if no one had been there for a long time. He drove around to the back, alongside another staircase, pulled the parking brake and cut the engine.

"Are you doubting your choice?" he asked, a bit of worry in his tone.

"I don't want to be different, Bill. I want to be ordinary, not special. If I go to Bobby's school, will this make me different?"

He reached over to stroke my cheek. "No different from anyone else going there. We're all different in our own way, and that's not a bad thing. Life would be awfully boring if we were all the same... I agreed to let you go to Newman because I believe you'll be happier there. That's all I want, Chère, for you to be happy here."

"Would it be better for you and Mama Bea if I go to boarding school?" I asked, worried that my choice would make things harder for them. I knew my presence alone was a complication.

He shook his head. "No, Désirée. Not if you're unhappy there."

I looked at him for a while, gauging his sincerity and finding only truth in his eyes. Then I took a deep breath and blew it out with a sigh, releasing my doubts.

"Okay, I will go to za Newman school and be an ordinary girl," I said, switching to English.

He stroked my cheek again, a tender smile in his eyes. "You are anything but ordinary, Chère. Let's go in and look around to see if everything is where it should be."

"Is zis your house, too?"

"This is our lake house. We used to come here every summer when it got too hot in the city. Pops and I spent a lot of time out here," he said as we stepped out of the car. "Look around while I check things out, then we'll grab a snack and head back. We've got a supper date tonight."

While he went up the back stairs, I walked to the front of the house, then climbed the front stairs to the covered porch to see the view. The lake was across the street, beyond the grassy parkway bordering it, and it was huge. That vast expanse of flat water extended forever. I knew the city was somewhere on the other side, but from that vantage point, it was completely invisible. And it was quiet. No city noise disturbed the tranquility. I stood on the porch, just taking it all in.

A while later, Bill came out onto the porch to stand behind me. "Do you like it here?"

"Yes. It is beautiful. It feels peaceful, like Papa's farm." The tranquility of the place soothed away any lingering doubts I might have had. It felt like a place I could call home.

"Maybe we can spend some time out here before school starts. Let's lock up and get going."

I followed him through the front door and took a quick look around the living room. Narrow beams of sunlight streamed in along the edges of the closed shutters, dimly lighting a room full of sheet-covered furniture. There was a thin layer of dust covering everything. Apparently, it had been some time since anyone had been there.

"Let's go, Chère. We'll come back," Bill said, taking my hand and leading me out the back door and down to the car.

"It doesn't matter how you wear your hair, Désirée. You're still only thirteen," I told my reflection after attempting several 'grownup' hairstyles I'd seen in magazines. I wanted to look older and more sophisticated for my first supper date with Bill, but it was a silly girl's fantasy. I was thirteen, and there wasn't anything I could do about it.

Blowing out a frustrated breath, I pulled the pins out of the French Twist I'd attempted, letting my blonde waves cascade over my shoulders. After a few strokes of the brush, I secured it up behind my ears with a couple of pretty combs Mama Bea had lent to me. Then a quick pinch to my cheeks and a bit of rouge on my lips finished the look.

"There, that's better. At least you don't look ridiculous trying to appear older than you are."

I chose a full-length peach-colored gown of embroidered chiffon with three-quarter length sleeves and a sweetheart neckline for this special occasion. Unfortunately, I didn't fill it out nearly as much as I would have liked to, but I looked pretty, even to my critical eye.

The different versions of me seemed to peek through the eyes of the girl staring at me in the mirror. No matter how hard I tried to put those versions away and lock them up beyond escape, I was never completely successful. They were always there, reminding me of who I'd been: Désirée Rondeau, Désirée Perot, Désirée Steigler-Lang, Marie Rondeau, and now Désirée Gautier. I wish I could forget them all and start fresh.

"*Be yourself, Désirée,*" Bill and Mama Bea had both told me.

"That's easy for them to say. I'm not sure I know who that is anymore," I told the mirror.

I knew *where* I wanted to be, but the question of who I was, or could be, was something I needed to figure out.

"Are you ready, Chère?" Bill called from the bottom of the stairwell.

"Coming," I said, turning away from the girl in the mirror.

Bill and Mama Bea stood at the bottom of the stairs, dressed up and waiting for me to come down.

My breath caught in my throat when I saw Bill. He was the most handsome man I'd ever seen. Clean-shaven, russet brown wavy hair and piercing deep blue eyes. He wore a dark suit, a crisp white dress shirt with a black tie tucked down behind the front of his dinner jacket, with a white handkerchief peeking above the breast pocket. When he heard me coming, he looked up, then watched as I walked down the stairs. As I reached the bottom, he held out his hand to help me from the last step, his eyes bright and smiling.

"You look beautiful, Chère," he said, lifting my hand to his lips. "Are you ready for supper?"

"*Oui, Je suis prêt*," I said, though I was as nervous as a kitten, or maybe it was giddiness.

"Ladies, our carriage awaits." Bill hooked his arms for Mama Bea and me, and we headed out the door for my first supper date in New Orleans.

Some moments remain forever vividly clear and richly textured with the sounds, tastes, and feelings embedded in the memory. That first supper with Bill and Mama Bea, at the Blue Room in the Roosevelt Hotel, became one of those moments for me, a memory I would re-live over and over in my mind, never tiring of how it makes me feel.

I had eaten in some of the best restaurants in Paris with Katarina and had lived for a year with one of the best chefs in that city, so I had some experience in fine dining. Despite all Bill said about New Orleans cuisine, the level of culinary skill I experienced that night was impressive. From the appetizers to the dessert, every bite was more delicious than the last. I was in heaven, my taste buds deliriously happy.

I spent most of the meal trying to identify the ingredients and preparation technique of each dish served, which amused Mama Bea and Bill. At the end of the meal, the *maître d'* came over to our table to inquire how everything was.

"Everything was excellent, George. Thank you," Bill said, then he looked over at me and winked. "I wonder, would it be alright if my young friend here took a quick peek inside your kitchen? She has a passion for cooking and would like to see how you do things in there."

Taken aback by Bill's request, the man's face displayed a measure of surprise, then curiosity, but he quickly recovered his composure. "Of course, Mr. Marchand. Follow me, Miss, I will show you around."

Bill and I followed him out of the dining room, stopping briefly for Bill to say 'Hello' and 'We'll catch up soon' to a couple of groups as we walked by. The *maître d'* led us through the double swinging doors at the far end of the room, and then we stepped into a totally different environment.

"Stay as long as you like, Mr. Marchand," he said, leading us to a small table that was out of the flow of traffic but from which I could sit and observe the activity.

It felt familiar, a place I understood and wanted to be a part of.

"What fascinates you about all this, Chère?" Bill asked in French after we sat there observing the organized chaos for several minutes.

"I like kitchens, restaurant kitchens especially, and you already know I enjoy cooking. There's music that plays in here. Can't you hear it?"

He laughed, shaking his head. "All I hear are clanging pans and yelling men."

"I hear a kind of symphony. Each person is playing a different instrument, separate but essential. Then, they come together in perfect harmony, creating something beautiful and delicious. I want to learn how they do it."

"I don't see any women in here, Chère. It doesn't feel like a place for a young girl to be."

I wrinkled my forehead at him. "Women have always cooked for men, Bill. I don't see why a restaurant kitchen should be any different. Madame

Brassart at *le Cordon bleu* said we need more women in this profession. I will be one of them."

Bill raised his eyebrows, looking down his nose with a skeptical expression. "Someday, Chère, but you need to be patient. Let's get back to Mama. I can hear actual music starting."

When we returned to the table, Bill ordered a bottle of champagne to celebrate his homecoming and my inclusion into the Marchand family. He even allowed me half a glass, despite Mama Bea's protest. She gave us both a look that spoke loudly of her disapproval of serving alcohol to a young girl.

"This will not become a habit, Désirée, regardless of what you're accustomed to. Is this understood?" She stared at me for a moment, then shifted her steely gaze to Bill, clearly wanting acknowledgment from both of us.

"Yes, ma'am," Bill and I replied in unison.

"Alright then, lift your glasses," she said. "I propose a toast. Here's to the Marchand family, together at long last. And a special welcome to our newest member, Désirée, who has brought an abundance of light back into our lives."

We raised our glasses, clinked them together gently and sipped the delicious champagne, smiling over the rims at each other. Tiny bubbles tickled my nose as I savored the wine, relishing the taste of my home for the first time since arriving in America.

The band started playing something that caught Mama Bea's attention, then Bill stood up, taking her hand. "May I have this dance, Mama?"

She nodded her head as he drew her to her feet, then he led her to the dance floor.

I loved watching them glide so gracefully around the floor to music and lyrics as tender as a son's love for his mother, their devotion to each other so clear, even a blind man could see it.

"Hello, Miss Désirée. What a delightful surprise to see you here," Carson Bentley said as he walked up to our table.

"Hello, Mr. Bentley," I said, quickly securing my Gautier mask firmly in place.

"Call me Carson. You and I should be friends. I'll just keep you company while Bill's cutting a rug with his mother."

He sat down in the seat Bill vacated, then scooted over closer, resting his arm across the back of my chair.

"Are you enjoying yourself in New Orleans, Désirée?"

I wasn't sure why, but I felt uncomfortable with him sitting so close to me, though I had no reason to distrust him. Carson was Bill's closest friend, but he was also Charlotte's brother. I subtly shifted on the chair, turning to face him straight on so he wouldn't be touching me.

"It is nice. Not as pretty as Montreal, but za food is delicious," I said as the music ended.

Bill led Mama Bea back to the table with a look on his face I couldn't quite decipher.

"Good evening, Carson. I didn't expect to see you tonight," Bill said with a chill in his voice.

"Well, I saw this lovely young thing sitting here all alone, so I thought I'd keep her company while you and Miss Bea were dancing," Carson explained, nodding to Mama Bea as she resumed her seat. "I'm meeting Joe Barone for drinks later, Bill. Maybe you can join us. I'd like to get your take on the man and his ideas for expansion. I'd consider it a favor."

There appeared to be a silent struggle between them, but evidently, Bill had no intention of letting it interrupt his evening.

"I'm out with my ladies tonight, Carson. We can talk about this later," he said, then he turned to me. "Désirée, I believe this is our song." He held out his hand for mine, then led me onto the dance floor.

"I do not know how to dance, Bill," I whispered to him, not wanting to make a fool of myself in front of the entire room.

"Don't you worry about a thing, Chère. Just follow my lead and I won't let you falter," he said, twirling me around once, then slipping his right hand around my back and gently pulling me closer.

With my hand in his, my other hand resting on his shoulder, and the gentle pressure of his hand on my back, Bill guided me through the steps of our first dance to a tune I would never forget.

*'There's a somebody I'm longing to see.*
*I hope that he turns out to be,*
*Someone to watch over me...'*

It had been a perfect evening. Not even the sudden appearance of Charlotte Bentley as we were walking through the hotel lobby could disturb my happiness.

"Bill, darling," Charlotte called out from across the lobby, and then she hurried over before we passed by. She took hold of Bill's available arm—I had hold of the other—then leaned in to kiss him on the cheek. "Carson said you might join us later. Please, darling, rescue me from the boredom of business discussions," she said, pouting and batting her eyes at him. From the look on her face, she fully expected his compliance.

Bill considered her for a moment. "You look lovely tonight, Charlotte. I'm sure you'll be fine. If you'll excuse us, we were on our way out. We'll talk soon."

I didn't turn around to catch her reaction as we walked away, but I could feel her staring at our backs as we exited the hotel.

Bill hadn't completely ignored Charlotte, but his greeting wasn't very warm either. So, a bit of hope bloomed inside me.

*Maybe what he told me about their relationship is true.*

I breathed a sigh of relief.

On the way home, I relaxed in the backseat, closed my eyes and dreamily re-lived each moment of the day. Not since I was little could I recall a time when I'd felt so content. I had a home now and a family, people who accepted me and wanted me in their lives. I hoped it would last, hoped this happy feeling would drown out every fear and doubt in my mind, but experience had taught me that time changes everything, no matter how much I wished it didn't.

Bill and Mama Bea talked quietly as Bill drove home, but I heard a serious undertone in their voices. My ears perked up when I heard who they were talking about.

"Carson's been pushing for a vote on his pending contracts. It seems his ultimate goal is a merger with Marchand Industries. Charles and Bertram won't make a move until they talk to you, Beau." Mama Bea sounded annoyed by Carson, and I wondered why.

"I'm not on the board, Mama, and it's not up to me what contracts the company enters into," Bill said, sounding frustrated by the subject.

"But you are William Marchand's son and a major stockholder in this firm. That carries a lot of weight. They will respect your opinion, Beau. You know Carson Bentley better than all of us. You know what kind of man he is. I think it would be a good idea for you to meet this Joe Barone and find out who he is. From what Bertram tells me, Mr. Barone has been sniffing around Bentley Company for the past six months. Carson has been struggling to keep his father's business together, apparently hoping these contracts with Marchand Industries will go through."

"Alright, Mother. I'll go back later and meet Mr. Barone and take his measure. When is the board meeting?" Bill blew out a heavy breath. He would do what she asked, but reluctantly.

"Friday morning at ten. They would like you to attend, Beau."

Another heavy sigh from Bill. "You can tell Charles and Uncle Bertram that I'll meet them Friday at 9:30 to give them my opinion."

I could sense we were close to home. The feel of the road and the sounds of the traffic were smoother and lighter, the deeper into the Garden District we traveled. I stretched and let out a sigh to signal my awareness.

"You awake back there, Chère? We're almost home."

"Get ready for bed, Désirée. It's late," Mama Bea said as we climbed the stairs together. Bill had stepped into her study when we got home, saying he needed to make a phone call.

"Yes, ma'am," I said. "Zank you, Mama Bea, for everyzing. For being my new family. Zank you." I wanted her to know I was grateful for what they'd given me.

"Oh darling, I'm the one who should thank you. You've given me more than you can know." She put her arms around me, placing a tender kiss on my cheek. "Be sure to hang up your clothes and brush your teeth. I'll be in to say goodnight later."

After following her instructions, I went out onto the gallery to re-live those special moments, the music and lyrics of 'our song' still playing in my head. I didn't want to let any of it go yet.

"Did you have fun tonight, Chère?" Bill asked, joining me on the moonlit gallery. He leaned against the railing, smoking a cigarette and watching me with a gentle smile curling the corners of his mouth.

"Yes. Zank you, Bill. It is a special memory."

"Someday, I hope you'll explain to me how you do it. How you keep it all sorted in your head." His expression had turned into one of curiosity and maybe a little admiration for my mental acuity.

I shrugged, pushing out my lips with a breath. "It is easy. A game Papa teach me long ago," I said, visualizing the game of cataloging and storing everything away. "He say to always end za day wiz an uncluttered mind."

Bill hadn't changed his clothes, which meant his evening wasn't complete. "You are going out again? To see Charlotte?"

"Not to see Charlotte, but she'll be there. I've got to meet Carson and a friend of his. It's a business meeting, Chère, but I won't be out long. I'll be here in the morning. Are you going to make me breakfast? Maybe try some of those new culinary skills you learned tonight?" he teased, deftly changing the subject.

"Zat food is not for breakfast, Bill. Zat is supper food."

"Well, if we're being traditional, then I like my eggs over easy, and prefer ham to bacon."

I pursed my lips and shook my head at him. "So ordinary. Not much of a challenge."

He shook his head and smiled. "You're the challenge, Chère."

I watched him for a while, wondering what he meant, what he was thinking. He finished the cigarette, then stubbed it out in the ashtray, apparently ready to leave.

"Bill?" I spoke before he could walk away.

"Yes, Désirée."

"Is zat what you zink?"

"What's that, Chère?" His brow furrowed a bit.

"Zat I need someone to watch over me?"

He didn't reply right away. He just stood there looking at me, his eyes tender and knowing. I could have bathed in that look forever, never needing his answer.

"You do, Chère, and I was hoping I could have the job for a while. If that's alright with you." He looked at me for a minute longer, then leaned down to kiss my cheek.

"Goodnight, Désirée. Sweet dreams. I'll see you in the morning."

# Chapter 11

## *What a difference a day makes*

### August 9, 1945

I got up early to execute the menu I planned the night before: toasted bread piled with thin slices of fried ham nesting two poached eggs covered with a hollandaise sauce and a sprinkle of chopped chives. A simple fruit compote rounded off the menu. Everything was almost ready by the time Miss Laila and Mr. Jefferies arrived.

"Miss Dezrae, whatcha doin?" Miss Laila asked, a grin lighting her face as she looked around the kitchen at the mess I made.

"I make za breakfast for Bill and Mama Bea, to zank zem for my new family. You want I make you some? You are my family, too. I will make you some." I scooped the last two poached eggs from the pot and finished plating the dish.

"No need, Miss Dezrae. We already ate. But thank you kindly for thinkin' of us. We're both real happy you're here. You put the light back in Miss Bea's eyes and I thank the Good Lord every day that He sent you here," she said, reaching over to stroke my cheek.

"You go call them down to breakfast, sugah, and I'll get this on the table."

"Hmm. What's this, Chère?" Bill asked, wide-eyed, as he examined the plate in front of him.

"Ham and eggs, but not so ordinary," I said, unable to stifle my smile.

"It looks good, Chère. Thank you," he said with a smile in his eyes.

"*Bon appétit.*" I watched anxiously as he sliced into the egg, the golden center oozing onto the ham and bread beneath. Then he captured the first bite on his fork and brought it to his mouth. I held my breath for his reaction.

"Mm, that is tasty," he said, licking his lips. "No grits, Chère? Laila usually has a pot of grits for me in the morning."

"Désirée isn't fond of grits, Beau," Mama Bea said as she sliced into her own serving.

"No? Well, you'd best learn, Chère. You've got the best teacher right here. Laila makes the best shrimp and grits in New Orleans. It's one of my favorite dishes. If you ask her nicely, she'll probably teach you how it's done." His eyes teased me, but I could tell he enjoyed what I made.

"That's right, Mr. William. I'll teach her all about Louisiana cookin', tho I tell ya, sir, she's already taught me a few things. Miss Dezrae is right handy in the kitchen," Miss Laila said as she breezed through the dining room, pouring fresh coffee for all of us.

"Okay, Bill. I will learn to make za shrimp and grits for you. And perhaps I will even learn to love zem like a souzern girl." That earned me two generous smiles.

As we ate in silence, I relished the satisfaction of knowing I made them something unusual and delicious.

"What did you find out about Joe Barone, Beau? You came in late last night," Mama Bea asked looking across the table at Bill, clearly seeking answers to the concerns she voiced the night before.

Bill took a deep breath, releasing it with a sigh as he closed his eyes. When he answered, his face looked tired, sad maybe, and I wondered why.

*Did you break the news to Charlotte? Is that why you're sad?*

"Barone isn't anyone we want to get involved with, Mama. The man throws money around like it's growing in his backyard, but there's the smell of the back street on him. The money isn't his. Someone is backing him, but I don't know who yet. I put in a couple of calls and may know more by the end of the day. I'm meeting Carson for lunch. He asked me to go by the warehouse and have a look around."

"I'm concerned this situation with the Bentleys could get messy, Beau," Mama Bea warned.

*Messy? What does she mean?*

"I know, Mother. That's what I'm trying to avoid. What the hell happened that made Carson think getting into bed with a man like Barone would be a good idea? Last I heard, Bentley Company was solid as a rock."

"You've been out of touch for a while, Beau. The war has taken its toll on everyone, although I suspect the Bentleys are suffering more from an extravagant lifestyle than anything else," Mama Bea said. "Apparently, Clayton Bentley neglected to teach Carson good sense. Use yours wisely, son."

They stared across the table at each other for a while, silently communicating something they either didn't need to verbalize or didn't want me to know. It was hard to tell which.

Mama Bea turned her attention to me after Bill gave her a barely perceptible nod.

"Désirée, I'd like you to write a letter to Mr. Henson, the principal of Isidore Newman. It should clearly state your desire to attend his school and your reasons for choosing Newman. You should also include what you hope to accomplish there. A few brief paragraphs will suffice. I would like to see a draft by the end of the day, dear. You and I have an appointment with Mr. Henson tomorrow at 4 o'clock."

Mama Bea gave me one of her looks that seemed to say if I wanted to go to Isidore Newman, I would have to take part in my successful acceptance into it. She would not do everything. She was always challenging me, but I didn't really mind.

I thought about it for half a second, drafting the letter in my head before responding.

"*Bien sûr*, Mama Bea. But did you like za breakfast?"

She snorted through her nose. "Yes, darling, thank you. It was delicious. I will need to start walking to class from now on so I can work off the extra weight I will undoubtedly be putting on. You go on and do your chores now. Have you finished the book report yet?"

'Little Women' by Louisa May Alcott was the book she was referring to, the latest in a series of books she assigned me to read once she realized I had read Alexander Dumas successfully. my assignment was to write a brief report about each book. She handed me the book last Friday when I got home from taking the test, but between being upset about boarding school, the atomic bomb dropping, and then Bill coming home, I hadn't even opened it.

"No, ma'am. I will do it today," I said, releasing a sigh. I hoped to spend more time with Bill, but that didn't seem to be on his agenda.

"Procrastination is not a study habit you should adopt, Désirée. When school starts, you will have daily homework in all your classes. You should develop good study habits now." Her look and the tone of her voice were enough to stifle any remark I might have made.

Bill chuckled over his coffee cup, the corners of his mouth twitching. "I never could get away with not doing my homework, Chère. That's part of living with a teacher. Education is always her priority. You best get it done before she asks for it again. Her second request usually earned me extra work."

"The extra work didn't do you any harm, Beau. It won't do her any either," Mama Bea said.

"I will do it, Mama Bea," I assured her as I cleared the table. "Will you be home for supper, Bill?" I hoped his answer would be yes. The thought of him spending more time around Charlotte felt like a huge stone in the pit of my stomach.

"So far, that's the plan. Right now, I'm going to talk with Bobby Easton, then I'm off to meet Carson. I'll see you both later. Thanks for breakfast, Chère," Bill said, rising from the table and kissing both of us on the cheek.

The phone rang, then Mr. Jefferies popped his head into the dining room. "Mr. William, there's a call for you from a Mr. Terrebonne. You want me to bring the phone in here?"

"No thanks, Jacob. I'll take it in Mama's study." Bill and Mama Bea passed another look between them I wished I could decipher.

Apparently, I was merely a child and could not be privy to adult information. It was so frustrating, and I knew it wouldn't be easy to get them to tell me things I thought I needed to know.

I spent most of my day reading about Jo, Beth, Meg, and Amy, and wondering if they accurately represented what northern girls were really like during the Civil War. I imagined southern girls would probably have behaved similarly under the same economic circumstances. Poverty makes people grateful for what they have, no matter the politics.

By the end of the story, they all married the men they loved and lived happily ever after, except for Beth, who died. Ordinary girls living ordinary lives, their fates dictated more by fortune and social status than by purposeful design, despite their intentions.

It left me wondering how much had really changed since then, if Evelyn Duret was an example of a modern southern girl. She was always talking about getting married, as if that were the sole purpose of women; to marry, preferably someone wealthy, and then have children. That was not what I wanted.

I finished the book report, then started on the letter to the principal.

*Dear Mr. Henson,*

*I would like to attend Isidore Newman school because my friend, Bobby Easton, goes to school there. He tells me Newman is a very good school. I hope you will allow me to join him.*

*My goal for the future is to become a professional chef and to have my own restaurant where I will make delicious food for everyone.*

*Yours truly,*

*Désirée*

I figured that summed it up—short and to the point. Maybe if I had met him, I'd have more to say, but it felt strange writing a letter to a man I knew nothing about, so I kept it simple. Mama Bea would have me change it, anyway. She loved her red pen.

"Désirée," Mama Bea looked up over the rim of her glasses, shifting her eyes between me and the pages I handed her. "Do I understand you correctly? You believe the March girls settled down and had happy lives because of social and economic pressures."

I might have rolled my eyes, but I heard her clear her throat, so I answered before she could add anything else.

"What choice did zay have? It was za time, no? Not so good for women zen."

"You are correct, it was not a comfortable time to be a woman or to be poor." She arched her brow, looking at me like she didn't quite know what to do with me.

"And then there's the draft of your letter to Mr. Henson. It appears to be written by a different person than the one who clearly expressed her opinion of Louisa May Alcott. It seems rather simple and brief. Can you explain yourself?"

With my lips pursed, I shrugged. "I not know him to write a letter. I just say za truth. Simple."

She leaned forward, resting her elbows on the desk, and pinched the bridge of her nose above her glasses, her eyes closed and head shaking. I thought she would make me rewrite it, as brief as it was, but she seemed to think better of it.

"Alright, Désirée. Take this stationery and an envelope. Write it again in cursive, and we'll take it with us tomorrow. Perhaps it's best if Mr. Henson gets to know you in person."

She handed me a sheet of her monogrammed stationery and a matching envelope, then reached behind her to the bookshelf, retrieving a book and setting it on the desk in front of me.

"Here is another book I think you'll enjoy. 'A Tree Grows in Brooklyn' by Betty Smith. It's a recent publication about a young girl at the turn of the century."

"Brooklyn is in za norz. I would like to read about girls in za south. Zis book, 'Gone with za Wind' is about a souzern girl, no?" I asked, pointing to the book on the bookshelf. I was eager to get my hands on it. Bobby and Evie told me about the movie, but I hadn't seen it.

"It is. However, I don't think it's an appropriate story for a girl your age."

"Why? Is she a bad girl?"

"No. Misguided, perhaps, but not essentially bad. The story is very rich in detail, but it paints a singular perspective of the time. That is my primary objection to Miss Mitchell's story."

"I would like to read zis book, to hear zis singular perspective of zat time. It is different now. No?" I wasn't sure she would let me read it; the shake of her head and furrowed brow seemed to imply my plea had failed.

Mama Bea let out a sigh of resignation. "Very well, Désirée, you may read it. It might give you a deeper understanding of Southern culture. Read it slowly, dear. Don't race through it as you did with 'Little Women.' Take your time, and if along the way you have questions about what you're reading, please ask them. Run along now. I have work to do."

"Zank you, Mama Bea," I said, snatching the book from the shelf.

"You're welcome, darling."

That night after supper, while Bill and Mama Bea retired to her study to continue their discussion of the upcoming board meeting, I went to my room to dive into Margaret Mitchell's perspective on the south.

The radio played softly in the background, the music pacing the story as I read. Around nine o'clock, an announcement came over the airwaves: President Truman's speech was being broadcast. I put the book aside and sat close to listen.

President Harry S. Truman spoke to America that night, reporting to his citizens what happened during his recent trip to Europe. As he described the devastation he'd seen, I heard the sorrow behind his words and then anger when he spoke of the reparations Germany owed the countries they had destroyed. Germany would have to pay—for all of it.

To me, it sounded eerily familiar, reminding me of De Gaulle's speech on the steps of the Hotel de Ville the day the Allies liberated Paris. It was a deadly call for revenge and retribution, although Truman's words sounded more economical than physical.

His talk turned to the war with Japan, and his tone became angrier and more intentional. He talked about the atomic bomb the Americans dropped on Hiroshima, which he described as a military base. He made it sound like there were only soldiers killed by that bomb. That wasn't true. I looked it up in one of the Encyclopedia Britannica volumes living in Mama Bea's study. It said 350,000 people lived in Hiroshima. I couldn't imagine they all were military.

What he said next chilled me to the bone.

"If Japan does not surrender, bombs will have to be dropped on her war industries and, unfortunately, thousands of civilian lives will be lost. I urge

Japanese civilians to leave industrial cities immediately and save themselves from destruction."

Then he said, "I realize the tragic significance of the atomic bomb."

*Do you really?*

"We have used it against those who attacked us... We have used it in order to shorten the agony of war, in order to save the lives of thousands and thousands of young Americans."

"We shall continue to use it until we completely destroy Japan's power to make war. Only a Japanese surrender will stop us..."

*He's going to do it again! All those people!* It horrified me to hear those words.

Then he talked about the bomb and keeping it out of the hands of America's enemies. That seemed a moot point to me. The genie would never return to the bottle.

What he said at the end struck a different chord, lighting up a dark corner with a glimmer of hope.

"... the worth and dignity of man is not a sentimental aspiration or a vain hope, or a piece of rhetoric. It is the strongest, most creative force now present in this world..."

*I hope you believe that about everyone, not just Americans.*

I found out the following day that even Presidents lie. By the time Mr. Truman made that speech, the bomb had already dropped on Nagasaki, undoubtedly killing tens of thousands of people.

The BBC reported it first, then it spread like wildfire over the airways and through the streets; US Drops Plutonium Bomb on Japan.

I was heartsick thinking about the innocent lives lost or permanently affected by Mr. Truman's decision to drop those bombs. Even at thirteen years old, I understood that war came down to choices, the choices of a few powerful men, and the willingness of others to follow. It didn't seem to me those choices ever considered the human cost, the lives forever altered or destroyed. I knew that cost firsthand.

Later that morning, I stood in line at the local grocery with Miss Laila, cringing at what I was hearing. The bomb and Japan's imminent surrender dominated all conversations around me. Mr. Langenstein was serving the man ahead of us, who seemed to want the entire market to hear his opinion on the subject.

"I hope old Harry drops a few more on them. Wipes every goddamn Jap and their whole damned country off the map. Grab me a couple of those T-bones, George. I'm celebrating tonight."

He looked to be in his late fifties, his face blotchy and red with the rage he felt toward the Japanese. Based on the nodding heads around him, he wasn't alone in his sentiments.

*I don't understand this kind of hate. How can you hate an entire race of people?*

The man took the wrapped package from Mr. Langenstein, then elbowed his way to the door just as a uniformed negro maid was entering. She quickly stepped out of his way, but not before he snarled at her.

"Get out of my way, nigger," he said with a hateful look.

Not one person in the market said anything about that awful remark. Not one.

*I don't understand Americans.*

That afternoon, I sat across from Mr. Henson at the Isidore Newman School with Mama Bea seated on my right and Bill on my left. Mr. Henson read my letter of introduction, then welcomed me.

"From what I see on your test scores, I believe you will fit in nicely here at Isidore Newman, Miss Gautier. We value the individuality of our students and celebrate their intellectual development. Young people are our future, after all. Tell me, Miss Gautier, what kind of world would you create for your generation?"

I hadn't expected such a question, and perhaps if I'd been in a lighter mood, my answer might have been different. As it was, my mood was a mixture of anger, confusion, and sadness. It was difficult sorting through it all, so my response came out without regard to who I was addressing. I just spoke my mind.

"I would have a world where men do not wage war, where zare are no weapons zat will kill zousands all at once, where people do not hate because of how ozer people look or what zay believe. I would have a world where za worth and dignity of every person is more zan a sentimental aspiration, a vain hope, or a piece of rhetoric. Zat is za world I would have."

I lowered my head, clasping my hands in my lap, and waited for his response. When I glanced up, three pairs of eyes were staring at me, making me feel more self-conscious than I already did. Mr. Henson leaned back in his chair, his hands across his middle, and he caught my eyes, holding them for a moment.

"Hmm. Yes, you'll fit in here quite well, Miss Gautier. Welcome to Isidore Newman."

# Chapter 12

## *Lies and Little Boxes*

School would start in a couple of weeks, too soon for me because I knew there would be little time to spend with Bill once it began. As it was, he seemed preoccupied with something, based on the looks he and Mama Bea kept giving each other across the table at Pascal's that night after our meeting at Newman.

Something was going on between them, some worry that had nothing to do with me. At least, I hoped it didn't. But I could feel it: a tension, an anticipation of something. Danger maybe? It was hard to tell. They'd known each other forever and could easily communicate without saying a word.

As we dined on plates of Barbeque Shrimp for Bill, Mama Bea's Veal Piccata, and my Chicken Marsala, very few words passed between us, but an abundance of communication occurred that I was not privy to.

I hated not knowing what was going on and was losing patience with the situation.

Mama Bea took a thoughtful sip of her wine, looking over at me and then at Bill, seeming to decide something. She lowered her glass, then dabbed her napkin to her mouth before neatly folding it into her lap.

"I've informed the university I won't be housing any students this year, or for the foreseeable future. Under the circumstances, I felt it was best to eliminate the ins and outs of a temporary guest. However, I have asked one of my older students to stop by. We will need someone to sit with Désirée on the occasions I'm out. I'd like you both to meet her."

"No one has to sit wiz me. I am not a baby," I said, feeling defiant that they thought I needed a nursemaid.

"Be reasonable, Chère. You're only thirteen," Bill said with a stern look in his eyes.

"Désirée, you're too young to be left alone. There will be occasions on weekends when the Jefferies are with their family, and I have an engagement. Marjorie Chandler is a sweet young woman and an English major. She can assist you in your studies."

"You will be here, Bill. I will not be alone," I said, not having considered the possibility he wouldn't stay with me now that he was home.

The look in his eyes almost broke my heart. I had become a child to him, someone requiring supervision, a responsibility needing a solution. He never treated me that way before, and it stung.

"I won't always be here, Chère. We need to make a plan."

My breath caught in my throat. *Are you leaving me? Again?*

His eyes confirmed my fear.

Later that night, when Bill came in to say goodnight, Scarlet O'Hara and her willful defiance lay open on my lap. I was sitting back on my bed, my knees pulled up with the book propped up against them.

"What am I going to do with you, Chère?" he asked as he came into the room. His tone was light, but the look on his face was serious.

I rolled my eyes at him. "Zare is nozing for you to do, Bill. You have your life, and I will go to school and become Désirée Gautier." Confused and angry, my response sounded surly, even to me.

"*Pourquoi es-tu comme ça*?" he asked, his use of French clearly a bid to get me to talk openly.

"How am I being?" I responded in French.

"Angry with me. Pouting about something... everything."

"Why do you treat me like a baby now? You never did before. I can see the worries and secrets you have with Mama Bea. You don't share these with me because I am only a child to you now." My accusation hit the mark based on the pinched look on his face.

"I'm sorry, Désirée. I don't mean to treat you like a little girl. I'm only trying to protect you from things you shouldn't worry about. I wish you could forget about everything and just..."

"It would be a lot easier if I could, but I never forget anything, Bill. Never." I turned away from him, unwilling to share the conflicting emotions racing through me.

"You said your Papa taught you a game to help you with your thoughts. Could you teach me the game, let me help you sort out your feelings?" he asked, trying to distract me from my frustration, from the hurt that might have escalated our argument further. His reminder of how Papa had always helped me at such stressful times softened my mood.

When he sat down on the bed, he reached out, touching my leg with a question in his touch. "Sometimes, I forget how different you are, how things stay with you that other people never notice. I know you're upset, Chère. Let me help you. Teach me how your Papa helped you."

I closed my eyes, recalling my memory of Papa. The vision filled my mind, replacing the hurt and anger with the feeling of safety that always came with Papa's love.

"It was a game we'd play when he'd come into my room to say goodnight. I was four when I learned to read, and as the new information built up in my mind, I became overwhelmed by it all. Papa sat on my bed one night and taught me the Game of Boxes."

"Papa said, 'Imagine little boxes with lids, *ma petite*, as many as you need. Each box will hold a memory or a new idea. At the end of the day, put everything you've learned away in its box. Clear up the clutter in your mind, so you can sleep and start fresh in the morning.' Papa gave me three small blue boxes to help me visualize them in my mind."

"We would talk about my day, about everything I'd seen and heard, and as we spoke, I'd store each new bit of information away inside a box, inside my mind. When I finished, Papa would say, 'Cover all the boxes now, *ma petite*. Now is the time for dreaming sweet dreams.' I miss Papa." Tears stung my eyes as the memory flashed crystal clear in my mind.

"What's troubling you today, Chère? Besides, my oafish need to treat you like a child," Bill asked, eliciting a reluctant smile from me.

"I don't understand Americans, Bill. Your President lied when he spoke last night. He warned the Japanese about the bomb, but by the time he made that speech, all those people were already dead. The bomb had already fallen. It fell on them yesterday morning, fourteen hours ahead of us." The look of sadness in his eyes told me he wouldn't deny my accusation.

"You knew, you knew it would happen," I accused him with tears stinging my eyes.

"No. I didn't, but I expected it. The Japanese would not surrender, and a lot more of our boys were going to die. Truman couldn't let that happen," Bill explained, as if this excused the lie.

"But why not tell the truth? Why say that all men have worth and dignity when the truth is, in this country, some people are more worthy than others?" Another accusation on target, based on his lowered, shaking head.

"You ask complicated questions, Chère." He was weighing his response, maybe stalling because he didn't want me thinking about such things.

"Presidential speeches are usually political. Last night was no different. But I know that in every leader there must exist a duality. It's the warrior's curse: having empathy for an enemy that you must stop at all costs." He let me sit with that for a moment, watching me.

"Laila told me about what happened today at Langenstein's. Mr. Ainsley lost both his sons to the Japanese, Chère. His youngest died at Pearl Harbor, the oldest died earlier this year at Iwo Jima. His feelings run deep regarding Japan, and he's not alone."

"He's not alone in his feelings about Negro people, either. Is he Bill? In America, Negro people have less value than white people. White people put signs in their business windows; 'Whites Only, except maids in uniform'. They are mean to people like Miss Laila, calling them awful names. This is what the Nazis did to the Jews; they isolated them, made people hate them. I don't understand how you can live this way when you know what the Nazis did." Another accusation he couldn't dodge.

"I see there's more than the heat I neglected to explain to you." He closed his eyes, apparently sorting through his own feelings, and then he blew out a heavy sigh.

"It's not the same, Désirée. I was there. I saw what the Nazis did. What you see here in the south is not the same. I'm not saying you're wrong about how you perceive our culture. There's a lot of inequity and prejudice here, but it took generations to create this situation, and it will take generations to heal it."

He touched me again, lightly on my knee, the worried look on his face hoping for my understanding. "We're going to the Beauly farm on Sunday. You'll meet someone there who can explain this far better than I can." He stroked my leg, giving my ankle a little squeeze. "Can you put these things away for the night and close the boxes?"

"I guess I can for now," I said, though troubling thoughts continued to swirl through my mind. "Bill, I will not be like them. I will not hate people that way."

"I know, Désirée. I don't expect you to." He stood up, reaching over to stroke my cheek. "I'll see you in the morning, Chère. Sweet dreams."

# Chapter 13

## *Bargains and the Beauly Farm*

Bill left before breakfast the following morning, apparently called away on some important task or mission or whatever it was he did. He never told me, and I knew better than to ask.

I tried diving back into the life of Scarlet O'Hara, but I found her obsession with Ashley Wilkes hit a bit too close to home. Instead, I spent my time in the kitchen, making several batches of cookies I intended to take to the Jefferies family the following day. Bobby came over in the middle of my baking spree, and I ended up making an extra batch to send home with him. Bobby liked my crispy oatmeal cookies.

"So, what do you think of Bill?" he asked as he snatched a hot cookie from the tray I'd pulled from the oven. "I think he's great. He sure knows a lot about baseball. Mm. I love these cookies. You could sell them and make a fortune."

"Bill is okay, but he treats me like a little girl." I said, shifting the conversation back to the subject at hand.

"Well, you are, Désirée. How's he supposed to treat you?"

"Ahh! I am not a baby. I know how to take care of myself."

"I don't see why you're so bothered by it. He's only looking out for you. He even asked me to watch out for you at school, to help you find your way around."

"Oh, so you will be my babysitter at school. Zis is what he wants?" I felt my frustration building again.

"Well, I wouldn't put it quite like that. It's more like he wants me to keep the boys away from you," Bobby said with a big grin. "From my point of view, I think the arrangement could work out pretty good for both of us."

"What do you mean?" I asked, curious where his mind was heading.

"Well, while I'm keeping the boys away from you, you can keep the girls away from me. Though I think you'll have an easier time than I will, based on how my baseball friends are around you."

"Don't you like za girls, Bobby? Zay like you," I said, teasing him.

The grin faded from his face. "Oh, they're alright, I guess. None of them understand what I'm talking about half the time. Most of them are like Evelyn, kind of silly, as far as I'm concerned. I'd much rather spend time with you. What do you say, Désirée? Is it a deal? Unless you don't want me to keep the boys away." He lifted his eyebrows up in question.

After shifting my cookies from the tray to the cooling rack, I checked on the batch in the oven. These cookies only baked for a few minutes, spreading out into thin, crisp rounds that could quickly burn with inattention. Two more minutes—enough time for me to consider Bobby's proposition.

Bill's protectiveness was about to spill into every part of my life, and his request for Bobby's help was another demonstration of that. I asked myself, why would he do that? Why would he bother?

My heart answered me, loud and clear. *Because he cares, silly, and this is how he can show you.* That would have to be enough for now. I wouldn't be thirteen forever.

The timer went off, and I pulled the hot tray from the oven, laying it on top of the stove to cool for a minute.

"I do not zink about boys or such zings," I said, rolling my eyes at Bobby. "But perhaps it will be better to have you wiz me, to show me za right way to be. And I will protect you from za silly girls. Okay. We have a deal," I said, offering him my hand across the countertop.

"Perfect," Bobby said, reaching across to shake my hand while snatching up another cookie with his other.

On Sunday afternoon, Bill, Mama Bea, and I went for a visit to Miss Laila's family farm, about an hour west of New Orleans. As Bill drove out of town, he talked about how he would spend summer days on that farm when he was a boy. He said the Beaulys were as much a part of his family as any Marchand member was. Mama Bea said I was going to meet her Granny Joliesse, "the woman who taught me the difference between right and wrong."

These new bits of information piqued my interest. This would be my first visit with Miss Laila's family, and a nervous excitement bubbled inside me. Plus, it had been five years since I'd been on a farm, and as we drove through the countryside, my mind flooded with memories.

The Beauly farm sat at the end of a road where a long dirt driveway curved up to the house. A humble two-storied building with dormered windows over a covered front porch, the well-maintained house looked like it had been there for a long time.

Two giant oak trees flanked the house in the front yard, where nearly a dozen children of varying ages played under the trees. A big swing hung from an outstretched branch, and the children took turns on the swing, some playing tag around the tree trunks. They all stopped their play when our car pulled up. A little girl, about eight years old, ran up the porch steps, calling out to the occupants inside.

"Thayz here, Mama! Thayz here!" she yelled, jumping up and down in her excitement. The other children surrounded our car, talking and laughing and running circles around us. Beautiful, smiling faces with bright eyes.

"Hello, children," Mama Bea said, stepping out of the car and finding herself among a sea of small, dark faces. "How y'all doing on this beautiful Sunday afternoon?" she asked, giving each one a quick hug.

"Skat, you rascals. Let them least get in the house before y'all set on them," Miss Laila said, as she hurried down the porch steps to greet us, shooing the children away with a wave of her hand as they scattered like birds.

"Sorry about that, Miss Bea. When they're all together, it's hard to keep them settled down, 'specially out here. Come in, come in. Miss Dezrae, Mr. William, thank y'all for comin' out to see everybody. Gran's been waitin' on ya."

Miss Laila led us up the front steps, then into the house where Millie (Miss Laila's daughter), Celia (Miss Laila's sister-in-law), and Addy (Celia's daughter) all welcomed us with warm hellos and shy handshakes. Granny Joliesse sat in a rocking chair in the corner with a sleeping baby in her arms.

"Jolie, come here an take dis bébé fore he make a puddle on my Sundy dress," Granny Joliesse instructed a girl who'd been standing out of the way. The girl came forward, shyly taking looks in my direction, before she gathered up the sleeping child, then took it down the hallway.

"Dat's betta. Come say hello to your Granny Jo, Miss Bumble Bea." She held up her arms for Mama Bea to enter her embrace, the two women hugging each other tenderly, then Mama Bea stepped back for Bill to greet the old woman.

"Mr. William, look at ya, all growed up an lookin' more like your father every time I sees ya. We're real glad you're home, safe an sound, sir. Bet your Mama is too."

Bill leaned down to kiss her cheek. "Thank you kindly, Granny Jo. It's good to be home, good to see y'all again. You're looking as beautiful as ever."

"Ah, go on with ya. I's nearly six years older den da last time I sees ya. We's all gettin older, son. Me 'specially," she said, a twinkle lighting her eyes. "Who dis ya got with ya, Mr. William? Dis da lil girl Laila tol me 'bout?"

Reaching out his hand, Bill encouraged me to step forward. "Yes ma'am. This is Désirée. She's come to live with Mama in the city." The look in his eyes told me I had nothing to fear with these people; they were family. "Come, Chère, say hello to Granny Joliesse, Laila's grandmother."

She was the oldest person I'd ever met, older even than Bisabuela, who I thought of as ancient. Her hair was pure white, not a trace of color, and she wore it tightly braided around her head, like a crown. Her skin was a deep rich brown, like polished oak, with wrinkles creasing the corners of her eyes, which were cloudy with age, but as alert as any child's eyes. She wore a blue floral dress with a crocheted shawl around her shoulders. The term 'matriarch' came to mind as I cataloged the family and her place in it.

"Come over here, child. Lemme get a good look at ya."

I stepped close enough for her to capture my hand, which she held for a lingering moment while our eyes locked. It felt like she could see through me—not like glass, but more like she could see into the dark places inside me. She squeezed my hand briefly, then let it go.

"You an I got things to talk 'bout, Miss Dezrae, but right now I needs to catch up with my Bumble Bea," she said as Jolie came back into the room. "Jolie, come take Miss Dezrae outside an show her round da farm.

Mr. William, the boys are out back workin' on that ole tractor. I spect you'll find 'em sharin' a bit of shine too. Run on you two, we'll see y'all at supper."

Jolie nodded to Granny Joliesse, turned without a word, and walked down the hallway to the backdoor. Bill and I followed her out, but I stopped briefly at the kitchen, the tempting sounds and smells urging me to investigate. Miss Laila and the other women were dancing around each other, chatting in a sing-song melody, while they each prepared some dish for the meal.

"Miss Laila? May I help you with za meal? I can help," I asked, wanting to learn how they did things, but mostly, I just wanted to watch and listen to the music I could hear in that kitchen.

"You's a guest, Miss Dezrae," she said, shaking her head. "You run on outside and meet the rest of the family. Jolie will show you around. Go on now. You can help set the table in a bit," she said, shooing me out of the kitchen.

"She always be wantin' to help me in the kitchen," Miss Laila said as I went out. "That girl knows more about cookin' than most white women I know."

I hurried after Bill and Jolie, equally excited to investigate the farm as I was the kitchen. A narrow porch off the back of the house led down to the backyard. Another big oak tree sat off to the right, shading two long tables set end to end, with benches along the sides and a chair at either end.

A well-worn pathway led across the yard to a big barn and work-shed where five men gathered around an old tractor, one of them lying underneath and only halfway visible. A boy, about eight or nine years old, crouched down next to the man, handing him tools from a metal box. Mr. Jefferies saw us coming and reached down to tap the knee of the man under the tractor.

"Come out now, Marcus. We can mess with this later. Mr. William is here. Welcome, Mr. William. Glad y'all could come out to see the family." Mr. Jefferies shook Bill's outstretched hand, then Bill moved to greet the other men.

"Clarence, Joseph, it's good to see you both. Thank you for inviting us out. Mama's been itching to see Granny Jo." Bill shook each man's hand with a firm grip, then he turned to the younger men.

"Bennie, you're looking good. Marcus, it's been a long time, brother," Bill said, patting Marcus on the back with brotherly affection. "I was so sorry to hear about Laura. I can't imagine how hard that must have been for you. If there's anything you need, you know where to come."

"Thank you, Bill," Marcus coolly replied, taking a step back. "You remember my son? Willie, say hello to Mr. William, Miss Bea's son. He's just come back from the war." The young boy reached out his hand for Bill to shake, though I sensed some hesitation, a wariness in his eyes.

"Very nice to see you, Willie. Anybody ever tell you that you look a lot like your father?" Bill asked, shaking the boy's hand.

"This the girl come to live with Miss Bea?" Marcus asked, looking at me standing out of the way behind Bill.

Bill took hold of my hand to introduce me to the men. "Gentlemen, this is Désirée." He didn't offer any additional information about me. I suppose they didn't need any because Miss Laila and Mr. Jefferies knew as much about me as anybody. Not everything, but enough.

The men each greeted me. Clarence was Miss Laila's older brother and married to Celia, and Joseph was married to Addy. The four of them, their six children, and Granny Joliesse lived on the farm. Marcus was

Miss Laila's son, and Bennie was Millie's husband. Marcus, Bennie, Millie, and their children lived together in the Jefferies home in the Broadmoor neighborhood of New Orleans. Once I got their names and affiliations straight and thanked them all for inviting me, offering to help wherever needed.

"Ain't nothin' needs doin', Miss Dezrae. You're a guest. Jolie, take Miss Dezrae and show her round the farm while we visit with Mr. William," Mr. Jefferies instructed the girl who'd been standing off to the side.

"What should I show her? It's just a farm. Ain't nothing she'd want to see," Jolie said, a testy tone to her reply.

"None of that smart mouth, missy. You mind your manners, ya hear?" This from Marcus, Jolie's father, who gave her a look clearly meant to curb her surliness.

"Yes, sir," Jolie replied, though she gave me a look that spoke a lot louder than anything she said so far. "Follow me, Miss Désirée." She took off down a path that led between the barn and the work-shed.

I hurried behind her, curious about the farm but also wondering why this girl seemed almost angry I was there. Jolie looked a little older than me, taller, and filled out way more than me, which tweaked my envy. I didn't think I'd ever grow taller or fill out like a proper woman. I watched the floral dress covering her straight back and swaying hips recede around the end of the barn. When I made the turn, she had stopped to face me.

"Why are you here?" She was clearly suspicious of me, though I didn't understand why.

My eyes flew open, surprised by the question, then I shrugged. "Zay bring me here, to meet za family."

She scowled at me. "I know that. What I don't know is why you came. Uptown girls like you never visit a colored home."

"Why?"

"It's just not done, is why. Where are you from that you don't know how things are around here?" She kept scowling at me like I had made a colossal error in judgment.

"I am from far away and have only been here a few months. What is zis 'Uptown girl' you say?" I asked, wanting to understand why my presence seemed to bother her so much.

Jolie stood there looking me over, her eyes traveling up and down, clearly assessing who she thought I was. I recognized the look immediately. People had always made some judgment about me. Usually, it was only partially correct. Typically, the real me lay hidden from view.

"You are," she snapped. "You live in one of them big mansions in Uptown, probably go to a private school, and you have lots of money. That's what an Uptown girl is, and they never associate with colored people except to give them orders."

When I realized that what I looked like on the outside classified me as a privileged Uptown Girl, my heart started racing because that was what ruined my life before, and it wasn't how I thought of myself.

"I live in a big house wiz Mrs. Marchand, and I will go to za private school, but I am just a girl like you. I am not special... I am new to zis place and do not know za rules," I said, testing the waters, wondering if she would explain things to me from her point of view. We were almost the same age and already had something in common: Miss Laila was her grandmother.

"There's rules alright, but mostly the unspoken kind. People like you don't mix with colored folks, socially, that is. The Marchand family is an exception, far as I know. Gran says she grew up around Miss Bea, and Daddy grew up around Mr. William." Her tone was softening, and I could sense she was curious, her eyes now holding more questions than suspicions.

"Zen you and I can be friends, like your fazur and Bill. I do not know zese unspoken rules. So, we can be friends, no?" I said, smiling at her, hoping for a positive outcome to this unexpected confrontation.

"Maybe. We'll see," Jolie said as she turned and walked behind the barn toward another building with lots of open windows.

As I followed her, I gazed out to the vast field of deeply furrowed rows topped with tall, wide-leafed plants. They were beautiful, and I wondered what they were. Rows of corn grew along the edges of the field, their stalks heavy with ripening ears sprouting from them.

Inside the windowed building, I found myself among racks and racks of drying plants, their broad leaves now withered and darkened to a deep bronze color. They were the same as the growing version in the fields outside, these now giving off the telltale aroma of tobacco.

Jolie stood in front of the doorway at the far end of the building, her fists resting on her hips and the look on her face telling me she was still suspicious. There was something else behind her angry eyes, some hurt that had nothing to do with me, but my presence seemed to remind her of it.

I walked towards her, admiring the racks of drying tobacco, inhaling the rich earthy smell. "Zese are tobacco, yes?" No confirmation was necessary. I just wanted to break through her distrust of me.

"I live... lived on a farm when I was a little girl. My Papa, he grew grapes to make za wine. It was a beautiful farm like zis." Visions of my home drifted across my mind, and I had to turn away to hide the tears instantly filling my eyes.

"What happened to you, Désirée?" Her tone had softened again. I thought perhaps she heard the loss in my voice, seen the tears I tried to hide.

I didn't want to hide from her, but knew I couldn't tell the whole truth, to her or to anyone. With a deep breath, I steadied myself before facing her.

"My family is dead, and I was alone. Mrs. Marchand, she send for me to live wiz her. I have nowhere else, no ozer people. Only zem." *And you, I hope,* I thought as I passed her, heading out the door toward the rows of growing tobacco.

"Jolie! Where ya at, girl? Table needs settin'. Supper's almost ready." Miss Laila's voice carried across the tobacco rows to the edge of the field where Jolie and I had stopped to pick a few ears of ripe corn. We looked at each other, smiled, and then headed back toward the house, walking side by side up the row.

"Do you miss living on a farm?" Jolie asked.

Her question was an opening, and I needed to give her something of myself, some truth she could believe.

"Yes. I was happy zen. It was a good life, a simple life. Not so different zan zis," I said, spreading my arms wide to indicate the farm and fields.

"How do you like living in that big house with Miss Bea?" There seemed to be an accusation in the question. Apparently, she was still unsure of me.

I shrugged, raising my eyebrows as high as I could, then rolled my eyes at her.

"Ahh. It is a big house, beautiful, but very big for so few people. It is not so simple as here on za farm. Za people in za city are more... how you say? Complicated."

"I suppose you'll have to get used to it, won't ya?" she said, the remark dripping with sarcasm combined with a touch of amusement as she led me into the kitchen.

*You're not going to make this easy, are you?*

I had met girls before who didn't like me, who decided things about me and then made my life miserable, but I didn't think Jolie was that kind of girl. It felt more like her anger wasn't directed at me specifically, but at what she thought I represented.

*I wonder what hurt you, Jolie.*

# Chapter 14

## *Dinner with Granny Joliesse*

Steamed rice, Crawfish Étouffée, bowls of cooked greens, a platter of crispy fried chicken, and a basket of hot biscuits went around the long table, hand to hand, as each person served themselves from the bounty.

Granny Joliesse sat at the head of the table with Laila on her right and Mama Bea on her left. She gazed down the length of the table at each member of her family, a smile lighting up her face. After everyone served themselves, they waited for her signal. Raising her hand toward heaven, she bowed her head to lead us all in a prayer.

"Thank ya, Lord, for bringin' my family together taday. Thank ya for all da years ya give me and all da blessins we've received. Bless dis food, dear Lord, and all da hands dat made it. We ask dis in your name, Amen."

A loud "Amen" came from everyone, and then the table erupted in the sounds of knives and forks and friendly chatter. Nearly two dozen people sat around that table: a dozen adults and almost as many children.

Bill and I sat across from Marcus and Jolie, who still eyed me with doubt. Bill and Marcus seemed to struggle in their own conversation. Marcus's responses sounded short and chilly. I didn't know anything about him or Jolie and scolded myself for not asking Miss Laila more about her family before coming.

*'Wake up, Désirée! Look around!'* A voice I hadn't heard in a long time whispered in my mind.

*Alex? What is it?* It felt like a warning, but I couldn't tell what it was about.

"I can have a word with him if you'd like," Bill said to Marcus, whose eyes darkened at the offer.

"I'll handle it on my own," was Marcus's swift response, then he added, "Thank you, Bill, but I'll take care of my own problems."

Bill stared across the table at Marcus, his eyes creasing with worry. "I understand, but if you need anything..."

The offer hung in the air between them, a promise unacknowledged and perhaps unwanted.

After supper, the ladies cleared the table and put away the food while the men washed the dishes. Then, all the children gathered around the dining table to listen to Mama Bea read from one of the many storybooks she brought them.

To the children's delight, I set out the box of cookies I brought. Jolie snatched one before they all disappeared, and after she took a bite, her eyes widened in apparent disbelief. I guess she hadn't expected me to make something she would like. It was satisfying to know I had surprised her.

"You an I gots some talkin' to do, Miss Dezrae," Granny Joliesse said, taking me by the hand and leading me outside onto the front porch. "Come sit here by me, child." She settled herself on an old settee facing the front yard, and I took a seat beside her, nervous but curious.

I wondered about her family history, about what happened to Marcus, about why people in America behaved the way they did. I had a lot of questions, and she looked like she would have the answers. She looked like she had seen and heard more than anyone.

"How old are you, *Madame*?"

Her mouth curled up on the ends. "I turn 90 years old dis summer, child. Seen a lot of things in my life."

"Were you born a slave?" I asked, calculating her birth year in my head. 1855.

She stared at me for a moment with the same look she had earlier, the one that made me feel exposed, visible. Still smiling, she shook her head, huffing through her nose. After reaching into her pocket, she pulled out a pouch and a corncob pipe, which she deftly filled with tobacco from the pouch. She struck a match on the side of the settee, put the flame to the pipe and drew in the pungent smoke, then released it with a sigh.

"Laila tol me you was smart." Her eyes bore into mine as she took another toke on the pipe and then blew the smoke out into the yard.

"Yes, Miss Dezrae, I was born a slave, not five miles from dis here farm," she said, gesturing toward the east.

"I was nearly ten years old when Mr. Beaulaurier give each slave he own dare freedom paper and twenty dollar. If'n day stay on the plantation, he give 'em each a plot of land to work, an a job doin what day'd been doin' dare whole lives; workin' the tobacca fields or at the plantation house. My family stayed an took his offer. Only difference after dat was, we got paid to work. But it weren't like dat for most colored folks. Most had it just as hard as before. Some even harder." She took a drag from her pipe, blowing out a puff of smoke before continuing.

"The Beaulaurier family been good to me an mine. Ain't never had no trouble with 'em. Dayz good people. My paw, he chose da name Beauly to pay respect to Mr. Beaulaurier." She leaned back on the settee, stretching like she needed to rid herself of a memory before taking another toke off the pipe.

"Is zis za land he give you? Zis farm?"

"Mr. Beaulaurier give my Pa an my brother each a small plot of land to sharecrop, plus we bought another plot from him with some of the money he pay us. All dat make up dis farm. Pa built dis house, he and my brother. My family been growin' Perique tobacca here for generations. After the South lost the war, nothin' much changed, ceptin' we got a share of the crop, by the good graces of Mr. Beaulaurier, and our hard work."

"I worked in the plantation house, carin' for the family. Whiles I was raisin' up Mr. Jean-Pierre, I started raisin' up my own chilren. Den I stayed on when he married Miss Nicole an took over the plantation. I raised up dare two chilren, Miss Bea and Mr. Bertrum. I always liked being round chilren. Day brings a smile to my face."

"I zink not everyone is so kind, like Mr. Beaulaurier or Mrs. Marchand. Za people here, zay separate from each ozer; white and colored. It not feel right to be zis way. It feel wrong to me." As soon as I'd spoken, I felt shocked at how freely I expressed my feelings to her, like I had known her forever and was sure of her understanding.

Granny Joliesse took a deep breath, then let it out, a sadness turning her smile to a frown.

"Dare's good people an bad people everywhere, child. Don't matter what color day is. It's what's in dare hearts dat matters. I teach my chilren, all of dem, to live with gratitude an generosity in dare hearts. Cain't never go wrong dat way."

With a rap against the edge of an empty coffee tin sitting next to her, she tapped out the burned tobacco from the pipe, then stored it away in her pocket. She reached over and took my hand, stroking the back of it, then turned it over and peered closely at my palm. Her finger traced over the lines etched there as she hummed softly behind her lips.

"I don' know what it be like walkin' in a white woman's shoes, but I've raised a few, an Beatrice Marchand is one of the finest women I know. Dare's no finer example dan her, of how to be in dat world."

She held my hand as she spoke, searching with her eyes and long dark fingers along the lines of my much paler palm. I wondered what she saw.

I wanted to ask her about Jolie and Marcus, about why they were angry, but it seemed too personal a question, so I couched it in an observation.

"Life is hard here, not so fair. for people like you and your family."

"Life's as hard as ya make it, child. Don't matter who ya are. Da Good Lord puts us on a path, den it's up to us to choose how we walks it. We can trip and fall over da troubles in our way, or we can step over 'em. It's always a choice. I see here, you've had to make a few choices yourself," she said, tapping my palm.

"What do you see? Are you a fortune-teller?" Bisabuela told me about the *Brujas;* gypsy palm readers who traveled through the Spanish countryside telling fortunes. I wondered if Granny Joliesse had such skills.

"I ain't no fortune teller, like da Voo-Doo women in da Quarter. *Ma Grand-Mère,* she teach me a few things, though," she said, pointing to a crease on my palm that began beneath my first finger and curved around my thumb nearly to my wrist. "Dis line tell me you gonna live a long life, an dis one say you gonna love real deep." Her finger traced another line, cutting all the way across my palm below the fingers.

"I don' need to be no fortune teller to see da hurt behind dose eyes of yours. Ya hides it well enough, but I sees it. No sense carryin' round sorrow for things ain't your fault. Best put dose ghosts to rest, child. Lock up dem monsters inside dose boxes. Ya gots a long life to live. How ya gonna choose to live it?"

*You are a Bruja.*

She could see through me, see into my mind, and it frightened me. I wasn't sure how to respond. I had only told one person about my boxes, but she knew. She knew about the monsters. She knew about Alex.

Shades of crimson and purple edged the darkening clouds, whipping and curling across the sky like a billowing blanket. A storm was coming. The tiny hairs on my arms tingled with electricity and anticipation.

As I stared across the yard, I tried to push away all the fear and regret, the sadness and loss, but knew it would always be there.

"I must make a life here," I said, a soft sigh escaping my lips. "But it is not so easy. Za people here are different, and I must learn to be like zem, but I cannot be za same. And... I must wait for what I want." I took a deep breath and blew it out with a frustrated sigh.

"Dat line on your hand tell me ya gots a long life ahead of ya, Miss Dezrae. Ain't no sense in rushin' through it. Ya might miss somethin' important," she said, squeezing my hand, a sensory reminder to heed her words.

Bill came out onto the porch, drying his hands with a towel. "Mama's finishing up, Chère. We'll be heading home soon. Are you about ready?" he asked, touching me lightly on the shoulder.

Granny Joliesse eyed him critically, as if needing to assure herself of something. She quickly snatched up his hand, examining the lines which told his fortune, then she released it with a satisfied smile on her face.

"Mr. William, I can see dare's somethin' powerful tween you and dis girl here."

Bill's eyes widened when he heard her, then he nodded. "Yes, ma'am. There is."

"Peers you're more like your father dan I thought. You do right by dis girl, Mr. William. She's precious cargo. Keep your eyes open. Ya never know what's comin' 'round da corner." There was a warning beneath the lightness of her tone, subtle but unmistakable. A chill rolled down my spine.

Bill nodded again, holding her gaze for a moment.

"Yes, ma'am. That *is* my intention."

# Chapter 15

## *Jolie and Marcus*

"Mornin' Miss Dezrae." Miss Laila looked around the kitchen, raising her eyebrows at the clutter covering nearly every surface, then she hung up her coat and purse on the hook by the door.

I had been up since dawn, making a mess in the kitchen, and hoped to have it cleaned up before they arrived, but the sink was full of dishes and the countertop cluttered with my cookbooks and journal.

"Good morning, Miss Laila. Do not worry, I will clean zis."

She pursed her lips, stifling a smile, her eyes twinkling with amusement as I gathered up my things from the countertop, making room for the groceries Mr. Jefferies brought in.

Miss Laila started unpacking the bags, laying everything out on the counter before systematically putting it all away. Her normally organized kitchen suffered from my chaotic methods, and I knew it sometimes annoyed her.

"I's not worried, Miss Dezrae. Did you enjoy yourself out on the farm, meetin' the family yesterday?"

"Oh, yes. It is so beautiful and very peaceful, like my home. Your grand-mère is old and wise, but Jolie, she not like me to be zare. She is angry and a little sad, I zink, but I want to be her friend," I said, hoping she could assist me in my quest to be friends with her granddaughter.

Mr. Jefferies stood behind his wife, listening, and when she turned to him, he gave her a look that seemed to communicate something. They were like Bill and Mama Bea, able to talk without saying a word, which severely hampered my ability to know what was going on. However, his message was obvious; she could tell me what I wanted to know.

"Jolie, she's hurting, Miss Dezrae. Ain't got nothin' to do with you. She and her father, they're holding on to somethin' they cain't do nothin' about, and it's eatin' them up." Miss Laila's face creased around her eyes as she spoke, her mouth turned down in a frown I rarely saw her wear.

"What happened to zem?" I asked, sitting down at the worktable, my hands curling around my cold cup of coffee. I wasn't sure she'd tell me more than she already had.

She looked at her husband once again, apparently seeking his approval to reveal further details. Mr. Jefferies stared at me for a long time, questions in his eyes, searching for the reason behind my interest. Whatever he saw on my face must have assured him of my sincerity.

"Go on and tell her, Laila. Might be Miss Dezrae is just what Jolie needs to start healing."

Miss Laila released a heavy sigh, her shoulders slumping and head shaking, not in refusal, but more like resignation and a reluctance to share the burden. She sat down across from me at the worktable, clasping her hands together in front of her. When she spoke, it was slow and measured; the sound of her voice was sad but layered with suppressed anger.

"About a year ago, Jolie's mama died. Sudden like. It was somethin' coulda been prevented, but Laura didn't say nothin' till it was too late. She'd been workin' for a woman here in Uptown, doin' fine, not havin' no problems, till the mister brought home a dog he found 'long side of the road. Musta been a mean dog, cuz Laura was usually real good with animals. Anyway, that dog bit her bad, but Laura never told Marcus about it. She hid it from him and the children, never got it tended to proper."

"A week or so later she was feelin' poorly, but she went to work anyway. By the time she got there, she was sweatin' with a fever. The missus sent her away, wouldn't let Laura inside to call to get a ride home. She coulda called us, coulda come here, but she didn't. She didn't want Marcus to find out about that dog. Laura was afraid of what he'd do."

"She walked all the way home to Treme. When she got there, she was burnin' up with fever and raving. When Jolie got home, Laura told her about the dog. Jolie called the plant where Marcus works and told the operator it was an emergency; she needed her daddy to come home, her mama was sick. The woman said she'd give Marcus the message on his next break. Then Jolie called us in a panic, and we rushed up there."

"We took Laura to the colored hospital, but by the time we got her there, the doctors say the poison from that dog bite was already in her blood, runnin' all through her body. She was unconscious when Marcus got to the hospital. Laura died that night."

I'm not sure I took a breath the entire time she was speaking. When I did, my throat tightened, and tears stung my eyes. It took me a minute to catch my breath as I pushed down the memories of losing my own mother.

"Jolie and I are za same. We boz have lost our mozers." I took a hankie from the pocket of my apron to wipe my tears away. Crying never helps anything.

"I will be her friend so we can comfort each ozer. You zink is possible?"

I wanted to believe it was, that there was a way for Jolie and me to 'step over' our hurts, like Granny Joliesse said. Some deep intuition told me I needed Jolie in my life. I would make her like me, somehow. My face must have signaled my hope.

Miss Laila stared at me for a moment, then a slow smile spread across her face, smoothing away the sadness and anger. She reached over to stroke my cheek, her touch warm and comforting.

"Anything is possible, Miss Dezrae. If you want it bad enough, anything is possible."

Bill came through the back door a short time later, tossing an old knapsack on the counter, then slumping onto the stool I just vacated. Gone since before I got up, I wondered where he'd been.

He looked like he'd been working on the docks: work boots, patched dungarees, an old plaid button-up shirt with the sleeves rolled up, a handkerchief tied around his neck, a cap on his head, unshaven beard. It wasn't his usual well-put-together look, but Bill was a chameleon, able to transform himself to suit his environment.

"Morning everybody. Is there any coffee?" he asked, glancing at me, then at Miss Laila, who was already pouring him a cup from the pot I'd made. She set the cup down in front of him, a worried look in her eyes.

"Thanks, Laila." He took a deep gulp and then set the cup aside. "Jacob, I picked up that carburetor Clarence needs for the tractor. It's in the trunk of the Ford. Do you think Joe can help him get it installed? If not, I can find somebody out there to help them."

"Joe knows as much as Marcus, Mr. William. He can do it. Thank you, sir. I'll take it out to Clarence later," Mr. Jefferies said, his expression matching his wife's.

Miss Laila stood next to Bill, her frown deepening, her hands on her hips, like she was about to scold him. "Mr. William, you been down to the docks? You're smellin' like ya just got off work down there. Marcus asked you not to do nothin', sir."

Bill looked up at her, shaking his head. "No, I didn't go into the plant, just met a few of the workers at a bar around the corner after the shift change. A few beers with the boys and I heard enough about Pat O'Leary to know Marcus isn't the only one having trouble with him."

"Marcus don't need no more trouble, sir. He makes enough of it on his own." Mr. Jefferies' parental concern was obvious in his tone.

*What kind of trouble?* I wondered.

"It's not only about Marcus now, Jacob," Bill said, looking over at Mr. Jefferies. "What I found out about O'Leary and what's going on down there concerns me. If what I heard is accurate, or even close to it, management doesn't know, Charles and Bertram don't know. That kind of trouble will eventually affect the entire company, if it hasn't already. I need to do a little more digging, but I promise you both, nothing I do will hurt Marcus."

Bill's face looked tired but calm and resolute, and his expression seemed meant to reassure them, though I'm not sure it did. They looked at Bill, then at each other, another silent communication passing between them, then they went about their daily work. It appeared they accepted Bill's assurance, but their parental worry remained unextinguished.

Bill sat slumped on the stool, his arms resting on the worktable, hands clasping the coffee cup. Lost in his thoughts, he absently reached for a scone. When he took a bite, the sensory experience seemed to bring him back to the room.

"These are good. Did you make these, Chère?" he asked, licking crumbs off his fingers.

"Yes. I make zem zis morning. You like zem?" I asked, happy he finally noticed me.

"I do," he said, reaching for another. He sat at the table, watching me as I finished cleaning up my mess, a tender smile on his face every time I looked at him.

"Laila? Does Carlos still work for us?" he asked.

"Yes, sir, Mr. William. He comes every other Tuesday. Should be here in the morning, with his son, Nico," she replied.

"That's good," Bill said, then he turned to me. "How about you and I walk the property later, Chère? You can show me where you want that garden, then we'll talk with Carlos tomorrow about getting it started. How's that sound?"

"We could do it now."

He shook his head, stood up and stretched. "No, we'll do it later. I need to speak with Mama, then I'm going upstairs to wash off the bar stink and maybe catch a couple of hours of shuteye. I'll see y'all later." He tossed back his coffee and handed me the empty cup. After stroking my cheek tenderly, he left in search of Mama Bea.

I was bored and needed a distraction. Bill was napping, Mama Bea was working in her study, and the Jefferies were busy with their work. Miss Laila wouldn't let me back in the kitchen, at least not till later, so I took my cookbooks up to my room, trading them for Margaret Mitchell's perspective, then headed down the back stairs to the gazebo.

"I'll scream out loud if you come near me. I will! I will—at za top of my voice! Get away from me! Don't you dare touch me!"

I was reading out loud, as I often did, so I could hear the words and feel them in my mouth. Scarlett's innocent protest on her wedding night seemed a ridiculous response. I found it hard to believe she didn't know what would happen; she was a lot older than me, and I knew already.

"Hey! Are you alright over there?" Bobby asked from the other side of the bushes.

"I am alright, Bobby. I was just reading."

"Well, it sounded like someone was about to hurt you. Don't scare me like that."

"I am sorry. Can I come over?" I didn't think I could stand one more moment with Scarlett and her selfishness.

"Sure. I was going to the workshop. Meet me there."

"I will tell Miss Laila, zen I will come. I have a treat for you," I said, grabbing my book and heading for the house.

A few minutes later, I walked into Bobby's workshop with a plate of scones in hand. He was sitting at his workbench, his head bent over in concentration, studying several tiny pieces of metal illuminated by the shop light directly overhead. I laid the scones down next to him and took a seat on the old loveseat by the open door, then waited for Bobby's thought to complete.

Bobby was like that; always needing to finish his thought process or at least write it down in his notebook before it disappeared. I envied his ability to forget things.

The workshop was Bobby's sanctuary, a place where he felt at ease, untroubled by anything outside those walls. He kept it neat, everything in its proper place. Hand tools hung on the wall behind the workbench, each slid neatly into their slot. Nuts and bolts, wires and connectors, and all the other tiny bits and pieces, lived in the small drawers of a metal cabinet sitting on the right end of the workbench. The left end of the bench, devoted to model building, held a partially completed schooner sitting atop a makeshift stand, the light above it turned off. Bobby's attention was elsewhere.

When he completed his thought, Bobby lifted his head, noticing the plate of scones. He grabbed one, then swiveled on the stool towards me.

"What were you reading? You scared the hell out of me," he said, raking his fingers through his hair with his free hand, a scowl darkening his face.

"Gone with za Wind, Scarlett O'Hara, who isn't very nice, I zink. Are za girls at school like zis, like Scarlett?" I asked, suddenly concerned I'd have to face an army of Scarletts when I got to school.

"No, not that I know of. I never met any like that, though it would be kind of funny to see them all dressed up in antebellum gowns on the first day of school." He grinned, lifting his dark eyebrows up and down in a funny expression.

"Not very comfortable," I said, relaxing into the loveseat, stretching like a kitten, then curling my feet under me.

I shook off the image of giant hooped skirts and incredibly tight corsets as I broached a subject that I hoped Bobby would talk about. "Bobby? Do you know any negro boys?"

The question took him by surprise, his smile fading and eyes darkening again.

"No, not really. No colored people live around here, no colored kids go to Newman. It's not allowed." He stared at me for a long time, like he was trying to figure out why I asked.

"Why are zay not allowed?" It seemed a pertinent question, but Bobby's look said he was uncomfortable, though I wasn't sure why.

"It's a law or something. Colored kids can only go to colored schools. Besides, they probably couldn't afford to go to Newman or any private school, even if there wasn't a law. Why are you asking about this, Désirée?"

His look told me it was a touchy subject, one he seemed cautious about exploring.

I didn't want to make him uncomfortable, but I needed to understand things, especially from a teenage perspective. I bit my lower lip, worried it between my teeth for a moment, then shrugged off my discomfort.

"I meet a girl, Miss Laila's granddaughter, and I want to be her friend, but she say I am an Uptown girl. She is angry wiz white people, I zink. So..." Another shrug and a shake of my head expressed my frustration at the situation.

"I know who she is," Bobby said, almost shyly, as if he had a secret that he was reluctant to share. "I never met her, but Millie told me what happened... to her mother, I mean. People shouldn't be allowed to have dogs like that. I'm sorry about the trouble we caused." He looked away quickly, glancing back at me, then away again.

"What do you mean? Why are you sorry, Bobby?" I tried to capture his eyes with mine, but he kept looking away. Finally, he faced me straight on.

"My friend Eddie lives next door to that old man where Jolie's mother worked. Eddie said there was trouble from the day that dog arrived. It terrorized everyone, barking and snapping at anyone who walked by. Eddie's little sister was terrified to leave their house after that dog jumped at the fence, trying to get at her. Then Millie told me what happened to her sister-in-law, and well..." He stopped himself, apparently still unsure if he wanted to reveal his secret.

"What did you do?"

When he looked up, I could see the memory flash across his face, and with it came an intensity I'd not seen in him before.

"Dogs that mean don't deserve to live. So, Eddie and I did something about it. I took a pound of ground meat from the freezer and let it thaw out, then Eddie got some rat poison, and we mixed it together, then we fed it to that dog. The greedy bastard ate it all up. He was stiff as a board by morning."

"We didn't mean to cause trouble for Millie's family. We just wanted to get rid of that dog. But that old man accused Millie's brother of killing his dog. I guess he went down to where Marcus works and took the police with him and caused some trouble. Millie told me that a dozen people vouched for Marcus. They all said Marcus was working in the plant when that dog died. The police didn't do a thing. They'd already heard complaints about the dog from the other neighbors. Nobody but that old man cared, but I guess he kept making trouble for Marcus. I'm sorry about that part," Bobby said, his head lowered remorsefully.

"Perhaps if Jolie knew zat two Uptown boys avenged her mother, she might feel better. I do not know, but I want to be her friend. It is important for me."

"Well, I don't know how you're going to do that. White kids and colored kids don't mix around here." His look held worry and a warning.

"Why do Americans zink you must be separated? Do you understand zis, Bobby?" I hoped he would give me a straight answer, give me his inner thoughts, but I wasn't sure he would.

He shrugged, clearly uncomfortable. The concerned look on his face said I was treading a hard path that he wasn't sure he wanted to go down.

"Not any better than you do, I guess. It's always been this way, far as I know. That doesn't make it right, but there's nothing we can do about it, anyway." He had a faraway look in his eyes, brooding pools of deep blue that held their deepest secrets close.

"What are you two doing in here?"

Bobby and I looked to the doorway where Bill stood leaning against the jamb, a grin on his freshly shaven face.

"I zought you were sleeping," I said. *But I'm glad you're not.*

“I couldn’t sleep. I kept thinking about that garden,” Bill said, a smile curling the corners of his mouth.

“What garden?” Bobby asked, munching on another scone.

“Désirée wants a kitchen garden. I told her I’d help make it. She was going to show me where she wants it.”

“I can help. I’m good at building things,” Bobby offered, his eyes brightening at the idea of spending time with Bill and me, but mostly Bill, I think.

Bill looked from me to Bobby, raising his eyebrows, and then he lifted his chin towards the house. “Alright then, show us where you want it, Chère.”

# Chapter 16

## *Gardens and Memories*

I walked the property with them, my protector and my friend, mapping out my dream garden: two wide beds along the side of the garage, separated by a walkway. Bill and Bobby marked out the areas with stakes of wood and string, taking measurements and discussing the finer points of construction. They reminded me of Papa and my brother, Jean-Michel, during that last spring when they walked the newly plowed field, their heads bent together, some mysterious discussion passing between them. I couldn't help but smile at the old memory, bittersweet as it was, and then delight at the new one unfolding in front of me.

"Miss Dezrae. Miss Bea says you need to come in and change. She's taking you somewhere right after lunch. Come on in now," Miss Laila called out from the patio.

"Where is she taking me?" I asked, turning to Bill for the answer.

*I hated surprises. They almost always turn out bad.* My stomach flipped over twice, a primal instinct alerting me to the possibility of change or danger.

Bill smiled, gently squeezing my shoulder, in what I supposed was a gesture of reassurance, but what he said made my stomach flip over again.

"She wants to take you shopping for school clothes, and then you have an appointment with Doctor Easton at his office to get your shots for school."

Besides surprises, I especially didn't like shots or doctors. Several horrible memories flashed across my mind, and I had to shut my eyes and slow my breathing to stifle the shudder rippling through me.

"Must I have za shots?" I asked, hopeful I could opt out and avoid the nightmare threatening to break loose.

"Yes, Chère. It's for your protection and the other kids, too," Bill gently explained.

"Aw, it's nothing, Désirée. Just a couple of pokes with a needle. You won't feel more than a pinch or two. It doesn't hurt. I promise," Bobby offered, trying to reassure me with a demonstration pinch on my arm.

It wasn't just the physical pain; it was the memory that pain evoked, a memory that sent another shudder rolling down my spine. I pushed it back as far as I could into the recesses of my mind, but some boxes refused to stay closed.

"You'll be fine," Bill assured me again. "Go on in and get cleaned up. Bobby and I will take care of this. While you're out shopping, we'll go down to the lumberyard and order what we need and have it delivered tomorrow morning. Then I'll call Carlos and let him know we'll need some soil for the new garden beds. We might even have this done for you by tomorrow afternoon. How's that sound?"

Bill knew me better than anyone, and from the look in his eyes, he could sense my anxiety. His lighthearted description of the garden project was his way of distracting me from my worries, and it almost helped.

"Darling, let me at least get you a few of these dresses. You can't wear the same thing all the time," Mama Bea said, handing me two more dresses to try on, one a muted floral in shades of peach and the other a red and blue check with three-quarter length sleeves.

It had been a battle of unshakable wills between Mama Bea and me, standing in the ladies' dressing room of the Maison Blanche department store. I refused to try on anything I thought might scream Uptown and had already settled on a couple of simple skirts and blouses. I didn't think I needed anything more and told her so.

"Please, Mama Bea, not so much. I not need zis many clothes." I wanted nothing that would make me stand out in the crowd, but Mama Bea disagreed. She thought I should look my best, especially on the first day of school. I relented and tried on the dresses to make her happy.

"All the girls dress up on the first day of school, darling. You'll see. Let's get the skirts and blouses you've picked out, but also these dresses I've chosen for you. I'm sure you won't regret having them once school starts."

She didn't understand how her easy generosity made me uncomfortable, and I was still shy about sharing my feelings with her. That wasn't something I did easily with anyone but Bill. I accepted the compromise, thanking her with as much grace as I could muster.

Already feeling uncomfortable, the ride to Doctor Easton's office added another layer to my anxiety.

"Doctor Easton wants to do a complete physical to establish your health record with him, then he'll give you a couple of shots to immunize you against the more serious childhood diseases. This is necessary for admittance to school, darling. It won't take long, and I promise it won't hurt," Mama Bea said, patting my jittery legs bouncing beside her.

Flashes of memory bombarded my mind, each one sending shock waves rippling through me. It was all I could do to hold myself still and control my breathing. Years of practice stifling my emotions allowed me to calm myself enough to don my Gautier mask as we headed through the doors of Doctor Easton's office.

The antiseptic smell immediately assaulted me, and I couldn't force the memory away any longer, no matter how hard I tried...

*'Anton, no. Please, she's only a child,' Katarina pleaded with the Kommandant as we stood waiting for the doctor in the examination room.*

*'We must have Doctor Gunters' confirmation that she is Aryan and unblemished. For our sake and Karls, there can be no doubt, Katarina. Or are you willing to risk Karl's future for this girl? If you are, I will dispose of her now and save us both the complication.'*

*Katarina turned to me, her eyes pleading for understanding and forgiveness. 'It will be alright, Désirée. Just do as you're told. It will be alright,' she assured me before walking out with the Kommandant and leaving me alone as Doctor Gunter walked in, snapping on a pair of rubber gloves and smelling like antiseptic.*

*'Let's get started, young lady. Remove all your clothes, then lay on the table with your knees pulled up and spread apart,' he ordered...*

I stumbled through the hall behind Mama Bea, hardly able to take a breath as we passed the patients waiting for care, their faces gloomy, worried, sad.

By the time we entered Doctor Easton's office, my breathing was fast and shallow, and my heart pounded hard in my chest. Fear coursed through me, and all I could think about was running and hiding, finding an escape.

"Right this way, Mrs. Marchand. Doctor Easton will be right with you," a nurse in a crisp white uniform said, leading us into a small examination room. "Remove your clothes and put this gown on, my dear, then we'll get you weighed and measured," she instructed before leaving.

"I want to go home. Please. I do not want to be here," I begged Mama Bea.

"Darling, you're trembling. What's upsetting you, sweetheart?" She pulled me into her arms, stroking my back, trying to comfort my distress.

"*S'il vous plaît. Je veux partir. Je ne veux pas être ici.*" I pleaded as tears fell freely down my cheeks and I tried to stifle the memories, push them back into their boxes. Then Doctor Easton came in, and the sight of his white coat hurled me into the nightmare again. I stiffened in Mama Bea's embrace, poised to run at the least provocation.

"Good afternoon, Désirée. What seems to be the problem, dear?" Doctor Easton asked, recognizing my emotional state.

I couldn't speak. My throat had tightened unbearably.

"I'm not sure what happened, Robert," Mama Bea said, her tone worried as she tried to comfort me. "She was fine earlier, but something has upset her. I don't know what it is. Perhaps we can reschedule the physical for another time. But we need her immunizations done for school."

"That's alright, Bea. She's certainly not the first young girl frightened by the doctor's office. Uncover her arm and we'll get the shots done as quickly as possible."

My mind shut down. As soon as we got home, I ran to my room, utterly overwhelmed by the memories. They hadn't assaulted me for a while, and rarely during the day. The residual fear and need to hide sent me cowering in the corner of my bedroom, tears still running down my face.

"I'm not sure, Beau. Something frightened her. I had to hold her in my arms while Robert and the nurse gave her the shots. She wouldn't talk to me all the way home," Mama Bea said, standing in the hallway outside my room.

Mama Bea was upset, and I was sorry about that. She was only trying to help, to do what any good parent would do, but she didn't know how broken I really was.

"It was probably a flashback, Mama. A memory triggered by something. It could have been anything, but that's the way her mind works. She remembers everything—everything she sees, hears, and experiences. She keeps it all sorted in her mind in tidy little boxes, but sometimes things don't stay sorted," Bill explained. He understood me so well.

"Is that what the nightmares are?"

"I imagine so. She's lived through some horrible things. Talking it through seems to help. I'll go in and talk to her."

"No, Beau. I'll talk to her. She needs to trust me the way she trusts you. I think that's important for both of you."

Mama Bea quietly stepped into my room, closing the door behind her, and found me still huddled in the corner, my face buried in my hands.

"Oh sweetheart, come here, darling," she said, lifting me to my feet, then she wrapped her arms around me and held me close. "I am so sorry. I didn't understand. Can you forgive me?"

It felt good being in her arms, it felt safe and uncomplicated. I didn't have to pretend with her, as I had with others. My tears soaked the front of her jacket as I shook my head.

"You did nozing wrong, madame. Zare is nozing to forgive. It is me. Sometimes I cannot stop it. I am sorry," I said, sniffling away my tears, attempting to pull myself together, but the residual fear lingered in my mind and trembling body.

"Come here and lie down for a while, darling. Doctor Easton said you should rest." She led me to the bed and joined me there. Reaching behind us, she removed the old woman's shawl from the headboard where I always kept it, then wrapped it around me, pulling me close.

I curled up next to her, needing her comfort and fiercely missing my mother. Mama Bea's gentle touch down my arm helped slow my breathing, calm my fears. We said nothing for a while, we just lay there together, each finding comfort in the other.

"Do I remind you of her? The German woman, Katarina?" she asked.

I looked up into eyes that searched mine for understanding, and I let go of my fears, opening my heart to her.

"Sometimes, you do. You are za same; your wealth and za way you live are za same. But she is different. She had a different life, a harder one zan you."

"Do you miss her?"

The question hung in the air between us, not a noose or a trap, but a simple query for clarity's sake and perhaps reassurance.

"*Oui*, I miss her and za ozers; Bisabuela, Tante Elsa, Sœur Louise Claire, and my mozer. I miss zem all." Tears filled my eyes again as I thought about the women who had saved me, protected me from the nightmare I'd been caught up in. They all had loved me, and I loved them, but love was no match for fate.

"Wiz Katarina, I could not talk to her. I must always hide how I feel. But now, wiz you and Bill, I can say my feelings, but sometimes zay are too big, too much." I took a deep breath, then released it with a shudder, sniffling away my tears.

She hugged me tighter, soothing my sorrow in her tender embrace. I wanted to stay there forever, absorb her strength and surety, so I could push the nightmares back into their boxes.

"Oh, my sweet girl, I know how that feels. Sometimes my sorrow overwhelms me too, and it's hard to step around it." She took a full breath, then let it out with a shudder, clearly remembering a deep hurt. "A good long cry can ease the sadness, especially in the arms of someone who loves you. It seems to help me."

"Do you miss him?" I asked, knowing she was thinking of her husband, who died five years earlier.

"Yes, darling. I miss him every minute of every day." She pulled me closer, hugging me tighter, perhaps to ease the sadness of her own loss in the comfort of my young embrace.

I fell asleep in her arms, feeling safe once more, and finally able to secure all the terrible memories back into their tidy little boxes.

# Chapter 17

## *My Dream Garden*

The next morning, I lingered deep in the dream-memory, unwilling to relinquish the happy feeling it gave me...

*I could feel the weight of the basket hanging from my shoulder, half-filled with clusters of ripe grapes, could smell the vines as I grasped the next bunch, holding it gently but firmly, and with a sure swipe of my knife, I severed it from the branch, dropping it into the basket. "Watch your fingers, ma petite," Papa said, even though it was my second harvest, and I'd never cut myself...*

Bang! Bang! Bang! — Bang! Bang! Bang!

The sharp sound of a hammer hitting wood pulled me from the dream. I threw off the sheet and ran to the gallery to see what was going on, though I had my suspicions. From the gallery railing, I looked down into the yard where Bill and Bobby were working in the garden, pounding boards together to make the raised beds. I watched them for a while, their heads bent over the task at hand, a quiet discussion passing between them.

A sense of peace washed over me, gratitude that they both were in my life. So many people I cared for had disappeared in an instant, leaving me lost and alone. I prayed it would be different this time. I hoped it would be.

Bill glanced up and saw me watching them, then waved. "Good morning, sleepyhead. Are you going to join us? I could use a cup of coffee, Chère."

"I will be right down with za coffee." I waved, then hurried inside to throw on some work clothes and join in the fun.

When I got downstairs, Miss Laila handed me a cup of coffee to take out to Bill. "Tell Mr. William breakfast will be ready soon. You can ask Mr. Bobby if he wants to join us. There's plenty, in case he does."

"Thank you, Miss Laila," I said, hurrying out the back door, coffee cup in hand.

Bill and Bobby had finished building one bed: a four by eight-foot cedar frame, sixteen inches deep. The planks needed for the other bed lay to the side. There were also four sturdy posts, about eight feet tall, two eight-foot-long boards, and a bunch of smaller pieces lying in the driveway. Those extra pieces puzzled me, and I wondered what the plan was for those.

"What do you think, Chère? Is it going to be big enough with the two beds?" Bill asked as I handed him the coffee. He was clearly proud of their achievement.

"It is perfect, Bill. Zank you. Zank you, Bobby. I love it." A deep breath filled my nostrils with the scent of cut timber, and I imagined all the things I would grow in those beds and the meals I would make from the harvest.

"We're gonna build a pergola that will cover the walkway and we're gonna put a bench at the back. Do you really like it, Désirée? It was super easy to build. Wasn't it, Bill? We'll have the other one done in no time," Bobby said, puffing out his chest with pride.

"As easy as Lincoln Logs, thanks to Bobby's expertise in design and measurement. The fellows at the lumberyard cut the pieces and delivered them last night. Bobby and I thought we'd get an early start on it this morning. It's going faster than we thought," Bill explained.

"I love it, Bobby. *Merci mon ami*. Will you have breakfast with us? It is almost ready."

"Sure. I'm starving. Got any more of those scones? Those were good."

"Sorry, Bobby. You'll have to get Désirée to make you another batch. I ate the last one last night," Bill said with a crooked smile.

"What is Lincoln Logs?" I asked as the three of us walked arm in arm into the house for breakfast.

Bobby and Bill looked at each other, rolled their eyes and laughed.

I should have been used to it by then. There had been countless days in the past five years that had started ideally, only to be ruined by some unforeseen eventuality. But I never got used to it, never lost the nagging feeling that something would pull the rug out from under me in an instant.

That day was no different, despite how happy those moments with Bill and Bobby were, the three of us working together to build my dream garden. The fickle hand of fate had lessons for me to learn that day, and they came in the guise of Charlotte Bentley.

After breakfast, we returned to the garden. The boys continued building the planting beds, and I stood around and supervised since they wouldn't let me swing a hammer, fearing I'd hurt myself. It was irritating that they thought of me as fragile. I wasn't, of course, but they were impossible to convince.

"Let Bobby and I take care of the heavy work, Chère. You can help with the soil when Carlos gets here. He's bringing a few plants to get your new garden started."

Señor Garcia and his son, Nico, arrived just as Bobby and Bill finished building the second bed of 'Lincoln Logs'. Their truck towed a small trailer, which they backed up into the driveway, all the way to the garage. The trailer held a pile of coarse gravel and several potted plants, and they had filled the truck bed with loamy soil. I wondered what the gravel was for.

"*¡Hola!* Señor William," Carlos called out as he climbed out of the truck with Nico not far behind. "*¿Cómo estás?* It's good to see you home, sir. We brought the soil and plants you asked for, plus a little gravel. We'll need it for drainage in the planting beds. All that Mississippi mud ain't no good for this kind of garden. Nico, pull those plants out so Miss Désirée can see what we brought for her."

Nico, who was a ruggedly handsome eighteen-year-old with dark hair and even darker eyes, set to extracting the pots from the trailer and setting them down in front of me along the driveway, a shy smile lighting his face every time he looked my way.

They brought a young rosemary plant, a cluster of chives, and small pots of thyme, marjoram, and sage. A young lemon tree with a few tiny flower buds ready to bloom filled a bucket at my feet. The scent of the blossoms instantly triggered a memory, one that was easy to save for later. Two other plants sat next to the lemon tree, but I didn't know what they were. I must have looked confused as I examined them.

"They're wisteria. Beautiful when they're mature and bloom. They smell good too," Nico explained.

"Is it an herb for cooking?"

"No. Strictly ornamental," he said, shaking his head. "Once they're grown, they'll cover the pergola walkway, and the blossoms will hang down beneath the canopy. Mr. William asked us to bring them."

"*Oye, mijo!*" Carlos called out from yard where the garden beds were going to live. "We have work to do. Let's get busy and get this sod cut back."

I followed behind, hoping to help, but they all refused my offer, which meant I had to stand back and watch while they did all the work. I moved my new plants out of the way so the manly men could do their manly things for me. It irritated me they thought I was too young or too fragile to help. I was just as capable as any of them, well, at least as much as Bobby, but I held my tongue and let them play the big, strong men.

But I did love watching them and couldn't help but smile at the sight of them working together to build my dream garden.

A little before lunchtime, I went inside to get them some iced tea and lemonade. It was a brutally hot day, even by Louisiana standards, and they were all sweating up a storm in the scorching sun. The front doorbell rang while I was in the kitchen, getting the drinks ready.

"You go get the door, Miss Dezrae. I'll take these drinks outside," Miss Laila instructed.

Typically, Mr. Jefferies would answer the door, but he had taken Mama Bea out to an appointment. I thought it might be one of Bobby's friends looking for him, but when I opened the door, Charlotte Bentley was standing on the doorstep, a fake smile plastered on her red lips.

Stylishly dressed, as always, her hair was impeccable, her makeup flawless. Everything about her looked perfect, and I hated her instantly. She was going to ruin my day.

"Hello, Miss Bentley. Can I help you?" I asked, even though I didn't want to help her with anything.

"Good afternoon, Désirée," she said, looking down her nose at me. "Don't you look sweet in your little summer outfit? It looks like you need to wash up, though. There's a bit of dirt on your face and some under your nails, too. Not very lady-like. Whatever have you been doing?"

"Working in za garden." I couldn't hold back the frown pinching my eyebrows together.

"Whyever for? Never mind, I don't care. Is Bill here?" she quickly asked, looking around for him.

"He is working in za garden. I will get him."

She looked down her nose at me again, wrinkling it up in distaste.

"He is? How domestic of him. Why don't you bring me a glass of sweet tea with a little bourbon in it while I go outside and see what Bill is up to? I know the way."

I hurried to do her bidding, albeit reluctantly. Initially, I thought about throwing the drink in her face the minute I got back with it, but knew that probably wouldn't go over well, regardless of how much pleasure it would give me.

Charlotte was sitting in a patio chair under the shade of the gallery when I returned with her drink. She was gazing across the yard at the half-naked men working there. I almost spilled the drink on her when I saw them standing around, their muscular torsos gleaming with sweat. I hadn't seen a sight like that since the last time I watched Papa and my brothers pull their shirts from their backs to rinse off at the pump after a day in the fields. My heartbeat raced, and I felt a flush rise to my face, unbidden and unstoppable.

"Now that's a sight, isn't it?" Charlotte said, taking the drink from my shaking hand.

"I always did like the look of a man working in the hot sun, especially one as attractive as Bill Marchand. From the look on your face, Désirée, he's captured your attention, too. You should close your mouth, sugar. You don't want to catch flies, do you?"

I clamped my mouth shut, blinking a few times, and trying to control my embarrassment. Charlotte Bentley wasn't someone I wanted to share any feelings with, so I attempted to excuse myself.

"I will get Bill for you."

"Don't bother. I'll wait till he's done. You sit here with me so we can talk a bit while I enjoy the view."

As much as I wanted to, I couldn't be rude, so I took the seat next to her and waited.

"You know, Désirée, I wasn't much older than you when I got my first crush on Bill Marchand. I knew even then we were perfect for each other. It took me a few years to capture him, but now that he's home and this silly war is almost over, I have every intention of sealing the deal. I thought you should know, so we understand one another." She looked at me like I was a bug she wanted to smash under her shoe.

There was nothing appropriate for me to say in response, so I just shrugged and rolled my eyes as if it didn't matter. Of course, it mattered, it mattered a lot, but I wouldn't let her see that.

Just then, Bill looked over and saw Charlotte and me sitting on the patio. His expression darkened a bit as he walked over to us.

"Charlotte, I didn't expect to see you today," he said, wiping his hands down his pant legs and putting his shirt back on. Sweat dripped from his forehead, his face red with exertion as he swiped his arm across it. The look on his face said he wasn't particularly pleased to see her.

Apparently, Charlotte was oblivious to Bill's mood, because her own transformed from the surly bitch she had been with me to the sweet Southern Belle that she showed him.

"Hello, darling," she said, leaning in to give him an air kiss. "I've missed you. We haven't seen each other in days. I thought I could entice you to take me to lunch today, but I can see you're occupied with a little project. I declare, Bill, I don't know what's gotten into you. I've never known you to be so... domestic." The words dripped off her red lips like poisoned syrup.

"I'm a little busy today, Charlotte. If you'd called..."

"That's alright, darling. I understand," she said, giving me a quick glance. "Take me to supper later? I don't think I could stand one more evening without you. Carson asked me to meet him and Joe Barone, but I'd much rather spend time with you. Please, darling," she pouted, sounding precisely like Scarlett O'Hara.

Bill stood there looking at her, his thoughts shielded from view. I wondered why he didn't just tell her he wasn't going to marry her and then send her away for good. But it was clear something else was going on, something I didn't understand between Charlotte and Bill, and it bothered me.

"Where are Carson and Joe meeting tonight?" Bill asked.

"The Carousel at nine," she purred. Her look had a kind of sweet, satisfied expression which told me she felt like she had him on the line.

"Let me walk you out, Charlotte. I'll call you later." He led her through the house to the front door, where she stopped to deliver one last shot while I watched from the patio door.

Charlotte turned, reached up with her gloved hands, and drew Bill's face down to hers, kissing him deeply, passionately. "I've missed you, darling.

Come by at eight. I'll have your drink ready for you," she said, loud enough for me to hear.

Charlotte smiled her Scarlett smile as she saw me standing in the living room. "Nice chatting with you, Désirée," she said, wagging her fingers at me before leaving.

When the door closed, Bill let out a heavy breath, then he looked over at me, shaking his head. He could see the questions behind my eyes, the ones I wouldn't ask him. *Why haven't you told her? Why are you still seeing her?*

He walked up and just stood there looking at me, his thoughts unreadable. Lifting his hand to my face, he stroked my cheek with his thumb, his gentle touch meant to be a reassurance.

"It's complicated, Chère," was all he said.

*I guess I'll just have to live with that.*

I didn't have a choice.

# Chapter 18

## *Friendship cookies and hard lessons*

"Mornin', Miss Dezrae. How you feelin this mornin'? Everythin' alright?" Miss Laila asked as I came down to breakfast the next morning.

"Come sit here, sugar. Tell Laila what's botherin' you." She pulled the stool away from the counter, patting the seat, then placed a glass of juice in front of me.

My eyelids were heavy with exhaustion, the result of a sleepless night spent waiting in vain for Bill's return. He hadn't slept in his bed. The clothes he'd worn the day before lay scattered across it.

It had been the longest night of my life, sitting in the dark, thinking about why Bill hadn't come home. I imagined a thousand different scenarios, each more horrifying than the last. My overactive imagination kept coming back to the most likely of possibilities: Bill had gone to Charlotte and stayed. The sting that thought left in my heart was almost unbearable.

"Ya still worrying 'bout Jolie, Miss Dezrae?" Miss Laila asked as she bustled around the kitchen. "She's fine. She asked me about you. Wanted to know if you'd write down that recipe for them cookies you made. The little ones was asking her to make them some. I told her I'd ask you."

Connecting with Jolie, even in this small way, was distracting enough to pull me out of the melancholy mood I was in. The possibility that Jolie and I could become friends, despite the social rules, continued to burn in my mind and right then I knew cooking might be the avenue to pursue that friendship.

"I will write za recipe for her and a letter, zen maybe she will write to me." Then another idea popped into my head. "Is it okay for Jolie and me to cook togezer? To learn from you? I would like zis."

Miss Laila gave me one of her brilliant smiles with flashing white teeth. "I don't know, Miss Dezrae. We'll have to talk with Miss Bea and Mr. William first. Need their okay before we make any plans like that."

"It will be okay. I will convince zem," I said with a renewed sense of purpose.

Tossing down the juice, I headed up to my room to write the letter, determined to secure Mama Bea's approval. Bill's permission would have to wait because he was busy pursuing his own interests.

Once I drafted the letter and recipe, I went in search of Mama Bea to begin phase two of my plan.

"What's this, Désirée?" Mama Bea asked as I handed her the letter to Jolie. She was sitting behind her desk, a folder of documents opened in front of her, and a cup of coffee nestled in her hands. "Have you finished 'Gone with the Wind' already? I told you to take your time reading it."

"I am not finish... finished wiz it yet. Zis is a letter I write to Jolie. Would you see it is correct for me?" My innocent expression apparently wasn't much of a disguise because Mama Bea's eyebrows raised up in two distinct arches above the rim of her reading glasses. I wasn't sure what that expression meant for the success of my plan.

"A letter to Jolie? Hmm. Alright, let's have a look at it." She perused the page for a moment, made some corrections with her red pen, then handed it back to me.

*Dear Jolie,*

*I was very happy to meet you and your family last Sunday. They were all so kind to me. It was ~~a~~ good ~~day for me~~* to be *~~being~~ in the country on a farm again, after such a long time.*

*Miss Laila said you would like the recipe for the cookies I ~~make~~* made *for your family. On the other page I ~~give you~~* have written *the recipe for ~~these~~ Florentine Oatmeal Cookies. Be careful when you bake them. They will burn ~~easy~~* easily.

*Do you have a special recipe you can share with me? Miss Laila ~~tell~~* told *me you like to cook ~~the same~~* as *I do. I want to cook with you sometime. Perhaps we can cook together with Miss Laila. She ~~say~~* said *she will teach me Cajun and Creole cooking. I hope you say yes to this idea, and ~~I~~ hope you will write to me about it.*

*Your friend,*

*Désirée*

Mama Bea looked up; her eyebrows still arched. "This is a lovely letter, Désirée. I'm sure Jolie will appreciate the gesture, but are you sure this is something you want to do? You'll be very busy with school once it starts. There won't be much time for trivial pursuits."

My lips pinched at the idea that cooking, or friendship, were trivial pursuits and told her so. "Yes, I do. I want to be friends wiz Jolie. We are za same. We both like to cook, we are almost za same age, and we boz have lost our mozers. You see, we are za same."

"Not quite the same, Désirée, as you well know by now. What you're asking is not as easy as you imagine it to be," she said, worry creasing her forehead.

"Why? Because her skin is darker zan mine? Zis is no reason not to be friends wiz her." I was adamant in my position, unwilling to accept the unspoken rules that dictated social etiquette in New Orleans.

Before she could respond, I added, "You are friends wiz Miss Laila and Mr. Jefferies, and zare family. How you do zis if it is so difficult?" I asked, hoping she'd give some sage answer which would solve the whole problem.

Mama Bea closed her eyes, pulling the glasses from her face, then pinched the bridge of her nose, exhaling her apparent frustration. When her eyes opened, she sighed, then stood up and walked to the front window, gazing out at something.

I knew I was making things hard for her. My presence alone was challenging enough, but my desire for friendship with Jolie wasn't something I would give up on, and it must have shown. She turned to face me, her shoulders straight and chin up with a look of resolve on her face.

"Eulaila and I have known one another since we were children, much younger than you, Désirée. Her family has worked for mine for generations, and our friendship developed over many years of being around one another, growing up together, so to speak. Eulaila is my closest friend. However, we are both keenly aware of the limits society places on our friendship. We've learned to navigate those limits over the years, which is something we could not have achieved at a distance."

"Jolie does not live far from here. I can visit her, and she can visit me. It is simple." That's how it felt to me anyway, but Mama Bea's expression said otherwise.

"No, darling. It is not that simple," she stated. "We'll need to speak with Beau about this before we decide. Send your letter to Jolie and we'll talk to Beau when he returns."

I assumed that to be my dismissal, but I had to ask.

"Where is Bill? When will he be home?"

Her look told me I shouldn't have asked, perhaps because she didn't know. I spun away, not waiting for her response, which never came anyway.

I spent the morning cleaning my room, rarely allowing Miss Laila to have any part in sorting through my mess. The mess was mine, and I preciously guarded my treasures. Not from a fear of them being taken—they had no value to anyone but me—instead, it was a fear of exposure, of someone finding out who I had been and what I'd done. That fear was ever present, always in the back of my mind, reminding me to stay vigilant.

*Who are you now?* I asked the girl in my mirror as I caught her reflection.

Bill and Mama Bea told me to just be myself, and I tried to figure out who that was, but I felt at odds with what New Orleans society expected of me. Becoming an Uptown Girl seemed to require my acceptance of the bigotry, both subtle and blatant, that the surrounding population willfully embraced.

I couldn't do it, couldn't force myself to swallow that pill. I had lived with that kind of hatred before and wanted no part of it again.

*Remember, be brave and strong and clever. Find a way, Désirée.*

"Knock, knock."

When I looked up, Bobby was standing in my bedroom doorway, munching on a biscuit Miss Laila had undoubtedly handed him on his way through the kitchen. He looked happy about something, with his eyes sparkling and a big smile on his face.

Bobby was a frequent visitor since we'd become friends, and Mama Bea didn't mind him coming up to my room, as long as the door stayed open.

"Hello Bobby, how are you?"

"Couldn't be better. I checked out our handy work on the way through the yard, and it's pretty nifty, if I say so myself. Can't wait to see what you grow in there." He plopped down, straddling the desk chair to face me. "Is Bill around? I didn't see him when I came in."

I shrugged, then rolled my head around, trying to release my frustration about Bill's absence. A heavier sigh than I intended escaped my lips before I answered.

"No. he is not here. He did not come home last night," I said, a little too petulantly.

"Oh... Did he go out with that pretty woman who came over yesterday? Is she his girlfriend?" Bobby asked, resting his chin on his crossed arms draped over the back of the chair. He just stared at me, like it was an interrogation or something.

I rolled my eyes, unable to hold back the frown tugging on the corners of my mouth.

"Charlotte Bentley is *not* his girlfriend. She is a Scarlett. Bill would never love a Scarlett," I stated firmly. I hoped that was true.

"I thought you said her name was Charlotte," Bobby said, his expression perplexed.

"It is... I do not want to talk about zem," I said with a huff, throwing my journal down on the floor by the armchair.

"Alright. Have it your way, but if you ask me, you're looking like the green-eyed monster has you by the tail." Blue eyes pierced mine with an intense curiosity and a bit of humor.

"What does zis mean? Green-eyed monster."

Bobby shook his head at me, chuckling under his breath. "It means you're acting like a jealous girlfriend. What's that all about, Désirée? Bill's old enough to be your father or uncle, at least."

"I am not jealous," I said, though I knew that was a lie. "I do not like her. She is like Scarlett O'Hara, very mean when she act so sweet. He should not be wiz someone like her."

I hadn't fooled Bobby for a minute.

"For someone who's only known Bill Marchand for what... nine days? You seem to care a lot about him. Come to think of it, he cares a lot about you, too. Why else would he do all that for you yesterday?" He stared at me for a while, patiently waiting for an answer that I wouldn't, or couldn't, give him. Bobby never pushed me for answers, seeming to understand my need to cling to my secrets. Bobby had his own secrets.

Then he shook it all off, changing the subject. "Wanna go to the movies? A bunch of us are meeting up at the Prytania this afternoon. Wanna go?"

Bobby and his friends had hatched a plan to invite some girls to go with them to the movies. The dilemma was what movie to attend. The boys would have preferred *Secret Agent X-9* with Lloyd Bridges or *Sherlock Holmes and the House of Fear* with Basil Rathbone and Nigel Bruce, but after some discussion, they all agreed that girls would most likely go with them if they saw *Anchors Aweigh* with Gene Kelly and Frank Sinatra, a much more girl-friendly film.

"Sure, I want to go. I need a distraction. Who will go?" I asked, always needing to know who I'd be with and what to expect; me being a habitually cautious person.

"Just Eddie and Jimmy and a couple of girls from school, Kaitlyn and Sarah. You might have seen them at the park. They come and watch us play sometimes."

"I see some girls zare, but we do not speak. I will tell Mama Bea about za movie. She will say okay." I was certain Mama Bea would give her permission for this social adventure. The Bridge Club was coming over and she would be busy all afternoon. Evelyn Duret was vacationing out of town and wouldn't be coming over.

Both Bill and Mama Bea approved of and even encouraged my friendship with Bobby. At first, I thought it was because the Marchands and the Eastons had been friends and neighbors for years. Mama Bea had known Bobby his entire life. But since Bill came home, it felt like there was some other reason they trusted Bobby so much while still warning me against the dangers of American teenage boys. There was something about Bobby they both found implicitly trustworthy, but I wasn't sure what that was. I just knew I liked him and was comfortable around him, so any opportunity to spend time with Bobby was fine with me.

"Super!" he said, climbing off the chair and heading for the door. "I'll be by to get you at 12:30. The movie starts at 1:15. See ya later, Désirée."

# Chapter 19

## *Movie Fiascos*

The Prytania Theater was only a few blocks away on the other side of St. Charles Avenue, close enough we didn't need Mr. Jefferies to drive us, but Mama Bea needed to assure herself of our safe passage. Bobby stood in front of her, thumbs hooked into the front pockets of his blue jeans, shirt almost tucked in behind his belt, and head bowed respectfully. He listened to her cautions, barely holding back a grin that mimicked my own suppressed laughter.

Bobby and I had walked the neighborhood lots of times, but this was the first opportunity Mama Bea allowed me to go with a group of kids to the movies. I suppose her extra caution was because Bill's approval was absent.

*Bill would say okay.* I mentally projected that thought to Mama Bea as she continued to lecture Bobby on good manners in the company of ladies.

"I promise, Miss Bea. I'll take good care of her, and we'll come home straight after the movie. On my honor." Bobby stood at attention, giving her a sharp salute with his right hand.

"I'll hold you to that, Robert," Mama Bea replied, a stern look marking her face. "Take a sweater, Désirée. It gets chilly in the theater sometimes. I'll be here all afternoon if you need me. Run along now. Have fun, you two," she said, waving her hand in dismissal.

A short time later, Bobby and I were walking through the doors of the Prytania Theater with Jimmy Wilcox, Eddie Berg, and their two dates, Kaitlyn Delaney and Sarah Edelstein. The girls were both older than me—well, everyone was older than me—and they seemed a little shy. I didn't understand why; I was the new girl, not them.

While Bobby and the boys conferred together about what to buy at the snack stand, Kaitlyn and Sarah whispered in each other's ears, their faces flushed with barely suppressed excitement. After observing them for a while, it became apparent it wasn't me they were nervous around; it was the boys. I was a simple curiosity, a new girl to question and then classify into the hierarchy of high school society. Bobby had warned me about it, but right then, the girls seemed more interested in Eddie and Jimmy than they did me.

"I was so happy when Eddie called. I've been hoping we could all go out together before school starts," Sarah confessed as Kaitlyn and I followed her into the ladies' room.

Sarah was a pretty, brown-haired girl with big brown eyes rimmed in a thick layer of dark lashes. She wore a white peasant-style blouse with puffed short sleeves trimmed with lace, tucked into a floral-printed skirt. The saddle shoes and bobby socks she wore seemed to be a staple among New Orleans girls. Kaitlyn and I wore the same style.

"Jimmy surprised me when he called. I didn't think he liked me. He's barely said a word to me all summer," Kaitlyn said as she leaned across the sink to check her hair in the bathroom mirror. "Where did you meet Bobby Easton, Désirée? You know he was one of the most popular eighth-grade boys at Newman last year and one of the nicest too." Kaitlyn adjusted her hair with her hands as she talked to my reflection in the mirror.

Just then, a woman with a young girl in tow pushed her way into the ladies' room, brusquely stepping around us. She guided the child into a stall, then stood guard while the girl did her business. "Hurry up now, Lizzy. I want to get a good seat," she told the stall door, her face lined with annoyance at the apparent delay.

Kaitlyn and Sarah gave each other a look that seemed to say we'd better rejoin the boys and take our own seats. I finished washing my hands and adjusting my Gautier mask in the mirror before following them out.

The boys were waiting for us with big smiles on their faces, their arms full of popcorn and snacks. When I saw Bobby standing there, my mind flashed back to the last time I'd been to the movies with friends. It was on a warm spring day last March when I'd gone to the cinema in Suresnes with Camille and the others. The war was still raging, but France was free and that was all that mattered to us.

*I wonder, do you ever think about me?* Chaz Maret's handsome face filled my mind, and a twinge of regret pierced my heart. *Don't think about him, Désirée. That's all over now.*

Bobby held the door for me as we followed the others into the dark theater. Eddie led our group a short distance down the aisle and into an empty row. Eddie sat next to Sarah, who sat next to Kaitlyn. Then came Jimmy, then me, and finally Bobby at the end of the row. We were a cozy group, chatting quietly about the upcoming movie while munching on our snacks.

Inside the theater, only a handful of couples and parents with children occupied the many rows of seats. A uniformed soldier sat next to a woman in the seats directly in front of Bobby and me, their heads bent together, sharing some quiet conversation.

When I looked up, the woman from the bathroom stood in the aisle next to the soldier, her daughter sheltering behind her. The woman had an ugly expression on her face, her brow pinched in a deep crease above her nose as she glared down at the soldier and his companion, like they were something distasteful she discovered in her seat.

"What the hell are you doing sitting here among decent folks, nigger? Get your black ass out of that seat and take your bitch with you. You don't belong down here," the woman said loud enough we all could hear her. Everyone in that theater could hear her. The little girl stood cowering behind her mother while the woman continued to rail against the Negro soldier, saying horrible things to him, as if he had no feelings and deserved her rebuke.

"We're just here to see the movie, ma'am. Same as you. We're not bothering anyone," the soldier said, with a lot more respect than the woman deserved.

"Well, you're bothering me, nigger. Now get out of here before I call the manager and have you and your whore thrown out." By then, the woman was almost screaming, and I had enough of it.

I stood up to confront her, unable to control myself. It made my blood boil just listening to her speak to him that way.

"Zese people were here first to watch za movie. Zare are ozer places for you to sit, madame. You should not speak like zis to zem," I said, looking straight at her as my Gautier mask slipped from my face.

She turned her hateful gaze to me. "This is none of your concern, girl. Sit your ass down and stay out of it."

Bobby pulled on my arm, trying to get me to sit down. "Désirée, come on. Let it go. Sit down, please."

"No, I will not," I said, yanking my arm free from his grasp. I was on a roll by then and Bobby couldn't stop me. "Zis man is a soldier who has fought for your country, and zis is how you treat him? As if he does not belong? You should have shame, madame, for being so hateful, for teaching your daughter such hateful ways. Shame on you. Are kindness and courtesy not valued in zis country?" I asked, spitting my own venom at the hateful woman.

No one in that theater offered an answer, but the woman became outraged at my assault on her character.

"How dare you speak to me that way, you little nigger-lover?" Then she pulled her arm back and struck me hard across my face. I grabbed the seat back in front of me to catch my fall.

"Hey, you can't do that! Leave her alone!" Bobby yelled at the woman as he jumped up out of his seat to pull me out of the woman's reach.

The soldier and his companion quickly stood up to exit the row at the opposite end. He hobbled up the aisle with the aid of a cane and his companion's help. Eddie Berg followed them out to the lobby, apparently to find the manager.

I just stared at the woman, my face stinging from the blow. "Does zis make you feel better about yourself, madame, zat you can hit a girl for telling you za truz? Shame on you."

"You little bitch. Who is your mother? I've got a few things to say to her."

"My mozer is dead, but she would never behave as you. She was a kind woman."

"Come on, Désirée. Let's get out of here," Bobby said, tugging on my arm to get away from the crazy woman. Then the theater manager hurried down the aisle to handle the situation before it got more out of hand.

"Young lady, you're going to have to leave," the manager said after he heard from the woman about my assault on her righteous position. Her physical assault on me didn't seem to matter to him or to anyone except

Bobby. Based on the looks I received, it was abundantly clear that I had broken a sacred rule; never publicly defend a Negro.

"I did nozing wrong. I only say za truz to her," I complained as the manager escorted me away. The implications and ultimate consequences of what I'd done slowly became apparent, but at that moment, I didn't care. Right then, the injustice of it was the only thing I could think about.

With crossed arms and a frown on my face, I marched out, more than happy to remove myself from the pervasive bigotry exhibited around me. The eyes of every person inside that theater followed me out, especially those of Kaitlyn and Sarah, who I suspected would never speak to me again.

I didn't care. I could never be like them, could never accept those kinds of rules. Every experience I had over the past five years taught me what happens when people hate like that, and what that hatred leads to when left unchecked. My mind railed against it.

Bobby and Jimmy Wilcox followed me out. Eddie stayed with the girls, hopefully to soothe their discomfort caused by my untimely disruption of their movie date. The theater manager pulled Bobby aside to discuss the situation while I stood by the outside door, gauging the timing of my exit. I wanted to leave immediately and had no intention of listening to a lecture on proper social behavior, least of all from these people.

"We're sorry, sir. My friend is new here. I mean, she's new in the States. She doesn't understand our ways, sir," Bobby told the manager, trying to convince him to allow me to stay.

"I'm very sorry, son. I can't allow this kind of trouble in my theater. I'm going to have to call her mother about this. Write her phone number down for me, son. You wait right there, young lady," the manager ordered before going into his office.

Bobby looked at me, his expression filled with worry as he wrote my phone number on a pad of paper and handed it to the manager. Jimmy stood close by, his own worry etched on his face.

"Are you okay, Désirée?" Jimmy asked. "That woman had no right to hit you—no right at all."

My face burned from the slap, a thousand tiny needles stinging my cheek. The sensation kindled memories of other times someone had hit me, filling my mind with unwanted images, sending shivers down my arms...

*"Now you have something to cry about," the Kommandant snarled...*

*"Tell me who you're working with! Where were you meeting them? Tell me!" the monster in the dungeon screamed...*

I had to leave, had to get as far away from there as I could. I needed time to think and fresh air to clear the nightmares away. Tightly held tears burned behind my eyes as I looked up at Jimmy. Shaking my head in response, I walked out the door and around the corner.

Going straight home was out of the question. There'd be a lecture waiting for me when I got there, and I didn't see any reason to rush into it. I needed to figure things out first.

"Hey, wait for me, Désirée," Bobby called out, running up behind me. "Miss Bea's sending Jacob to pick us up. She said we've got to wait here."

"I do not want to go home, Bobby. I want to walk to za park, to zink for a while." I couldn't meet his gaze.

"Well, let's wait for Jacob to get here, then we'll tell him. Okay?"

"Excuse me, miss," said a woman's voice behind us. I looked back and saw the negro woman and soldier standing at the back of the building. The soldier was leaning hard against the wall, balancing himself with a cane held tight in his right hand. The woman took a few shy steps toward Bobby and me.

"I just want to thank you for what you did for my husband back there. We're very sorry for the trouble we caused you."

I shook my head, realizing they felt responsible for the hatefulness that awful woman unleashed on them, and I couldn't let them hold on to that idea.

"It was not your fault, Madame. It was not mine. Zat woman was wrong in what she say to you. I am sorry you do not see za movie."

The woman lowered her head. "We should have tried walking up the stairs, but Nathan's only just got his new leg, and it pains him climbing stairs. I didn't think anyone'd mind us sitting down below, Nathan being a soldier and all. We're real sorry, miss."

"Where you go now? Your husband, he must sit, no? For his leg." I asked, looking around for somewhere the soldier could sit down and get a respite from what was obviously a painful condition.

"My brother is supposed to pick us up after the movie, but that's not for a couple of hours. I guess we'll try to catch the bus up Magazine," she said, worry creasing her face as she gazed up the long blocks towards the bus line.

"I have a better idea. You wait here," I said when I saw Mr. Jefferies pull the car up to the curb in front of Bobby. I went up to the car to speak with him.

"You alright, Miss Dezrae? Look like there been some trouble," Mr. Jefferies said as he climbed out of the car and got a good look at my cheek. "Miss Bea's not gonna like it that someone laid hands on you."

"I am okay, Mr. Jefferies. I explain to Mama Bea about zis when I go home. But first, I want you do a favor for me, okay?"

His face darkened with deeper worry. "Whatever you need, Miss Dezrae. I's here to help."

"Zank you, Mr. Jefferies," I said, then I motioned for the soldier and his wife to come over to the car, which they did, but not without nervous faces. Bobby stood back and never said a word, just watched me take charge.

"Mr. Jefferies will take you home. No need for you to walk so far," I explained to the soldier and his wife. "Come, get in za car and he will take you home. Okay, Mr. Jefferies? You do zis for me, okay? Now I walk a little wiz Bobby, zen we go home. I will explain to Mama Bea."

Mr. Jefferies gave me a long hard look, like he wasn't sure he should comply with my unusual request. Then he looked at the soldier, who was leaning hard on his cane, trying to steady his stance. My pleading eyes must have convinced Mr. Jefferies because a moment later, he was helping the soldier and his wife into the backseat of the car.

"I'll take them home, Miss Dezrae, but you need to get home too, or Miss Bea's gonna worry herself."

"I promise. I will walk a little and zink a little, zen I go home. I promise."

"I'll be with her, Jacob. Don't worry. I'll make sure she gets home safe," Bobby assured him.

Before the car pulled away, the back window rolled down, and the soldier leaned out. "Thank you, miss, for your kindness."

"May I ask, sir, where you lost your leg?"

His gentle smile seemed meant to reassure me that he was okay, then he just shrugged as if the entire experience was in the distant past and totally forgettable.

"German machine gun fire tore it off me in a little town outside Caen. I'm lucky to be alive and back home, miss."

Tears stung my eyes and my breath caught tight in my throat. He had lost his leg and nearly his life fighting for my country's freedom, and his own countrymen had shunned him. I didn't understand Americans at all.

"*Merci beaucoup, monsieur. Adieu.*"

I watched as Mr. Jefferies drove up the street into the heart of the city.

# Chapter 20

## *Unforeseen Consequences*

The entrance to the Audubon Park was straight down Prytania Street, less than a mile away. My eyes fixed in front of me as I hastened towards it. Bobby kept pace beside me, making good on his promise to be quiet and let me think for a while.

The hot and muggy weather did nothing to amend my mood. Sweat trickled down my back beneath the sweater I put on in the theater and, in my haste to leave, had neglected to remove. Impatiently pulling it off, I tied it around my waist with the sleeves, allowing the warm breeze to dry off my clammy arms.

The temperature cooled by several degrees once we stepped under the canopy of the huge live oaks living in the park by the lagoon. I found an empty bench under the tree and deposited myself onto it with a heavy release of breath.

"Is it always so hot here?" I asked Bobby, who seated himself on the grass in front of me, his knees bent and legs crossed like an Indian.

With his elbows upon his knees, his hands clasped together under his chin, he just stared at me for a while without responding. I didn't really need an answer. I only asked to ease the tension between us.

"It's always this hot in the summer, but it cools down come winter. You'll see," he said. He had a probing look in his eyes, like he was trying to figure something out, something about me. “It sure must be different where you come from,” he said, clearly a bid to open a dialogue.

“Not so hot as here,” I replied, not yet willing to open up further, though I knew I owed him an explanation and an apology.

“You know that’s not what I meant, Désirée. Why did you do that?”

I buried my face in my hands, taking deep breaths and releasing them through my nose. My hands dropped to my lap as I tried to find the right words to explain myself, to make him understand my point of view, without revealing the why of my opinion. I couldn’t tell him about the years I lived with the Kommandant, the countless lectures on racial superiority I listened to, the echoing moans coming from boxcars filled with Jews destined for the camps. I couldn’t say anything about any of it.

“She was cruel, and zare was no reason for her to say such zings. I could not listen to her speak zat way any longer.” I could have gone on, but felt myself getting worked up again, so I left it at that.

“Don’t think I’ve ever seen anyone do something like that,” Bobby said, his brow pinched with a concerned look.

I gave him a hard stare, gauging his response to my reply. “Perhaps if more people would speak out against such hateful behavior, zen it would not happen. Zen people would be kind to each ozer.”

“Maybe, but folks around here don’t take kindly to their shortcomings being pointed out to them... especially in public,” he replied, a warning behind his words.

“I am sorry, Bobby. I ruin your day wiz your friends. I am sorry.”

“You didn’t ruin it. You made it a lot more interesting, that’s for sure. I’m not a big fan of musicals, anyway. Now if you’d made me miss *Secret Agent X9,* then I might have something more to say about it.”

“But I embarrass you and your friends. Zay will hate me now.”

"Nah. They're not gonna hate you. Far as I could tell, Jimmy even admired your courage at standing up to that woman. Don't worry about the rest of them. I'll explain things. Besides, you've got a bunch of built-in excuses."

"What excuses?" I asked, hopeful I hadn't totally ruined all possibility of friendship once school started.

"Well, you're foreign, only been here for a few months, you barely speak English properly, you're a girl and you're only thirteen. I figure that should be enough to excuse just about anything," he explained, a devilish grin on his face. He rose to his feet in one smooth move, reaching for my hand. "Come on, Désirée, let's start walking back. Jacob will probably beat us home by the time we get there. God, Miss Bea and Bill are gonna kill me."

"No, zay will not kill you, Bobby. I will not let zem."

We entered the house through the back door, stepping into the kitchen where Mr. Jefferies was sitting at the worktable talking with Miss Laila. Female chatter filtered in through the dining room door, evidence the Bridge Club was still in attendance and giving me a temporary reprieve from what I knew would be an uncomfortable meeting with Mama Bea.

Mr. Jefferies and Miss Laila looked up from their conversation when Bobby and I entered, relief coupled with concern marking their faces.

"It's about time you two showed up. Miss Bea's been asking after you," Mr. Jefferies said.

"You alright, Miss Dezrae?" Miss Laila asked, taking my face into her hand to examine my bruised cheek. "Do it hurt?"

"I am okay, Miss Laila. It not hurt now," I replied, shaking my head. "Is she very angry wiz me, Mr. Jefferies?" My heart was racing with nervous anticipation of Mama Bea's reaction to the day's events, but I didn't regret what I'd done. Not one bit.

"She ain't angry with you, Miss Dezrae. Though I spect she ain't gonna be happy once she gets a good look at your face. I'll go tell her you're home."

"Miss Dezrae, you and Mr. Bobby go on outside and wait till Miss Bea calls for you. She gots to finish up with the Bridge Club fore she does. Won't be too long," Miss Laila instructed.

"Maybe I should go home," Bobby said.

"Miss Bea wants to talk with you too, Mr. Bobby. Both of you go on outside and I'll come get ya when she's ready." She handed us each a glass of lemonade as she shooed us out to the garden.

Less than an hour later, Miss Laila and Mr. Jefferies escorted Bobby and me into Mama Bea's study. She was sitting behind her desk with her elbows perched on top, her hands covering her face. The sound of heavy breathing filtered through her fingers, deep sighs of what I could only imagine as disappointment with my behavior. Her hands dropped to the desk when she heard us come in.

Her expression transformed several times as she looked at me. First frustration, then shock marked her reaction, and then a slow burning anger made its way behind her eyes. She stood up and came around the desk to stand in front of me.

"Does it hurt?" she asked, reaching up to touch my cheek.

"No."

"I'm real sorry, Miss Bea," Bobby said nervously. "If I thought that woman was going to hit her, I would have stopped her, but it all happened so fast. You know how some people can be. It wasn't Désirée's fault, Miss Bea. Don't be mad at her."

"I'm not angry with her, Robert, nor am I holding you responsible. Mr. Monroe, at the theater, gave me an account of what happened today, and Jacob has told me what the soldier and his wife told him about the incident. Mr. Monroe said I should expect a call from this woman regarding your behavior, Désirée. Apparently, she has some issues she wants to bring to my attention. And now that I see your face, there are a few things I would like to say to her. But first I want to hear from you, Désirée. Tell me exactly what happened." She walked back around her desk and sat down, waiting for my explanation.

Moment by moment, word for word, I recounted the scene for her, leaving nothing out. By the time I finished, the anger behind her eyes had deepened, leaving little doubt as to her feelings. Then the phone rang, and Mr. Jefferies answered it in the hallway.

"Miss Bea, there's a Mrs. Edgars asking for you," he announced at the door to the study.

"Thank you, Jacob," she replied, reaching for the phone on her desk. Bobby and I sat with rapt attention, both of us wondering what would happen during this call.

"This is Mrs. Marchand," Mama Bea said; then she listened for a moment. "Yes, Mrs. Edgars, I am aware of what happened at the theater today. Perhaps you can tell me your version of this unfortunate event."

Mama Bea sat patiently listening for several minutes, her eyebrows lifting in response to what she was being told. While she listened, she looked over at Bobby, then to me, her thoughts unreadable, then she interrupted the woman. "Yes, I hear what you're saying, Mrs. Edgars. However, I find it very interesting that neither you nor Mr. Monroe thought it important to mention that you struck my daughter in anger."

She waited for the woman's response, which came swiftly, the sharp sound of her denial coming through the receiver.

"I beg to differ with your assessment, Mrs. Edgars. The severe evidence of your action is marking my daughter's cheek, right in front of me. Frankly madam, I am very tempted to contact my attorney regarding this unwarranted assault," Mama Bea said, her tone steely but calm.

The woman must have softened her stance after hearing that, because Mama Bea relaxed back in her chair. "Yes, I understand the heat of the moment, Mrs. Edgars, but let me give you a bit of friendly advice. In the future, I suggest you curb your tongue and stay your hand, lest you find yourself standing in front of a judge." Another pause followed, then Mama Bea said, "Yes, I will tell her. Good day, Mrs. Edgars."

Mama Bea placed the receiver in its cradle and released a sigh. "Loathsome woman," she whispered to the phone, then she looked over at me. "She asked me to tell you she was sorry for striking you, Désirée."

"But not for what she say to za soldier. She is not sorry for zat," came my swift reply. The statement was a fact, and we all knew it.

"No, she's not sorry for that."

Mama Bea sent Bobby home and me to my room to await Bill's return.

As I was leaving her study, she had one last parting remark. "When Beau gets home... Lord knows what he's going to say about this... when he gets home, we'll sit down together to talk. In the meantime, Désirée, I want you to think about the consequences of what happened today, what effect your actions had, not just on you, but on that soldier and his wife, your friends, all of us. Actions have consequences. You need to think about that."

The only response I offered was a lowered head and shrugging shoulders as I walked up to my room and closed the door.

The consequences were obvious and unfair. While that awful woman sat enjoying the movie, Bobby and I, along with the soldier and his wife, had to leave for disturbing her peaceful entertainment. There was nothing about the situation that felt right to me, no matter how I looked at it.

Before I came to America, I had heard all kinds of things about this country: how wonderful it was, how everyone was free to pursue their dreams. The land of the free and the home of the brave was how people described America. After nearly four months, I discovered that description to be a lie. That slogan was no different from the endless propaganda messages Hitler fed to the German people, convincing them they were superior to everyone else. It was an illusion of greatness hiding an ugly truth. In America, not everyone was free to pursue their dreams, and, as far as I could see, no one was brave enough to stand up to expose the lie.

It was obvious why Bill said nothing about what it was really like in New Orleans, about how the people really were. If he had, I might not have agreed to come. I might have taken my chances in France, where at least I understood the way people lived.

As it was, I was stuck here with no options, too young to make my own way in life, and dependent upon people I didn't understand.

# Chapter 21

## *Lectures and Choices*

Not long before suppertime, the heavy tread of Bill's footsteps on the stairs signaled his return. My stomach turned over a few times in anticipation of what I knew would be a night of lectures.

"Is that you, Beau?" Mama Bea called up from her study. "Come in here, son. I need to speak with you."

"I'll be right down, Mama." I heard him go into his room, then head downstairs a moment later.

Rather than face the consequences straight on, I retreated to my bathroom, where I inspected the physical consequence of my actions. The woman's blow had left a dark purple mark across my cheekbone and under my eye. It looked uglier than it felt. It felt like a badge of honor, but I wasn't sure Bill would see it that way.

"What does it matter what he thinks?" I told the girl in the mirror, reverting to French. "He has more important things than you to think about." I stared at myself for the longest time, frustrated and angry at the powerless situation I was in.

Miss Laila tapped on my bedroom door before peeking her head in.

"Miss Dezrae, supper's almost ready. You want to come down and help me get it on the table?"

She'd never had to ask since I'd been there. I was usually in the kitchen with her, helping with the meal. Shame flushed across my face as I realized how thoughtlessly I had neglected this basic chore.

"I am sorry, Miss Laila. I forget about..." The words choked up in my throat as tears filled my eyes when I looked up at her. Any control I might have had was swiftly fading as I became overwhelmed by all the conflicting emotions running through me.

She came to me with open arms, pulling me into her embrace. "Ah, sugar, come here to Laila. Let those tears out right here with me, child. Let 'em all go." She held me close, stroking my back, letting me spill my misery into her chest. "It gonna be fine, sugar. After a time, it gonna be fine."

She led me back into the bathroom to stand next to the sink. "Let's get your face washed up 'fore Mr. William sees you been cryin' and gets hisself all riled up again."

She pulled a cloth from the rack, wet it, then rung it out. With my face gently in one hand, she held it up for a closer view, then wiped the cloth over my cheeks and eyes, ending with a swipe across my forehead. She examined the scar snaking across the hairline, gingerly tracing the length of it with her fingers.

"Looks like you've had this for a while," she said, searching my eyes for answers.

"Za Nazis give me zis when I was eight."

I sniffled back my tears, swallowing down the feelings threatening to consume me.

"I am okay, Miss Laila. Come, I will help with za supper," I said, leading her out the door and down the back stairs.

As I entered the kitchen, the spicy aroma of Miss Laila's Creole sauce filled the air, savory warm scents that calmed my troubled mind as I helped her complete the meal.

"You lay out them plates, Miss Dezrae, while I cook up these shrimps. Won't take but a minute. We'll serve em up in here, then we'll take em out to the table."

She was giving me time to compose myself before facing Bill and Mama Bea, and I was grateful because I didn't know what to say to either of them.

We filled the plates with mounds of fluffy white rice topped with steamy Shrimp Creole and a side of sauteed greens. A basket of hot cornbread rounded off the meal. Typical Louisiana comfort food that I had learned to love, but right then, I didn't feel very comforted.

"I'll take these two plates. You take the other one and that basket of cornbread. And you best take that frown off your face, Miss Dezrae. Things will go better that way," Miss Laila said, giving me a gentle smile as she headed for the dining room.

I would rather have eaten in the kitchen with the Jefferies, but that wasn't an option. So, I schooled my face—as I'd done a thousand times before—took a breath and calmed myself for what was to come.

With my head bowed, I stepped through the door, put the plate and basket down on the table, then took my seat like the obedient child they expected me to be. I waited for Bill or Mama Bea to give some kind of signal or make a comment or something, but neither said a word. They just started eating as soon as Miss Laila left the room.

Ella Fitzgerald's silky voice filtered in from the living room, past the tick, tick, tick of the hall clock, both sounds punctuating the uneasiness at the dining table. The tension floating around that room was thick enough I could cut it with a knife. The three of us just sat there silently, eating, thinking, and waiting. I had no idea what they were waiting for.

While I waited, I examined the content of my plate, counting the grains of rice, the uniform pieces of chopped peppers, anything to avoid looking directly at either Bill or Mama Bea.

I mentally wagered which one would be the first to speak. Suspecting it might be Bill, I stole a glance at him. His expression held a scowl of suppressed anger that I'd never seen him wear before. Mama Bea kept her attention on the meal until her plate was nearly empty.

"I spoke with Julianna today, Beau," Mama Bea said, winning my mental wager with a casual opening remark. "She and Charles are planning a birthday celebration for Uncle Henri at Antoine's on Saturday afternoon. I hope you haven't made plans," she said, putting her fork down on the plate, then folding her napkin and laying it aside.

This simple end-of-meal routine was a clear signal the lecture would soon begin. I took a deep breath to steady myself, calming my nerves. I wondered what Bill was going to say, what he was thinking. The scowl hadn't lifted from his face, which made me wonder if his anger was at me.

Bill shook his head when he looked up, his expression softening. "I have no plans, Mama. It'll be nice to see the family." His eyes caught mine and held them, not with a scolding look, but a worried one, tinged with regret.

"Before we go to see the family, Mama, you'll need to use some of your cosmetics to hide that black eye Désirée is sporting." His lighthearted comment—obviously meant to ease the tension at the table—didn't work.

"Undoubtedly," Mama Bea replied, turning to me. "About that black eye, Désirée. Do you suppose this was the only consequence of your actions today?"

I couldn't look at her. "*Je ne sais pas*," I replied with a shrug. It didn't matter, anyway.

"This entire unfortunate event need not have occurred, Désirée. Neither you nor Mrs. Edgars handled the situation appropriately. She *was* within her rights to object to the soldier and his wife sitting where they were. The theater has a policy regarding Negro patrons and has provided seating for them in the balcony. Rather than taking her complaint to the management, as any reasonable person would do, Mrs. Edgars made a scene and voiced her bigotry publicly. You then pointed out her inappropriate behavior in an equally public manner rather than taking your complaint to the manager. And how did that turn out for you?"

"She hit me and za manager, he zrow me out for making trouble. It is not fair. I did nozing wrong," I said, crossing my arms across my chest.

Mama Bea shook her head and furrowed her brow. "The concept of fairness plays little part in our society, Désirée, especially for the Negro people. Your defense of the soldier today, while honorable, could gain you a reputation as a troublemaker, which is something you do not need for several reasons. I do not disagree with what you said to Mrs. Edgars, however, it is never acceptable for a child to speak disrespectfully to an adult, regardless of the circumstances." Mama Bea held my gaze while she spoke, clearly attempting to impress upon me her version of social etiquette.

"I was as respectful as she deserved. Ze truz is... zat here, it is not acceptable to defend a Negro. Zat is what I do wrong, no?" By then I was incapable of holding back my exasperation. I wanted an honest answer from them both. I wanted to hear them admit the truth of it.

Mama Bea dropped her forehead into her hand with a sigh. Bill's concerned eyes held mine while both his hands covered his mouth as if trying to stifle his response. I wished he would just say it, whatever it was. I was tired of all the waiting.

"Defending that soldier wasn't wrong, Désirée, but it was dangerous," Bill finally said. "People around here remember things like that, and they'll mark you as a troublemaker if you do it again. That is something you do not want. It will make your life here much harder than it already is." His warning was clear.

"Why do you live zis way, accept such zings? You are all American, no? Why do you treat each ozer zis way?"

Mama Bea finally lifted her head from her hand.

"Those questions deserve honest answers, but that will require many more conversations. Right now, you need to make sure your conduct in public is beyond reproach. We don't want people asking questions about you, Désirée. I'm sure you understand why." Mama Bea held my gaze with a firm look, reminding me of my circumstances.

My face and hands met with an anguished sigh. I was done. No more talking, no more listening. There was nothing more to say. Clearly, they both expected me to be like the other Uptown girls; follow the rules, mind your manners, and whatever you do, don't make a scene. All because I had to hide who I'd been and how I got here.

I needed to leave… the dining room, at least.

My hands dropped to my lap as I lifted my eyes to hers, dutifully acknowledging her directive, albeit with a surly sigh. "*Je comprends.* May I be excused, *s'il vous plaît*?"

Without waiting for a response, I rose from the table, turned my back on them, and headed upstairs to my room. I didn't even take my plate to the kitchen. Facing the Jefferies felt too hard right then.

*"Soixante-cinq, soixante-six, soixante-sept..."* The rhythmic strokes of the hairbrush usually calmed me by the time I reached this point in my nightly one-hundred-stroke ritual. Avoiding the girl in my dressing-table mirror, I attempted to release some of the stress accumulated by the day's events with this simple hair-brushing routine. It was useless; nothing seemed to calm me.

I ignored Bill's tap on my bedroom door, hoping he'd go away and let me just... I didn't know what I wanted right then but it certainly wasn't more lectures. My mind was already a chaotic mess, and I could tell it was going to be a tough night of tidying up.

"Can we talk, Désirée?" he asked, standing at the door, waiting for my invitation to come in.

"*Non. Je ne veux pas,*" I said, turning away from him. I didn't want to hear any more about proper behavior or reputations, or anything.

"S*'il te plaît, Chère.*" His French response proved he knew my language would be the path to our communication.

He stepped into the room with his hand outstretched. "Come outside with me, Chère. Let's sit and talk."

My frown revealed an unwillingness, but the touch of his hand softened my resolve. I let him lead me out onto the gallery, where the evening breeze rustled through the oak trees, cooling everything off. A gentle brush of wind across my cheek calmed my troubled mind.

He seated me on the chaise, then sat down next to me, putting his arm around my shoulder. I didn't resist. It felt good being close to him, tucked under his arm with my head on his chest.

"I'm sorry, Désirée. I didn't think being here would be this difficult for you." He gently stroked my arm.

"I didn't either." I lifted my head from his chest to look into his eyes. "Why didn't you tell me what it's really like here?"

He held my eyes with his, then pushed out a heavy breath before answering.

"You wouldn't have come, Chère. I see that now. And as shameful as this sounds, it never even occurred to me to mention this part of who we are. I thought I could give you the kind of childhood I had. I didn't think about what our culture would look like to you. I'm sorry." A profound sadness deepened around his eyes.

I hadn't told Bill all the details of my life with Katarina and the Kommandant, what it had been like for me during those years. I hadn't been able to tell anyone, but I needed him to understand how I felt.

"The Kommandant talked all the time about the superior Aryan race and how they would populate the world to make it better. He hated anyone he thought of as impure or imperfect; Gypsys, anyone deformed or crippled, people he called deviants, but he especially hated the Jews. He said there was no place for such rabble in the new world that Germany was creating.... The whole time I was with him, I pretended to agree, to accept his stupid idea as the truth. I could never say what I really thought or show my feelings to anyone... I thought it would be different here. I thought Americans were different." I straightened up in the chaise, turning away from Bill's worried expression.

"We're not all like Mrs. Edgars or Mr. Ainsley, Désirée. Most of us live our lives paying little attention to the bigotry you see so clearly. It's been there for generations, like a nagging sore that never heals, but we've become accustomed to the discomfort."

I turned around to challenge his explanation. "I might be young, Bill, but even I know that if you ignore a wound, it can get infected and make it a lot worse."

Recognition of truth flashed in his eyes. He closed them, shook his head in apparent frustration, then took slow, deep breaths through his nose. "You speaking out about this won't fix anything, Chère. The only thing it will accomplish is to make your life here a lot harder."

"I can't be like the people here, Bill. I don't want to ignore something I know is wrong. I don't want to pretend I don't see it. That's what I did before, so I could survive the war, but I lost everything anyway." My lips quivered as I spoke, the loss still so real.

"I told you I would find a safe place for you in France. If you're really unhappy here, Chère, I'll take you back. Your safety and happiness are all I care about. If it means taking you back to France, I will... if that's what you want." There was sadness in his challenging offer and perhaps fear I would accept it.

My breath caught in my throat. Tears filled my eyes at the thought of seeing France again, and then it hit me, the realization of what going back would mean. I would have to start over again, be someone new with different strangers, and I'd lose Bill and Mama Bea.

"All I want is to feel like I belong, where I can be me and not have to pretend anymore," I said through tearful sobs.

Bill pulled me close, wrapping his arms around me. "Ah, baby girl. You belong here with me and Mama. We're your family now, if you can give us a chance. I know Mama can help you if you let her. She navigates our society better than anyone I know."

"This is so much harder than I thought it would be." I buried my face in his chest, seeking the comfort I hoped would be there.

"I know, baby girl. We're a flawed people, no doubt, but is there anything about us that you like? Something that might make it worth your while to stay?"

There were plenty of reasons to stay out of France, but mostly, I wouldn't go because, as much as I missed it, I would miss Bill more if I went back.

"I like the food and the music here. I like the Jefferies and Bobby, and I like you and Mama Bea." There were lots of things I liked and lots of things I didn't.

"Is that enough to keep you with us?"

I nodded. "I don't want to leave, Bill. That would be too sad." I sniffled back my tears, cuddling close to him.

"It would be sad for me too, Chère. I never want to lose you," he said, stroking my cheek as he placed a kiss on my head.

"Beau? Is everything alright?" Mama Bea asked, coming out onto the gallery.

"Everything's fine now, Mama."

"It's getting late. Désirée should be in bed." Her motherly concern was evident in her voice.

I shook my head in his chest, showing my unwillingness to abandon his comfort. With a stroke on my arm, Bill let me know he understood.

"We're going to sit out here for a while longer, Mama. We'll be alright."

I fell asleep in his arms that night, barely waking when he carried me to my bed and tucked me in.

# Chapter 22

## *Friends, Family and Well-Laid Plans*

"O*h non, c'est pire aujourd'hui.*"

I hoped the bruise would look better when I got up but found it had changed from the lovely shades of red and purple the day before, into a deep indigo and black. I looked like a one-eyed bandit. There was a tiny cut on my cheekbone where the crazy woman's ring had scratched me.

Normally, I wasn't vain about my looks, but the face staring back at me wasn't very pretty. I hoped I wouldn't have to explain to Bill's family what happened, but if the bruise didn't fade before Saturday afternoon, that might be an uncomfortable conversation.

After helping Miss Laila with the breakfast dishes, I went outside to my garden to think for a while. Shears in hand, I began clipping back the dead blossoms from the flower plants surrounding the lawn, a simple task not requiring focused attention. Maman taught me long ago to give the garden tender care, to nip back the dead flowers, so to signal the plant to make new ones. My new garden beds were still getting settled in and required little more than sun and water.

While I nipped my way around the established flower beds, I thought about the choice I made the night before. It was the right decision to stay here with Bill and Mama Bea, but I was still unsure of how to be myself here, of how I could live among these people without giving up my sense of fairness and justice, without giving up my newfound voice.

I needed a plan, and right then, I couldn't think of one beyond staying home and never speaking to anyone again. That was definitely not an option.

"Miss Dezrae, you have visitors," Mr. Jefferies said, leading Bobby, Eddie, and Sarah into the garden. My bandit's face couldn't have been more shocked.

"Hi, Désirée," Sarah said, walking up and peering closely at my face. "Oo! Your cheek. Does it hurt?"

"Course it hurts. No one gets hit like that and it don't hurt," Eddie said, taking a close look at my face. "Yeah, you got a shiner, alright. It don't look too bad, though. I've seen worse."

"Hey, Désirée. We wanted to see how you're doing. Did you get in trouble with Bill last night? Is he mad at me?" Bobby asked, looking around to see if Bill was nearby.

"*Bonjour, mes amis.* No, it not hurt, but it look terrible. I hope it will go away before school begin. Bill is not angry too much, but not wiz you, Bobby. It is okay now," I explained, answering all their questions as best I could. "Come, we will sit and talk in za gazebo. You want somezing to drink or eat? I can get you somezing."

"No, that's alright, Désirée. We just came over to talk with you," Sarah said, following me into the gazebo and taking a seat. She had a curious look on her face, like she wasn't sure of herself or how to begin the conversation. She looked over at Eddie sitting next to her, who just shrugged, apparently deferring to her to speak for them. Their nervousness only amplified my own.

"Well, it's about school and a little about yesterday," Sarah began. "Eddie and I had a long talk about it after the movie, and we decided we should talk to you and Bobby." She nervously grabbed Eddie's hand, seeking his support. He nodded, giving her hand a gentle squeeze.

"I am sorry I embarrass you yesterday," I said, wanting to get that part out of the way before they said anything else.

"Oh, don't worry about that. You didn't embarrass us. Well, most of us anyway. Kaitlyn got a little upset about the whole thing, but don't mind her. I told her you were new here and didn't know how things are in the South. That woman was just awful. She should never have hit you."

"Tell her about school, Sarah, and what we talked about," Eddie said, looking from me to Sarah, then to Bobby, who appeared to know what was coming. From the anxious looks on their faces, my nerves took over and my stomach started doing backflips.

Sarah looked at Eddie with raised eyebrows, as if to say she *was* getting to the point.

"The thing is, Désirée, when kids start high school, everything changes. We've all seen it happen. Kids, like me and Kaitlyn, Bobby and Eddie, who've been friends all through grade school, suddenly get separated into social groups, Jews and Christians." She stopped to gauge my response, her eyes widening with nervous anticipation.

I clamped my teeth tight to my bottom lip, stifling my alarm at this new information. It was another example of how different Americans were, and all I could do was shake my head in dismay.

"Social status is a big thing in high school," Sarah continued, "and certain kids are expected to join certain groups. Kaitlyn wants to be a Delta because her sister was. That's the Delta Beta Gamma sorority, but there are others. It's always a big rush at the beginning of the school year for the sororities and fraternities to choose their new members from the freshmen class, the ninth graders. The Jews have their groups, and the Christians have their own, but once school starts, they never do anything together outside of school."

Hearing this made my brow wrinkle up and my stomach clinch tight for another flip. America had turned out to be nothing like people in France thought it was.

"Americans are strange. You zink it right to separate from each ozer, but I zink zis way is more... uncomfortable. It is not right. Why do you do zis?"

They all gave me blank stares, but at least Bobby offered a feeble explanation.

"It's just how it is. Kinda like how adults around here do things. Jews and Christians don't mix socially," he said, then he turned to Eddie and Sarah. "I told you she would understand."

Sarah's expression was sympathetic. "When that happened yesterday, I remembered how hard it was for me when I first moved here. Everything was so different."

"Where do you come from, Sarah?" I was a lot more curious about this girl who seemed to understand what I'd done the day before and didn't seem bothered by it.

"Papa and I moved here five years ago from New York City, and believe me, it was the hardest thing I'd ever done. Everything here is so different. And I hated the weather when I first got here. I still don't like it much."

"Ah, za weazur is... *Oof, il fait toujours trop chaud,*" I agreed, waving my hands to cool off my face.

"You'll get used to it," Bobby and Eddie offered in unison.

"No," Sarah and I both said, shaking our heads, then we all laughed.

"Anyway, Désirée, after what happened yesterday, we thought we should let you know what to expect when school starts. Eddie, Bobby, and I made a pact to stay together in high school, and Bobby said you might want to join us. Maybe we could start our own group, one that lets anybody join, as long as they're nice. Bobby said Jimmy Wilcox might want to be part of it, and I know a few girls I could ask. What do you think, Désirée?"

The tightness in my stomach relaxed into a soft ripple of joy as I scanned their hopeful faces. Unwittingly, they had just solved my immediate problem, and a great big smile curled up the corners of my mouth.

"I zink we have a plan, *mes amis.*"

Two days later, Bill, Mama Bea and I were heading into the Quarter for Uncle Henri's birthday celebration at Antione's. I felt a flutter of excitement at the possibility of looking inside the kitchen while we were there. At least I hoped I could if Bill remembered his promise.

"I see Uncle Bertram is here, Mama. I'll let you out in front. Looks like I'll need to park around the corner," Bill said, pulling the car up to the front of the restaurant.

"I will walk wiz you, Bill," I said from the backseat, not intending to miss a walk through the Quarter, however short it might be. It wasn't often I got to go there, and then only to the French Market and the Café du Monde, whenever Mama Bea yearned for beignets and chocolate milk.

"Alright. Don't be long, you two," Mama Bea said, stepping out of the car to greet her brother and his wife at the entrance to the restaurant.

Bill drove to the end of the block, then turned right onto Bourbon Street, which was alive with sights, sounds and smells combining to excite and tingle my senses. He turned right at the next corner, then right again onto Royal Street, parking halfway down the block.

There was something about the Quarter that sang to me in ways no other place I'd ever been had done. Those few square blocks of the old city had a mystery about them, one begging for discovery, and currently beyond my grasp, without the accompaniment of a responsible adult. In these situations, I hated being young. My youthful curiosity wanted to investigate without limits.

"Can we explore? I want to see more. Will you show me, Bill?" I asked, squeezing his hand and slowing my pace as we passed the shops.

He didn't stop or slow, he just tucked my hand into the crook of his arm, patting it tenderly as we walked. "Maybe later, Chère. We'll see if Mama is up for a stroll through Jackson Square after lunch. Let's not keep her waiting."

A few moments later, Bill and I were walking through the front door of Antione's and into a large, brightly lit dining room. The walls were painted white and mirrors hung on every wall to reflect the light from the gaslight chandeliers and the tall French windows along the front of the restaurant. Filling the room were almost two dozen linen-covered tables, most of them hosting happy diners enjoying the offerings.

"Welcome home, Mr. Marchand. It's nice to see you back with us," a distinguished gentleman greeted us with a shake of Bill's outstretched hand. He looked to be in his forties with thinning dark hair neatly combed back from his round face. He wore frameless glasses perched at the top of a very French-looking nose, long and straight. Impeccably dressed in a dark three-piece suit with a black bow tie over a crisp white shirt, he was either the owner of the restaurant or the maître d', I wasn't sure which.

"Thank you, Mr. Alciatore. It's good to be home for a while. How's the family?"

"Mary is doing very well and little Yvonne is almost eight now. Thank you for asking. Who is this with you today, Mr. Marchand?" the man asked, giving me a curious but friendly look.

"This is Désirée. She's come to live with Mother and finish her schooling here in New Orleans." I was grateful Bill hadn't used the fake surname they'd given me. I didn't want to use it, anyway.

"Well, she is certainly with the best teacher. Welcome to Antoine's, Miss Désirée."

"*Bonjour, monsieur,*" I said, smiling up at him and adding a little curtsy.

Bill glanced down at me and winked. "Désirée would like to look inside your kitchen, Roy. If that wouldn't be too much trouble."

Mr. Alciatore gazed down at me, his forehead pinching above his glasses. "*Pourquoi, mademoiselle?* The dining rooms offer a more pleasant view."

I could see the same resistance in his eyes that I received from the head chef at the George V in Paris when I attempted to enter his kitchen for the first time. My determination to succeed in my quest was undeterred by this man's obvious reluctance to allow me entry into his domain.

I answered him in French, hoping my use of the language would soften him to me. "Because I like to cook. I enjoy watching how the food is prepared. I like the music I hear inside a restaurant kitchen," I said as demurely as I could.

"*Quelle musique, mademoiselle?*" he asked, seemingly more curious about me now.

"The symphony of ingredients and technique that only happens inside a restaurant kitchen. *J'adore cette musique.*"

With wide eyes and youthful innocence, I tried looking as unsuspicious as possible. Adults were generally willing to comply with a childish request, if made respectfully enough, but I could sense his reluctance.

"I'd consider it a favor, Roy," Bill said.

Mr. Alciatore looked past me and over to Bill, his brow still pinched as if weighing his response, then he nodded. "I'll see what I can do, Mr. Marchand. Your family is in the Rex Room today. Leonard will take you back."

"No need, Roy. I know the way. We're going to stop and freshen up first."

Bill took my hand, leading me through a wide entry into another vast dining room. This room was darker than the first, with a more intimate feel to it, despite its size. The walls were painted red, ornate brass sconces lit the dark wood wainscoting encircling the room. A thin pall of smoke lingered momentarily along the ceiling above the chandeliers before drifting away through the ceiling vents. There were easily as many occupied tables here as in the main dining room. It was a busy restaurant.

On a side wall, I spied a pair of swinging doors with windows at eye level, obviously leading to the kitchen, as evidenced by the wait staff's comings and goings. I knew sneaking through them unseen wouldn't be easy, so I sent up a little prayer that Mr. Alciatore would look upon my request favorably and allow me entry through those doors.

We crossed the dining room and passed through another doorway into a long hallway, going left and right. Directly ahead were the restrooms.

"Go wash up, Chère. Do a little touch up on that eye before we see the family. I'll wait here," Bill instructed as he walked me to the Ladies Room door.

As soon as I stepped inside the ladies' room, I dug into my purse to retrieve the compact Mama Bea had lent me. The reflection in the mirror above the sink revealed my blackened eye needed attention. With an unpracticed hand, I leaned into the mirror, applying the compact puff with several pats across my cheek.

"It looks alright, Miss Dezrae," the negro attendant said shyly.

I turned around, surprised she knew my name. "Do I know you?"

"No, Miss... Laila Jefferies, she told me you was comin in today. She ask me to watch out for you. Laila's my neighbor. She told us what you did for that soldier and his wife the other day. I just wanted to say thank you for your kindness."

I rolled my eyes, shaking the memory of that day back into its box. "Zis is what I get for my kindness." I gave my cheek a last pat with the compact puff.

"It don't look too bad. It'll go away in a few days. You won't ever know it was there," she assured me.

"Zank you... Betty," I said, noticing her name tag. "I will use za toilet, and zen I must face za family."

As soon as I closed the stall door and sat down, I heard two voices enter the restroom.

"I don't know, Mother. I talked to Charlotte yesterday, but she didn't say a word about coming here today. She told me she and Bill had a little tiff the other night, but they were working things out. If she's not here with him today... well, that might mean the door is open for someone else to step through. I wouldn't mind having Bill Marchand's arms around me," the voice said over the rush of water.

"Maybe Bill got wind of what Charlotte's been up to while he's been away," said the second voice, sounding older than the first. "One thing is for certain: no one gets through that door without first going through Beatrice Marchand. It appears Charlotte forgot that. Ready, Emily?"

The women exited the restroom, and I left the stall with a million thoughts flying through my head. Evelyn Duret's voice spoke loud and clear from my memory. "*He's the most eligible bachelor in New Orleans, maybe even the entire South.*" I realized then that if Bill and Charlotte were really through, there could be an army of Charlottes waiting to take her place. That was a troubling thought.

I quickly washed my hands and thanked Betty once more before following them out.

Bill stood in the hall speaking with two women, who I assumed were the same two I'd just overheard, the younger gazing up sweetly at him. When he saw me come out of the restroom, he reached his arm between them to take my hand.

"Excuse me, ladies. It's been nice talking with you. We'll see you inside. Ready, Désirée? Mama's waiting," he said, pulling me through the opening between the two women and leading me down the hall.

"Who is that girl, Mother?" I heard the younger woman ask.

"I'm not sure, dear, but I believe she's the young girl Beatrice has taken in. I'm rather surprised she's here today. Let's go find out why."

The Rex Room was another of Antoine's large dining rooms, this one private and lavishly decorated. Gilded mirrors filled the gold-trimmed, emerald-green walls of the space. An enormous, gilded mirror hung at the far end of the room, with the insignia *REX* carved beneath its crown. Three long elegantly set tables filled the space, configured in a U-shape, with the head table set beneath the large mirror. I counted thirty seats around the tables, twelve down each side and six at the head table. Only a few seats remained vacant when we entered.

Bill and I walked down the left side of the room to the two empty seats closest to the head table where Mama Bea sat at the end, next to Aunt Adele and Uncle Bertram. The guest of honor, Uncle Henri, sat in the middle with a full view of the room and guests. On his left sat his son, Charles, and daughter-in-law, Julianna. Bill led me over to introduce me to this branch of his family.

"Happy Birthday, Uncle," Bill said, taking the old man's hand in a firm grip.

"It's about damn time you showed up, Bill. I was beginning to think you forgot about your old uncle." The old man frowned at him, returning Bill's handshake with equal strength.

"You about done with that nonsense overseas? We need you back here to settle down and help these two run things, like your father did. I need you here, Bill." Uncle Henri looked up into Bill's eyes with intensity. He looked like Bill, an older version, but clearly still a man of strength and vigor.

"I'm not quite done yet, Uncle. There are still some things they want me to do over there, things I need to take care of," Bill said, drawing me forward. "Uncle, this is Désirée. Mama may have mentioned her."

"Happy birzday, sir," I said, offering him my hand, which he readily took.

"*Enchanté,* Désirée. What happened to your eye?" he asked, peering closely at my face.

"Ah, it is nozing," I said, making sure I didn't touch the bruise with my free hand. "I was clumsy, and somezing hit my face. It is better now," I said, proud of my explanation. I told the truth, with none of the uncomfortable details.

Uncle Henri squeezed my hand, then released it. "You best be more careful in the future, young lady. You don't want that kind of 'accident' happening again."

That was a clear warning and from someone I'd never met. I couldn't help but wonder how many people had already heard about my mishap.

"Yes, sir. I will be more careful."

"We'll take our seats, Uncle, so Charlie can get this party started for you," Bill said, taking my hand.

"I'd much rather he didn't. I'd rather be out on the bayou fishing, but neither of them asked me, so here we all are," Uncle Henri said, reaching across the table for his drink, a bourbon on the rocks that looked like it needed replenishing. Tossing back the last swallow, he raised his glass, and almost instantly, a full glass appeared in front of him, courtesy of the waiter.

Bill chuckled under his breath as we took to our seats, along with the rest of the guests. The food service was about to begin.

Waiters streamed into the room, carrying plates of appetizers, placing them around the room, first on the head table, in front of Uncle Henri and then the other tables. Once the food was in place, Charlie stood up, tapping his water glass with a knife and bringing everyone to attention.

"Thank y'all for joining us this afternoon to celebrate my father's 75$^{th}$ birthday, a milestone for the Marchand family. I'm sure we can all agree that Henri Marchand has led our family and company with unmatched skill over the past four decades. We've all benefited from his fierce determination to continue the legacy his forefathers began generations ago. Please raise your glasses in a toast to my father, Henri Marchand, a man among men." Charlie lifted his glass to his father, and everyone in the room followed suit, toasting the old man with a raucous cheer and impromptu rendition of 'For He's a Jolly Good Fellow.'

Uncle Henri sat back in his chair, calmly looking around the room at his family, friends, and business partners, a satisfied expression on his face. He appeared to be enjoying the attention despite what he said earlier.

"That's enough, Charlie," he said. "Let's not let these oysters go cold. Eat up, y'all. No sense in wasting good food." He grabbed an oyster, tipped it into his mouth, and sucked the shell clean in obvious enjoyment.

I tried to decipher the ingredients and cooking techniques of the food placed before me. The Oysters Rockefeller, a signature dish at Antoine's, was a bit of a mystery. I could taste the butter, shallots, garlic, a few spices and breadcrumbs, but there was another flavor I couldn't identify, and it occupied a good deal of my time trying to figure it out.

Following the oysters, the waiters served an entrée of *Petit Filet de Boeuf Marchand de Vin aux Champignons*, consisting of perfectly cooked slices of beef tenderloin with mushrooms in a red wine sauce. A green salad, topped with a ripe cheese dressing, and crusty bread, rounded out the meal.

The entrée recipe wasn't too hard to figure out. I had once made a similar wine sauce when I lived with Julian in Suresnes. It was the method of cooking the beef I was unsure of. There were several options to consider, and consequently, I became impatient for my visit to their kitchen so I could discover how they did it.

Realizing we were only halfway through this family/friend/business event, I settled back to listen to the surrounding conversations. Being the youngest person in the room can be an advantage. Adults usually ignore children, especially if they're well-behaved. I knew how to be that perfect child, present but invisible and therefore ignored.

During my years with Katarina, I had accompanied her to several luncheons and a few dinners hosted by the Nazi Military Command in Paris. She would take me as insurance for her easy departure to avoid becoming embroiled in their intrigues. I would sit next to her, quietly listening and remembering every conversation I heard, while constantly being mindful of my precarious position among them. They talked freely across the table about politics, business, and the war, favorite subjects among the high-ranking Nazi officers.

This gathering of New Orleans movers and shakers—an expression Bill used to describe them—felt very familiar. What I heard around the tables in the Rex Room that afternoon could easily have been translations of the German conversations I heard in Paris during the occupation. Business, war, and politics dominated their discussions, and an uncomfortable feeling swept over me as I listened. The only difference between these men and the Germans who had controlled France was that these men weren't Nazis. At least, I hoped they weren't.

Besides the male-dominated discussions in the room, there were several more intimate chats among the women in attendance. Mama Bea never shifted her seat during the entire affair, holding court at the head table all afternoon. Every time a chair would empty in her vicinity, there'd be a woman waiting to fill the vacancy, wanting to sit and have a quiet chat with her. She introduced me a few times, but I suspected the younger women who came to chat were only interested in Bill's company. He sat close by, rarely leaving my side.

By the end of the party, I'd lost all hope of my wish being granted. Mr. Alciatore had come and gone from the room during the dessert service and never said a word to either Bill or me. Disheartened and impatient to leave, my crossed legs bounced restlessly beneath the table.

If I'd been even slightly willful, I might have used the pretense of going to the ladies' room to go exploring. Had I been braver, I would have slipped out of Antoine's altogether to go explore the Quarter on my own. I imagined myself doing it, but I couldn't make myself take that first step.

'*Brave, strong, clever.*' the old woman's words echoed in my mind.

*I've never been brave. I've always been a coward.* Frustrated with my inability to act on impulse I scorned myself for letting fear stop me.

My bouncing legs kept a steady beat beneath the table and by then my composure was nearly gone. With every bounce, the heel of my shoe brushed against the carpet, making a soft, rhythmic sound. Bill interrupted his conversation with our waiter to lean over to me, reaching his hand under the table to still my leg.

"Are you ready, Chère?" he asked, a smile curling the corners of his mouth.

I wasn't sure what he meant but had no time to think about it because at that very moment, Carson Bentley strutted into the Rex room carrying a bottle of something tied with a bow.

He strolled between the tables as if he were an expected guest arriving late. After he greeted several people, he purposefully walked up to Uncle Henri and set the bottle down in front of him. The room went silent while everyone watched and listened.

"Happy Birthday, Henri Marchand. I couldn't let this day pass without paying my respects, sir," Carson said with feigned deference, and loud enough the room could hear.

Uncle Henri slowly turned from his conversation and towards Carson, his eyes traveling up from the bottle on the table and coming to rest on the younger man's face.

I could feel the tension in the room as Carson waited for Uncle Henri's response. It felt like everyone was holding their breath. Bill stood next to me, still as a statue, tense and clearly unsure of his friend's reception. As I watched the scene unfold, I wondered why everyone seemed so... uncomfortable.

"Carson Bentley..." Uncle Henri said, then silence ensued as he took his time assessing the man in front of him.

From Carson's shifting stance to his furtive glances around the room, it was clear he was as uncomfortable with the silence as everyone else. Before he could offer any further greeting, Uncle Henri spoke up.

"Your father, Clayton Bentley, was a good man, a good friend. You'd do well to remember that. Thank you for the bourbon, Carson," Uncle Henri said, nodding his dismissal, then he turned back to his previous conversation, leaving Carson in standing there in awkward silence.

Bill took me by the hand. "Come on, Chère. Leonard is going to take us on a tour of the restaurant," he said, leading me out of the room.

We followed Leonard through Antoine's many dining rooms, listening to the history of each, and the stories of the important guests they'd hosted. Impatient to get to the kitchen part of the tour, I pestered him about it.

"Monsieur, may we go to za kitchen now?" I asked as we walked from one room to the next.

"We will see the kitchen at the end, mademoiselle," Leonard assured me, but he took his time as we toured the restaurant.

By the time we entered those swinging doors, the lunch service was over. The only sounds heard inside that kitchen were those of cleaning: a coal-fired stove being scrapped clean, prep stations being scrubbed and made ready for the dinner service later that day. The chef was nowhere in sight, so Leonard walked me around, describing the different stations but avoiding my questions about the food preparation and recipes.

I was extremely disappointed. Mr. Alciatore had granted my wish but denied me the music I sought. I hoped the other restaurant owners in New Orleans didn't share his view of girls in the kitchen and that Bill would help me discover them. With a last look around, I followed Bill out.

Once I thought about it, I realized the tour hadn't been a total waste of time. After hearing the 105-year history of Antoine's, I understood four things were essential to the successful operation of a restaurant; exceptional food, superb wine and alcohol, excellent service, and a comfortable setting, all offered and delivered with a consistent attention to detail. I couldn't wait to get home to make some notes in my journal about this experience.

Just as Bill and I returned to the Rex room, Carson was leaving. With his head down and a frown pulling on his mouth, he nearly collided with Bill in his haste to depart. Bill pulled me behind him to shield me from any jostling.

Carson recovered his previous swagger when he realized who he'd run into.

"Where did you run off to, Bill?" he asked. "I could have used your help in there. Charles wouldn't give me the time of day."

"What did you expect, Carson? Did you think a bottle of bourbon would fix things after that stunt you pulled last week?" Bill asked.

"I made a point of apologizing for that little indiscretion the next day, but the son-of-a-bitch wants to hold a grudge. He won't even give me a meeting with the board to discuss the project. Marchand Industries would be foolish to pass up this opportunity, Bill. I guarantee you this hotel-casino project is going to make this town into a mecca." Carson was apparently sure enough of their friendship to express his less-than-flattering opinion of Bill's family.

Bill laid his hand on Carson's arm, a gesture of friendship and goodwill. "It's not the project, Carson, it's who you're partnering with that concerns Charles and the others. I've already told you what I think about Barone."

"Joe's money is as good as anyone's. It's not like the rest of them haven't cut corners when they needed to. The self-righteous bastards," Carson swiftly replied, shrugging off Bill's hand. His face darkened with obvious resentment that he'd not received the support he thought his due. He stared at Bill, silently assessing him.

I stood back, listening, but thought it best I move away lest I somehow become part of their argument. "Excuse me," I said, stepping around Bill to return to the Rex room and the rest of the family. Carson's eyes shifted to me as I passed.

"What's going on between you and my sister, Bill?" he asked, still looking at me, then he turned back to Bill. "Charlotte said she wasn't feeling well today, but it seems like things have changed between you two. You and I had a plan, Bill. What happened?"

I'd only gone as far as the dining room doorway, waiting for Bill, wanting to hear his reply.

"Maybe you should ask Charlotte that question, Carson," Bill said.

"I'm asking my friend."

Bill gave him a long, hard look, like he was trying to decide how far to take this conversation. He took a breath, releasing it slowly, his expression resolute.

"Plans change, Carson. People change," Bill said as he walked past his friend and toward me.

"Apparently, some people more than others," Carson replied, as Bill and I rejoined the family in the Rex room.

# Chapter 23

## *Family Revelations*

The following evening, Bill, Mama Bea, and I went to Charles and Julianna's for an intimate family supper with Uncle Henri. They lived together in Marcel House, which Uncle Henri's great-grandfather built for his bride in the Uptown neighborhood.

As soon as we stepped into the house, Julianna Marchand pulled me into a warm embrace, as if I was a long-lost child who had returned home.

"Welcome, Désirée. We're so happy to get a chance to spend some quiet time with you," she said, sliding her hands down my arms to capture my hands and squeezing them gently. Her sea-green eyes gazed down at me with soft sincerity.

I couldn't help but stiffen a bit in her arms. We'd hardly spoken the day before, so the warmth of her reception surprised me.

I nodded shyly. "Zank you, madame."

"Please, call me Julianna."

Two small children, a boy and a girl, were bouncing up and down behind her while their father attempted to settle the restless five-year-olds with a stern look.

Julianna released one of my hands, turning to her excited children. "Henry, Madalyn, this is Désirée. Mind your manners and greet her properly."

Both children stopped in mid-bounce, grabbing the other's hand and standing perfectly still, beaming smiles up at me. They were nearly identical. The only things telling them apart were their hair and clothing. He had short brown hair trimmed neatly around his pert little ears, and she looked like a life-size doll in her pink nightgown and robe, and her long brown hair braided down her back.

"Nice to meet you, Désirée. Welcome to our home," they said in well-rehearsed unison. The formalities attended to, Henry and Madalyn resumed their bouncing, clearly excited about something.

"Mommy, can Désirée come up to read us a story before bed? Please?" Henry asked, his sister's head nodding in agreement.

"Well darling, she's only just arrived. Perhaps...," Julianna began.

"I don't mind," I quickly offered, realizing the company of these two children felt far less complicated than the evening of adult conversation ahead of me.

"Yay!" little Henry squealed. "Come on, Maddie. Let's show Désirée our room."

They each took hold of one of my hands and began pulling me toward the staircase, a grand sweeping structure leading to the upper floors.

"Aren't you two forgetting something?" Charles said with a stern but gentle look.

Henry and Madalyn halted in their tracks. "Oh! Sorry, Papa." They released my hands and turned to Uncle Henri, Bill, and Mama Bea. "Goodnight, Pawpaw," they said, each giving him a hug and a kiss. Then they repeated this with Mama Bea and Bill, then finally with their father, who was clearly proud of his progeny, based on his wide smile and shining eyes.

"Darling, please get Aunt Bea and Bill something to drink. Désirée and I will join you once the children are in bed," Julianna said, leading me up the stairs, Henry and Madalyn bouncing and giggling behind me.

After two chapters of *The Wonderful World of Oz*—a book I had not read but mentally added to my reading list—a couple of singing rounds of *Frère Jacque,* followed by a nighttime prayer, little Henry and Madalyn finally settled down for the night.

"You have a way with them," Julianna said as we walked down the hall from the nursery. "Maddie isn't usually so open with new people. Henry is the one to convince her to do things. But she took to you right away." She gave me a look I'd seen before.

"Were there other children... where you lived before?"

It was going to be a night of questions; that much was clear. I kept my gaze straight ahead as we went down the stairs, not answering until we reached the bottom. "No, madame. Zare was no one younger zan me." Which was the truth, except at La Maison, but I only lived there for a few months before the Kommandant took me away.

When we entered the living room, the tension between Bill and Charles was palpable. Both men stood with crossed arms, facing each other, hard looks marking their features.

"Damn it, Bill," Charles snarled. "Your recklessness left us with a public relations nightmare that we're still dealing with. And now you bring this to our door?" Charles threw his hands in the air, turning away, clearly frustrated with his younger cousin.

Bill's head hung low. He looked like a schoolboy who'd just received a dressing down by his elder. When he lifted his head, his eyes caught mine. Sadness, and perhaps humiliation, seeped through them when he looked at me.

"Supper is ready, everyone," Julianna said cheerfully, attempting to lighten the mood in the room. "Let's all move to the dining room, shall we? We can discuss this later, Charles. Aunt Bea, Father Henri, Justine has promised a special treat for us tonight," she said, guiding them out of the living room.

I didn't follow them, mostly because I could feel Bill's discomfort and it troubled me. He seemed to carry a weight, a secret that was shameful and burdensome.

"Coming, Désirée?" Charles asked as he walked away from Bill.

"I'd like to speak with her alone, Charlie. We'll join you in a minute," Bill said, holding me in place with his eyes.

Charles sought my agreement with a quick look in my direction. My nod convinced him, though suspicion still filled his eyes when he gave Bill one last look before leaving the room.

Bill sat down on the sofa, patting the place beside him.

"Sit with me, Chère. I need to talk to you." He still had that uncertain look in his eyes, like he was reluctant to speak.

I sat beside him, nervous and unsure, my heart thumping in my chest.

"Your family, zay are angry wiz you because of me?" It was the only thing I could imagine that would make Bill so uncomfortable.

"No, it's not you, Chère. It's me. They don't understand how things are for me now." He leaned back, crossing his legs, resting one arm across his body. His expression was grave, like he was about to face a battle.

"I wasn't always the man you know," he confessed, now speaking in French. "I was different before... before Pops died. Before the war. Charlie called me reckless. I was reckless, selfish, and cocky. I was all those things and probably a lot worse." He took a breath, blowing it out with a heavy sigh before he continued.

"Carson and I called ourselves the future kings of New Orleans. We were the privileged, rich heirs to the Marchand and Bentley fortunes, and we wielded that power all over town. There were more than a few sticky situations our fathers had to pull us out of. In college, we made plans for what we would do when we took over the companies, all the things we would accomplish that our fathers were too conservative to attempt. Then Charlotte stepped into the picture. And well, she was just icing on the cake for me."

"Things changed my last year of college. Pops died that year. He had always been there, and then he wasn't, and I was rudderless. I knew I had disappointed him; hadn't become the man he thought I could be. After graduation I enlisted in the Army. They sent me to officer training. I was searching for something there, redemption maybe. I needed a purpose, something I could believe in that would make my father proud."

"By the time I got to France, I was a changed man. Then something happened the night I met you. I didn't understand it then, I still don't, but I knew you were important to me, that you were the reason I was there. You, Chère, gave meaning to everything I've done since that night."

"I've been away for a long time. My family doesn't know who I've become. They don't trust that I'm not being reckless again. They don't know you, and I need you to tell them, Chère. Let them know you the way I know you, so they can understand why I made this choice."

"They are like the Laurents. They are afraid I will cause trouble for them. Will they send me away, Bill?" My bottom lip quivered as tears filled my eyes.

"No, baby girl. I'd never let that happen, and I don't think they would do that. They just need to understand. Can you help me, Chère? Will you tell them your story, just this once, for me?"

"Do you trust them, Bill?"

"I trust them more than anyone besides you."

"Okay, I will tell them if it makes things easier for you." I couldn't hold back the sigh escaping my lips.

Since the day I walked into the Laurents home, fifteen months earlier, I had told no one but Bill what happened to me during the war, and I hadn't told him everything. The thought of reliving my history unsettled my stomach. By the time Bill and I rejoined the family, I had lost my appetite completely.

"Glad you finally decided to join us," Uncle Henri said gruffly as we joined the family in the dining room.

"Sorry to keep you waiting, Uncle," Bill replied.

The elegantly appointed oval table was relatively small for the size of the room, offering a more intimate setting for the small gathering. Bill held my chair, seating me between Uncle Henri and Julianna, then he took the other empty seat between Mama Bea and Charles.

The meal was a leisurely affair, casual conversation across the table while dining on the tempting offerings of Justine, the family cook. Julianna regaled us with the antics of little Henry and Madalyn during their summer with Julianna's brother and his family in Boston. Eventually, their focus turned to me and my sudden appearance among them.

Julianna was refilling the wine glasses when Uncle Henri turned to me with a fixed stare.

"I'm not one for beating around bushes, girl, so I'll ask you straight. Who are you and why'd my nephew need to sneak you into the States?"

His question wasn't totally unexpected, though the directness of it surprised me. Henri Marchand was a formidable man, clearly accustomed to and requiring honest answers.

As I watched Julianna fill Uncle Henri's glass and then set the carafe down in front of him, I thought about the first time I told my entire story. It was to Picasso, in his studio, and he had given me a glass of wine as a fortification.

*There's nothing to lose by asking.*

I looked up at Uncle Henri and politely asked, "May I have some wine, *monsieur*? It is a long story."

Uncle Henri's raised eyebrows and piercing look sent a jolt through me. He had decided who I was, or rather what type of girl I was, and my request seemed to take him by surprise. His eyes searched mine for any insolence. Finding none, he took the empty wineglass that had been sitting in front of me all evening, then filled it himself before passing it over to me.

"Here's your wine, girl," he said with a nod.

"Henri, she's too young," Mama Bea objected, reaching for the glass, but she stopped when Bill spoke up.

"Let her have the wine, Mama. Go on, Chère, tell them."

"*Merci, monsieur,*" I said, tipping my head to acknowledge Uncle Henri's permission before lifting the glass to my lips.

As with Picasso's wine, the heady Malbec hit my near-empty stomach and then blossomed into a warm glow, lighting up all the dark places and exposing the secret boxes holding my memories. I sipped the wine slowly, lamenting that a dreamless sleep would not be my reward, as it had been with Picasso.

It was Uncle Henri I must win over, so I focused on him, never looking away. I spoke as calmly and dispassionately as my memories would allow, telling him everything that had happened to me over the past five years, with a few omissions. Only the occasional tremble or quivering lip betrayed the depth of my feelings.

*Memories can't hurt you,* I reminded myself as I restored each recounted moment back into its box, hopefully sealing them forever.

"You took an enormous risk, Bill," Uncle Henri said at the conclusion of my history.

"It was necessary, Uncle. I took advantage of an opportunity to get her out of harm's way. I believe my father would have done the same, under the circumstances," Bill replied, steel-blue eyes unwavering.

Uncle Henri held Bill's gaze for a while, the two men sending silent messages to each other across the table. It looked like Uncle Henri was taking Bill's measure, taking time to reassess his opinion, as if he were seeing Bill for the first time, new, yet vaguely familiar.

"I'd say that's a fair assessment," Uncle Henri said. "My brother always had a keen sense of honor, and you're looking more like him every day. Wouldn't you agree, Bea?"

"Yes, Henri. The resemblance is... uncanny," Mama Bea replied, looking at me the entire time.

I didn't think she was referring to Bill's resemblance to his father, though that was plain enough, based on every photograph I'd seen. No, her remark held some other meaning that was as unclear to me as it was unsettling.

"Who'd be looking for her, and is there any chance of them looking in this direction?" Uncle Henri asked.

"The Laurents are the only people in France who know where she went. There's nothing to fear on that front, guaranteed. My team knows she was on the transport, but they believe she was part of the mission cargo. That's as much as I can say about how Désirée got here. As for who'd be looking for her, I suppose that would be the French police. There was a warrant issued for her arrest last December," Bill said as small lines appeared around his eyes and his mouth pulled down in a frown.

"They won't be looking here, but what about the Germans, that Nazi officer, and the woman? What happened to them?" Charles asked.

Bill held my eyes briefly before answering, the worry deepening in his own. "We traced Katarina Lang to Laredo, Spain, and then to Portugal, where she took a flight to Buenos Aires. Last report was, she's still in South America."

For the past year and a half, I tried not to think about the Steiglers and what had happened to them, but right then, I could hear Karl Steigler's warning ringing loudly in my head: *"They'll be looking for you. Mother, Father."*

"What about the man? What happened to him?" Uncle Henri asked.

Bill closed his eyes, and when he opened them, sadness leaked out. He seemed to want to spare me any distress, but there was no help for it. He must answer.

"There has been no trace of Steigler since late February '44. He's not listed among the dead or captured. His name is on a list of escaped Nazi officers."

My throat tightened with a gasp. Tears fell with each ragged breath.

"Any reason that man would come looking for you, girl?" Uncle Henri asked me.

"I do not know," I choked out my answer, chills running down my back. "Karl, he say zay boz will look for me. I zink za Kommandant is very angry wiz me for deceiving him. He will blame me for Karl's death, and perhaps Katarina will too." I sniffled back my tears, trying to hold my fear in check.

The thought of the Kommandant being out there somewhere, plotting his revenge, sent another wave of trembles down my spine and more tears falling down my cheeks. I was sure he would never forget or forgive, and that nearly paralyzed me with fear.

"Oh, you poor thing," Julianna cried, throwing her arms around me and pulling me into her embrace. "No child should have to suffer so. You're safe here with us, darling. Isn't she, Charles?"

A fresh wave of guilt coursed through me as I struggled to compose myself and pull away from her.

"No, madame. It was za French people who suffered, not me," I said, wiping my tears away with the napkin and lowering my head. It was a shameful admission, my lack of any physical suffering, but it tortured me the most. I lived through those years well-fed and tenderly cared for by Katarina and Tante Elsa, given every luxury available, and it cost me my identity.

"Of course she is, Julianna," Charles replied. When I looked at him, his eyes held mine with the same honesty I'd known with Bill. There was no hesitation there, no cautious expression of distrust.

It had all been too much for me, the questions, the revelations. I was ready to go home. I looked around the table as I sipped the last of the wine, trying to gauge their acceptance of my tale, and if they heard enough. Bill looked as if he felt the same, ready to leave, but he was waiting for something.

"If I understand all this correctly, no one will look for you here, as long as you stay out of trouble." Uncle Henri gave me a hard look to impress that order upon me. "Get her into school, Bea. The nuns will keep her busy."

"She's not going to Sacred Heart, Henri. She's going to Newman," Mama Bea said.

"Whose brilliant idea was that?" Uncle Henri asked, turning his stare to Bill and Mama Bea.

"Mine," I answered. "I do not want to live in za school. I want to live in my new home wiz Mama Bea." My lip quivered, so I bit down hard on it, stifling any additional remark I might have added.

He shook his head, clearly unhappy with this decision, and I worried he would overrule what we had already decided.

"You agreed to this, Bea?"

Mama Bea sighed, tilting her head. "I did... reluctantly. Newman is an excellent school, one of the best in the city. She'll get a good education there. I'll see to it."

Uncle Henri gave me another piercing look, assessing the risk I might pose. After a couple of minutes of that silent scrutiny, he relaxed back into his chair.

"Alright, young lady. You're part of the Marchand family now. From this moment on, make sure you conduct yourself with dignity. I will not have a repeat of the Prytania incident. Am I understood?"

He wasn't being mean or anything. The look in his eyes didn't frighten me like the Kommandant's had, but I knew I must obey his orders, just the same.

"*Je comprends, monsieur.* I will remember," I said, swallowing hard and nodding my head.

"As for you, Bill," Uncle Henri said, turning back to his nephew. "You've got some cleaning up to do around here before you go off and take care of business for Mr. Truman. You get this Bentley situation handled, once and for all."

"Yes, sir, I'll take care of it," Bill said, keeping eye contact with Uncle Henri.

"See that you do. And get a handle on that Steigler fellow. I don't like loose ends. They always come back to bite you in the ass. Make sure this one doesn't."

Bill looked from Uncle Henri to me, his face drawn with more worry lines than I'd ever seen on him before. My stomach clenched again.

"I'm working on it, Uncle," he replied solemnly, his clasped hands resting on the table.

"You've set yourself a mighty task here, Bill. Are you up to it? Are you the man your father was, the man he thought you'd be?" Uncle Henri asked, glaring across the table at his nephew, challenging him.

"Yes, Uncle. I believe I am," Bill answered with steadfast conviction. He was looking at me when he said it.

"Let's hope you're right," was Uncle Henri's reply.

By the time we got home that night, the wine had fully kicked in, and I was unsteady on my feet as we came in the door. Bill swept me into his arms and carried me up the stairs to my room, Mama Bea fussing behind us.

"I told you she shouldn't have had the wine," she scolded.

"She needed it, Mama. She'll be fine. Won't you, Chère?"

"*Bien sûr*... I am fine... hmm... Bill... I must tell you somezing... hmm." It felt like I was drifting in a warm, soft blanket of comfort, and I couldn't seem to pull my thoughts together.

"You can tell me in the morning, Chère," he said, laying me down on the bed. "Mama is going to get you ready for bed now. I'll be in to say goodnight when you're tucked in."

Before he left, I levered myself into a sitting position, trying to get them to listen to me.

"No, Bill. I must tell you... za Kommandant... he had a plan... wiz Heir Himm... had orders to... hmm..." That was all I could get out of my foggy brain before falling back onto the bed.

# Chapter 24

## *My Revenge*

Bill was sitting in the overstuffed chair in the corner of my room, smoking and reading a newspaper that lay open across his lap. The sheer curtains covering the opened gallery door billowed gently in the morning breeze, freshening the room. His face showed signs of weariness as he scanned the newspaper, then his eyes met mine when he heard me stretch along the bed.

"Good morning, Chère. How do you feel?" he asked, one eyebrow arching over a tired eye.

"Thirsty." I reached for the glass of water I always had by the bed, and once I quenched my dry mouth, I sat up, sensing his apprehension.

"Did you sit zare all night?" I asked. The final moments of the evening were still a little foggy.

He shook his head. "No. I went to bed, then I heard you moaning around two thirty and came in to check on you. You settled back down, but I stayed to make sure. Laila brought me up a pot of coffee a while ago. Do you want some?"

When I nodded, he poured us each a cup, adding a cube of sugar and a dash of cream to mine. He knew the way I liked it.

"*Merci,* Bill," I said, taking the cup from his hands.

"*De rien,* Désirée."

He stood at the end of the bed for a moment, as if deciding whether to sit there. His eyes scanned the rumpled covers, then he reached down to straighten them, resting his hand there briefly. Decision made, he walked back to the chair, picking up his coffee cup as he sat down.

When he spoke, it was in French, our preferred language. "Before I say anything else, I want to thank you for being so brave last night. I don't know many adults who can stand in front of Henri Marchand and undergo that kind of scrutiny without coming away shaking in their boots. My uncle is a tough man to impress, but I think you accomplished that, Chère."

"He isn't so tough," I said, remembering Uncle Henri's nod of approval when I asked for wine. "He didn't really frighten me, except now I know I must follow his rules, or he'll be angry with me. I think if I make any trouble, he'll send me to a boarding school." Bill probably wouldn't let him, but the threat was enough to stifle any rebellious need I might have.

Bill's wry smile and the look in his eyes showed my assumption was probably correct. "You might be right, but you won't let that happen. Will you Chère?"

"No, I won't," I said, even though I knew it would be a challenge to conform to their expectations. Being an Uptown girl wasn't who I wanted to be.

"You go freshen up. I'll take the coffee outside. Laila's bringing us up a bite to eat. You and I have a few things to talk about this morning." His look became serious, and I knew immediately what was coming next.

I threw aside the covers and scurried into the bathroom to relieve my bladder and gather my thoughts. Re-living any of those memories wasn't something I wanted to do, but I had to tell Bill about the Kommandant, about what I'd done before I ran away.

I brushed the morning tangles out of my hair, pinned it back with a clip, and then splashed cool water on my face. When I looked up into the mirror, I expected to see the girl I had seen in Picasso's mirror—maybe a braver version of that girl—but that's not who looked back at me. The face looking back at me was the same face I saw in the bathroom mirror on the day I ran away from the Kommandant, frightened and nervous, bruised cheek and all.

*Tell him what you did,* she said.

I didn't want to, didn't want to think about the Kommandant ever again, but now that I knew he might still be alive somewhere, everything I knew about him fell into place, painting a clear picture of who he was... until the moment I ran away from him.

*Tell him,* the girl said again.

I took a deep breath and walked out onto the gallery to share my memories of Anton Steigler and my last act of revenge upon him.

Bill was sitting on one of the wicker chairs, a small table in front of him. A tray laden with coffee, cups, and a plate of biscuits and jam sat on the table. He leaned back with his legs crossed, obviously waiting for me. As I approached, his look was cautious, as if he were gauging my mood.

"Are you alright, Chère?"

"I'm fine, and you?" I replied, taking the chair across from him.

"Yeah, I'm fine too." He sat quietly for a while, smoking and sipping his coffee while I helped myself to one of Miss Laila's delicious buttermilk biscuits, filling it with strawberry jam before taking a bite. When I had finished half of it, he spoke again, reverting to French.

"I'm sorry you had to find out about Steigler that way. I thought I could spare you that information." He looked sorry, as sorry as he had the night before.

My voice was shaky when I spoke. Ripples of remembered fear began running down my back. "I thought... imagined he was dead. I hoped he was. But now..." I couldn't finish the thought. It was too frightening.

Bill took a deep breath, then blew it out. "You said something last night before you fell asleep. You said you needed to tell me something about the Kommandant. Do you remember what it was?"

I rolled my eyes at him. It always struck me as funny whenever he asked if I remembered things. He was the one person who really knew how my mind worked, knew that I remembered everything.

"I don't like thinking about him, Bill."

"I know you don't, but I need you to." He wrinkled up his forehead, giving me the same look Uncle Henri had given me the night before, the kind that demanded a response.

"After you fell asleep last night, it occurred to me you might know something about Steigler, something that might help me find him." He locked my eyes to his, like he was trying to penetrate my thoughts, my memories.

"He is dangerous, Bill." Visions of the monster I lived with for three years flashed across my mind.

"That's why I need to find him. Can you help me, Chère? Will you tell me what you know?"

I closed my eyes and hesitantly brought up my memory of that last day, the worst day of my life.

"We were leaving, Katarina and me, and the Kommandant was... nervous, unhappy about Katarina leaving, and angry with me for crying. He didn't like change. There was chaos in change, and he liked things orderly, predictable. He carefully planned everything he did, leaving nothing to chance. That day, the house was in chaos, and he was angry about it."

"He had received orders to move his troops toward the coast. He was to leave the next day, same as us. Then early that morning, a courier came with a message from Berlin. As soon as it arrived, his mood changed. He became excited and told Katarina they would be together sooner than he thought, and that their plans were going to work out. He didn't see me watch him put the message into the secret drawer under his desk."

"After they left to take Tante Elsa to the train station that day, I went into his office and opened the secret drawer. I knew he kept valuable things in there, things he didn't want his men to know about, or even Katarina. I was scared, but I wanted to hurt him as much as he hurt me. Destroying what he valued was the only thing I could do.

"I emptied the drawer onto the desk and read everything. There was the message from Berlin, the envelope Himmler gave him at Berchtesgaden, and two identification cards, one Swiss and one Spanish, each with a photo of him in different guises. There was some money, a little booklet from a bank in Switzerland, and a funny little key. I read everything, and then I burned it all in the fire, except the key. That wouldn't burn, so I kept it and tied it to Jean-Michel's ribbon and tied that to my doll as an ornament. I put the drawer back, completely empty. Then I left."

Images of the stolen house filled my mind, the sound of the Kommandant's voice, the feel of his slap across my cheek, and the smell of burning paper all combined to send another jolt of fear flowing through me.

"What did the message from Berlin say?" Bill asked as gently as he could, but he needed to know.

"It said, 'Commence Operation Tango Bariloche' and it had a rendezvous; March 1st, 01:00, Kriegsmarine, Brest. The signature at the bottom was only the letter H."

"Shit.... What was in the envelope from Himmler?"

"A map and a list of names. The Kommandant's name was on the list."

"How do you know Himmler gave it to him?"

"In November, before I ran away, the Führer ordered us to come to Berchtesgaden. The Kommandant said we must go as a family, but Katarina didn't want to take me. He insisted I go because Karl couldn't. Karl was a guard at Auschwitz in Poland. The Kommandant wanted to present a complete family to the Führer, and I was a part of it."

"Heir Himmler presented us and four other families to the Führer. All the men went off to a meeting while the wives and children visited with Ava Braun outside in the gardens. When the meeting was over, and we were getting ready to leave, Heir Himmler came over and thanked the Kommandant for his contribution. Then he slipped the letter into the Kommandant's breast pocket and said, "Good man." When we returned to Châlons, I saw the Kommandant put the letter into the secret drawer.

Bill shook his head, though not in disbelief. "Jesus, Chère... I wish I'd asked you about this a year ago."

"No one ever asked me about him. And I didn't want to think about him."

"I'm going to need something else. I need you to write down everything you saw on those papers. All of it. Can you do that for me?" His brow remained furrowed, obviously worried the request might be too much for me, yet I could hear his excitement at finding a trail to follow. If it meant I could finally put that nightmare away forever, I would write an entire book for him.

"I'll do it, Bill, but then I don't want to talk about this anymore."

"Do you still have the key you took from him?"

I nodded, leaving him to contemplate that last bit of information.

While I sat at my desk, writing everything I had seen on those papers, I heard Bill and Miss Laila talking out on the gallery.

"I brought y'all up a fresh pot of coffee, Mr. William and a glass of juice for Miss Dezrae. The two of you been talking a long time. Oh, and Miss Bea ask me to remind you that she has a meetin' at the university today. She'll be home round two."

"Thanks, Laila. I remember her saying something about it. How's the family? Marcus?" Bill asked.

"Thayz fine, Mr. William. Marcus, he be doing better now that O'Leary fella's gone from the plant. Was that your doin', Mr. William?"

"Nah. O'Leary made that bed himself. I just helped him into it. I'm glad Marcus is doing better. You give him, and the family, my best."

"I will, sir. Thank ya, Mr. William. Miss Dezrae doing alright? Miss Bea said Mr. Henri give her a hard time last night."

"Well, you know how Uncle is, but she held her own. Better than most. She's a strong girl, our Désirée."

"That she is, sir. That she is," Miss Laila said, her voice trailing off down the gallery stairs.

When I returned, his eyes were closed, and his face relaxed, but I could see his eyes moving behind the lids as if he were searching for something. He heard me approach, lifted his eyes to meet mine, and smiled the way he always did when he saw me.

"*C'est tout*," I said, handing him several sheets of neatly written pages. "This is everything I saw in the secret drawer, everything I burned."

He flipped through them with an astonished look in his eyes, occasionally glancing up at me.

"Are you sure about these dates and numbers?" he asked, holding up the page with the Swiss Bank booklet entries.

"I'm sure, Bill. I remembered some of those dates when I was writing them down. Those were when he took trips with *Le Soldat Jouet*, his aide."

When Bill finished looking over all the pages, he folded them carefully, then put them aside. His movements were slow and deliberate, like he was thinking hard about something. He wasn't looking at me, his gaze fixed on something over my right shoulder, one hand stroking the stubble of his morning beard thoughtfully.

"This is my satchel, where I keep my special things," I said, breaking into his thoughts and handing him the bag.

He shifted his eyes to mine and hesitated to take the satchel from me. "Are you sure you want me to look in here? You don't have to show me everything. Some things might be private, and that's alright, Chère."

"You know me better than anyone, Bill. I want you to know... to see what I kept from before. It's okay to look." I leaned back in my chair with the juice in my hand and watched as he opened the satchel.

One by one, he pulled out my few precious treasures and odd keepsakes, laying them out on the table. First came the letters from Mama Bea, then the photo of my friends taken the day the Allies liberated Paris, then a folded piece of crumpled up newspaper, a capped leather tube, and the doll Grand-Mère had made for me. He held up the doll to examine it.

"See the key tied around her waist? The ribbon was from Jean-Michel's box. I saved it."

He looked closely at the key without detaching it from the doll. He seemed to know what it was for, his fingers thoughtfully rubbing along the edge, like it was familiar to him. Then he tucked the key back into the doll's pocket and laid it aside.

"What's in the tube?" he asked.

"Two drawings. Mine and Picasso's."

"Picasso's?"

"He drew it while I was sleeping on his couch, the night he saved me." I carefully withdrew the delicate sheets from the tube, unrolling them for Bill to see.

He examined Picasso's drawing, then looked at my doll and satchel, comparing the details. "This looks more like his earlier style, but it's his signature, alright. If anyone had any doubts about that part of your story, this would shatter them. It might be worth a lot of money to the right collector if you ever want to sell it."

I shook my head firmly. "I would never sell it, Bill. He gave it as a gift."

After putting Picasso's drawing aside, he picked up my drawing and held it carefully, as if it might break in his hands. He said nothing, just stared at it for a while. It was a child's drawing of a family standing in front of a farmhouse. There was nothing to say that would change anything.

"We could have them framed, if you like."

I shook my head, looking down at the drawing I'd done so long ago. "No, I don't want to. It's too hard to look at them. Maybe someday, but not now." Carefully rolling up the drawings, I restored them to the safety of the leather tube.

"Do you want the key, Bill?"

"No. Leave it where it is. I can't use it, though I sure would like to know what's in that safe deposit box. If I need it, I'll ask for it, alright?"

"Okay. Are we done talking about this now?" I started repacking my treasures into the satchel.

"We're done for now," he said, a tender look in his eyes. Then he held up the folded newspaper and asked, "What's this?" When he opened it up and saw what it was, his look darkened, worry lines creasing the corners of his eyes.

It was the official notice of the warrant for my arrest printed in the Paris newspaper last December, the public declaration and catalog of my sins.

"Why did you keep this?" he asked as the creases on his forehead deepened.

"I don't know. I was going to burn it that day, but that wouldn't make any difference. I just kept it," I said with a shrug.

He spent some time reading the list of people I had hurt by my choice to escape the Kommandant. I would carry that burden forever. Destroying the paper wouldn't change anything.

Bill put one hand to his mouth, pinching it and stroking his chin. He tapped a finger on the paper. "Do you know who added Alex's name to the warrant? It had to be someone in Châlons," he asked cautiously.

It was my turn to stare beyond him, unwilling to meet his gaze. "It doesn't matter who it was, because it doesn't change what happened." Some secrets are best left unexposed.

My teeth were gnawing into my bottom lip, an unwelcome response. From the look in his eyes when I finally looked back at him, he knew I was hiding something, but he said nothing and wouldn't push me to say more.

After a minute or two of mutual silence, Bill lowered his eyes, shaking his head. He let out a deep sigh, refolded the newspaper, returned it to my bag, then handed it to me.

"Thank you for sharing your things with me, Désirée, and thank you for this," he said, holding up the pages I'd written. "You'd make a hell of a spy, Chère," he said, tucking the pages into his robe pocket. The look in his eyes held more questions and concerns.

"No. I don't think so. It's too dangerous and not as much fun as cooking."

"You're right about that," he said, the smile returning to his eyes. "Speaking of which, how about I call Charlie and ask if he can recommend a restaurant in town that might let you into their kitchen? He knows all the good places to eat in New Orleans, and all the best chefs."

My eyes lit up at the suggestion, but then I remembered my experience at Antoine's. "That sounds wonderful, Bill, but do you think the other restaurant owners will be like Mr. Alciatore? He didn't want me to watch them cook."

"Well, Roy's an old-fashioned fellow, set in his ways. I even heard he doesn't much like taking telephone reservations. He prefers the old method of handwritten requests delivered by mail or messenger." He raised his eyebrows in an expression clearly meant to suggest that I might expect the same from the others. "I imagine a few of the more established places might share Roy's point of view of women in the kitchen," he added, confirming my suspicion.

I gave him as scornful an expression as I could muster, and before I could protest, he asked, "Do you really have your heart set on doing this, Chère?"

"Of course, I do. How else will I learn that type of cooking? I can't go to cooking school until I'm eighteen, and that's too long to wait," I said, a hopeful look replacing my previous frown.

"Alright. I'll see if Charlie can help. But you need to promise me you won't go inside any restaurant kitchens alone."

"I promise, Bill." I didn't think a restaurant kitchen was any more dangerous than our own kitchen downstairs, or anywhere else, for that matter, but I'd keep the promise.

"Can we go today?"

"Not today, Chère. I've got some calls to make and some unfinished business to take care of. If I don't handle it soon, Uncle Henri might just send *me* back to boarding school," he said, standing up in one smooth move. He reached for my hand, lifting me from the chair.

"I'll call Charlie and ask him to set something up for us. You go on and get your day started." He planted a tender kiss on my forehead before walking around the corner of the gallery to his own room.

# Chapter 25

## *A good day at the symphony*

Two days later, Bill, Charles, and I were walking into Gaston's, a local Uptown restaurant and a favorite of Charles and Julianna's. Sitting on a quiet little street was a simple two storied building that had initially been an apothecary shop but was now a restaurant. It didn't look like much from the outside, but the location was perfect for me. It was right around the corner from the Isidore Newman school, and therefore, within easy access for frequent visits.

The restaurant wasn't open for lunch, but once inside, it was apparent we were expected.

"Mr. Marchand, welcome back. We have everything ready for you, sir," a friendly woman greeted Charles as we stepped inside.

"Thank you, Felicia. I appreciate you and Parker doing this," Charles said. "Let me introduce my cousin, Major Bill Marchand, and this is Désirée, the young girl I told you about."

"Very nice to meet you, Mrs. Landry," Bill said, shaking her hand. "Charlie has told me how much he enjoys coming here."

"We love hosting Julianna and Charles. They have been so helpful in spreading the word about Gaston's. Welcome, Major Marchand, Miss Désirée. Parker is in the kitchen. Please follow me."

As we trailed her through the restaurant, I took in the surroundings. The main dining area was relatively small and decorated in simple elegance; white linen-covered tables set discreetly apart, soft lighting and beautiful carpeting, all creating an intimate atmosphere.

The transition from the dining room to the kitchen was as expected, though it lacked the retreating noise of diners. We were the only ones there. As soon as I stepped through the swinging door, the musical sounds of an active restaurant kitchen filled my ears, and I was in heaven once more.

"*Bienvenue, mademoiselle Désirée,*" a man in a chef's hat and uniform said, reaching out his hand for mine. Older than his wife, late thirties maybe, he wasn't tall, but was stout in stature, and he had a crooked smile which made his brown eyes sparkle. He seemed genuinely pleased to meet me.

"*Enchanté, monsieur,*" I replied, taking his hand with a firm grip. I wanted him to take my interest in cooking seriously and thought a firm handshake might convey that message.

"I'm pleased to meet you, Major Marchand. Welcome to Gaston's," Parker said, shaking Bill's hand.

"Gentlemen, we have a table here for you. Felicia will get your drinks while I take Miss Désirée on a tour of my humble kitchen. Shall we, *mademoiselle*?" he said with a sweeping gesture for me to follow.

I looked to Bill for his approval, which he gave with a wink and nod, then he took a seat at the table tucked into the corner. Bill and Charles ordered their drinks and watched as I followed Parker around the kitchen.

It wasn't a big kitchen, not really needing to be to serve the number of guests they could seat. The stove and ovens were along the wall, and the prep station was situated directly across. A cold room lived on the other wall, cooled by large blocks of ice. Outside the cold room, a rack with shelves held cans and jars of different things. Bags of potatoes and onions occupied the bottom shelf. A rack of spice jars lived on a shelf above the prep table, along with bottles of oils and vinegars. Stacks of clean plates sat waiting on the end of the table within easy reach.

"May I ask, Miss Désirée, is cooking a hobby of yours?" Parker asked as he guided me through the kitchen, his expression kind but curious.

"No, not a hobby, sir. It is what I love to do. Someday, I will have my own restaurant, like yours, and I will make delicious food for everyone who comes." He seemed like he would understand my dream, maybe better than anyone else. At least, I hoped he would.

"I know what it's like to have that dream," he said with a gentle smile. "If there's anything I can do to assist you, it would be my pleasure."

"Will you teach me how to cook like you? I will be a good student, and I learn very quick." I hoped my expression matched how much I wanted this.

His expression darkened a little, as if my request concerned him. "Do you plan to go to culinary school?"

I shrugged. "I cannot go until I am eighteen. Five years is too long to wait, *monsieur*."

"You're thirteen?" he asked, his bushy eyebrows nearly touching the edge of his cap.

"Yes. I will finish high school when I am seventeen, zen I must wait anozer year for cooking school. It is too long, *monsieur*. Will you teach me? Please?" I gazed up at him as guilelessly as I could, praying he would say yes.

"That would require your guardian's approval, Désirée. Perhaps that question can wait until after they've eaten. Things always go better after a good meal," he said with a conspiratorial wink.

"May I watch you prepare za meal? I will stand here, out of za way, okay?" With his nodded affirmation, I stood at the end of the prep table, close enough to Bill and Charles that I could overhear their conversation as I watched Parker prepare the meal for us.

"How'd it go with Charlotte?" Charles asked.

I wanted to know the same thing, so I listened closely while keeping one eye on Parker as he prepared the appetizers.

"As well as I expected. She called me every name she could bring herself to utter, and a few I hadn't heard before. I wished her well and said goodbye. That was that," Bill explained.

"Have you heard from Carson?"

"Not yet, but I'm sure I will. He's in Chicago, talking with some investors. Why?"

"Well, Carson probably isn't too happy right about now. I don't know if it was you breaking it off with Charlotte, or losing those contracts, but his vengeful nature has come back to bite him in the ass," Charles said.

"What do you mean?"

"Carson placed every share he owned in Marchand Industries up for sale this morning. He probably thought he could trigger a selling frenzy with a large sell off, along with a few well-placed rumors about illegal business practices. The rumors are completely unfounded, of course. My broker called me as soon as the exchange opened. I bought every share back at $114 a share. A couple of hours later, I issued a press release about the Senate's approval of the Trade Agreement with South America and our joint venture with PanAm Freight, which will open the entire southern hemisphere to us. Senator Overton's office called me early this morning to give me the good news. Last I checked, our stock was trading at $231. I imagine Carson's feeling like a fool today. But he's a vengeful fool, Bill, so you'd best watch your back."

"I can handle Carson."

*At least Charlotte's gone.* But I wondered what Bill meant by handling Carson, so I glanced over to gauge his mood. He smiled at me, seeming to take pleasure in seeing me so happy.

"Are you sure about all this, Bill?" Charles asked, following Bill's gaze.

"This is what she loves. It makes her happy, and I want her to be happy here," Bill replied, still looking at me.

"That's not exactly what I was talking about, but I can see she loves this. What I meant was..."

Bill cut him off, turning to look at him. "I know what you meant, Charlie, but it's not like that. Have you ever had a moment when all the stars aligned perfectly, and you knew with absolute certainty that you were exactly where you were meant to be? That's what it was like the night I met her. Believe me, I'm surer of this than anything."

"Are you sure it's worth it? This isn't a game, Bill, one of your adventures you can just decide you're done with. We're talking about your life... and hers," Charles said, uneasiness in his voice.

"I'm not doing this for myself, Charlie, and I know it's worth it."

"I hope, for both your sakes, that you're right about this."

"Have a seat, Miss Désirée. The appetizers are ready," Parker said, carrying two small platters to the table. "You'll be able to observe the entrée preparation from the table. Gentlemen, *bon appétit.* Miss Désirée can describe these dishes as well as I." Parker held my chair for me as I sat down next to Bill.

"Look Bill, he has made us two appetizers," I said as Parker served us from each platter. "Zis one, Baked Armagnac Dates wrapped wiz bacon. It is so simple to make. Try one," I said, snagging one of the delicious dates on my fork.

"Yum, so delicious." I purred as I savored the tasty bite.

"And za other is crepes wiz goat cheese and a red onion marmalade. Za crepes have herbs in za batter. I did not see how to make za marmalade, but I zink I can know, can learn how to make it." I hadn't had this much fun in a very long time, and it was difficult to contain my excitement.

"It's delicious, Chère. What's he making next?" Bill asked, his smile letting me know he understood how pleased I was.

While Parker prepared the entrée, I enthusiastically described what I observed, watching him carefully, making mental notes on how he did things, the specific moves he made, the timing of his steps eventually leading to the finished plates.

"Now he makes za *legumes;* asparagus, oyster mushroom, and za... how you say... fingerling *pommes de terre*, potatoes. He sautés zem togezer with butter and garlic," I said, carefully describing each dish being prepared. "Now he cooks za snapper fillets. And he make a sauce for za fish, a Beurre Blanc; white wine, minced shallots, lemon juice, a little cream, and zen he stirs in za butter, *et Voilà, une sauce,*" I finished with a flourish.

Parker plated the entrées, then brought them to the table, setting them before us.

"*C'est beau, monsieur. Comme une œuvre d'art,*" I said. The colorful food was so artfully displayed against the bright white plates, it was like being presented with three beautiful and nearly identical paintings.

Parker smiled at me, taking pleasure in my compliment. "Presentation is essential, *mademoiselle*. We must win the eyes first, and then the mouth."

"Gentlemen, *mademoiselle*, I hope you enjoy what I've prepared for you today. If you require anything, please let us know." Parker nodded his head, then discreetly stepped back into the depths of the kitchen, leaving us to delight in his culinary skills.

And delight I did, relishing the sensory experience. He had won my eyes, and when the first morsel hit my tongue, the rest of my senses fell in line.

The moist, flaky fish, seasoned delicately with a hint of Louisiana spice, coupled perfectly with the traditional French sauce, made my mouth tingle in the most soothing way.

As we ate, I silently recounted the steps of the recipe, visualizing myself preparing it. I thought about how I might do it differently, use a different fish, or a richer sauce, different vegetables.

"Are you enjoying yourself, Chère?" Bill asked, breaking into my thoughts.

I pulled my mind back to the table with a satisfied sigh. "I am. Zis is a good day, Bill. Zank you, Mr. Marchand, for bringing me here," I said to Charles, with a sweep of my hands to indicate the entire experience.

"It was my pleasure, Désirée. But please, call me Charlie. Let's leave the Mr. Marchand for my father, shall we?" he replied with a wink.

"Okay, Charlie," I said, testing the name on my tongue. "Za chef, Mr. Landry, he is very kind. He say he will teach me cooking." As long as I was testing things, I figured I had nothing to lose by inserting that idea into the conversation. The possibility of training with Mr. Landry was just within my reach, if only I could convince them to allow it.

"Did he?" Bill and Charlie asked with two sets of raised eyebrows.

"Yes, he say he will, but first I must have permission."

"It's not just our permission you need, Chère," Bill said. "I believe Mama and Julianna will have an opinion about this. Don't you agree, Charlie?"

"Without doubt, cousin. Let's speak with Parker first, before we mention this to the ladies," Charlie said, followed by a chuckle just as Parker returned to the table.

As the table was being cleared and fresh spoons set by his wife, Parker brought out three servings of *crème brûlée* for our dessert, a delicious concoction of burned sugar atop a creamy custard. It was a perfect ending to a perfect meal.

"I hope you enjoyed your time with us today. Was everything to your satisfaction?" Parker asked.

"Everything was wonderful, Parker. As usual. Thank you for doing this," Charlie said. "Désirée has mentioned that you might be willing to give her cooking lessons. Is that right?"

Parker gave me an understanding smile before answering. "I said I would teach her a few things, but only with your permission. It is an uncommon request after all, and I wouldn't want to go against your wishes in the matter."

"I appreciate that, Parker," Bill said. "May I ask, since this is unusual, what are your thoughts about women being in your profession? I'm not aware of any women cooking in the finer restaurants."

"That is true, Mr. Marchand. There aren't many, but there are a few, and good ones too. I believe food is akin to music. We all need to eat, just the same as we all can appreciate a beautiful melody, maybe even hum along. But only a few of us can truly hear the musical nuance, can pick out the different instrumental sounds, understand the tempo, and read the notes in order to recreate the music. That takes a special person, one passionate about what they do."

Bill regarded him thoughtfully for a moment. "I appreciate your candor, Parker. From what you've seen in this short time, do you think Désirée has that quality?"

"I believe she does, sir, and it would be my honor to teach her what I know," Parker replied without hesitation.

"Were we to approve of this arrangement, would you object to a chaperone accompanying her during her lessons? I understand you fellows hold your secrets closely." Arranging for my safety seemed to be a constant theme with Bill.

"I have no problem with that, Mr. Marchand. In fact, given her age, I would insist upon it."

"Good. We'll get back to you about this, Parker. Excellent meal, by the way. Thank you." Bill shook his hand, then held my chair as Charlie paid the bill.

*Please say yes, please say yes.* I mentally chanted the phrase all the way home.

# Chapter 26

## *Shattered Plans*

I kept mentally chanting *Please say yes,* all the way to Saturday, waiting for Mama Bea's approval, while memories of Lucia and Julian Laurant spilled out of their box. Lucia said I was too young to work in the kitchen at Le Catelan, but I knew her denial had more to do with her fear of me being recognized and the danger that posed to them, than it did my age. I prayed things would be different this time.

"We should wait before adding this to your calendar, Désirée," Mama Bea said at lunch that afternoon. "Let's wait until you get settled in school and accustomed to the new routine of homework and social obligations. This will be a busy time for you, darling, and I'd like to see how you handle the assimilation before agreeing to any extra-curricular activities."

It wasn't a firm no, like Lucia gave me, but it wasn't a yes either. I would have to prove myself to her, but Bill was on my side, and I felt sure he'd help me convince her.

Bill dashed that certainty when he added, "Mama's right, Chère. Let's wait and see how things go. Gaston's and Parker aren't going anywhere. They'll be there when you're ready."

"But I'm ready now, Bill," I objected, scrunching up my face in a pouty frown, though I knew it wouldn't do me any good. Adults always got their way.

Bill lowered his head, looking down his nose at me with a stern expression in his eyes. "You must wait, Chère. We'll see how things are when I get back at the end of September. You'll be settled in school by then."

That night Mama Bea went out to dinner with Mr. Austin, a professor at Loyola. She'd gone to supper with him a few times before Bill came home. I could tell Mr. Austin was interested in Mama Bea, because he was so attentive, like he wanted to be more than colleagues. He always came bearing gifts, usually flowers or some small trinket he thought might interest her.

I didn't think she was interested in anything more than friendship with any man, though several sought her favor, she an attractive middle-aged woman, and one of the wealthiest widows in the city.

"David, I've told you before, it's unnecessary for you to bring me gifts, but I appreciate your thoughtfulness. Such a lovely bouquet." Mama Bea sniffed the flowers before handing them to Mr. Jefferies to deal with. "Shall we go? We don't want to be late." Then she turned to Bill. "We'll be home around ten, Beau. Have a pleasant evening, you two."

Mr. Austin reached out his hand to shake Bill's. "Goodnight, Major. I'm pleased we met at last. Miss Désirée, good luck with school next week. Goodnight."

Bill gave him a friendly smile and shook his hand. "It was my pleasure, Mr. Austin. We'll see you later, Mama," he said, giving her a kiss on the cheek.

When Bill closed the door, he turned to me with a funny look on his face. He seemed perplexed at the notion of his mother being with a man who was not his father. He looked as if he'd never seen such a thing, and I wondered how he felt about it.

"What's Laila making us for supper, Chère?" Bill asked, shaking off whatever thoughts he had about his mother. Apparently, he didn't want to talk about it.

The doorbell rang a moment later and when Bill opened the door, there was a uniformed soldier standing on the doorstep, holding a large yellow envelope.

"Major Marchand?" the soldier asked.

"I'm Major Marchand. Do you have something for me, Corporal?"

"Yes, sir." The soldier saluted smartly, then handed the envelope over to Bill.

"Thank you, Corporal." Bill took the envelope, gave the soldier a salute, then closed the door. "Let's go have supper, Chère." Evidently, he didn't want to talk about the envelope either.

After supper, we retired to the living room. Bill sat in his father's favorite chair, nursing a drink, and reading the papers he pulled out of the envelope. The scowl on his face said he wasn't happy.

I lay on the floor next to the phonograph player, going through Bill's collection of records while Billie Holiday crooned softly in the background and not feeling much better than Bill looked. Ever since that envelope arrived, my stomach began aching in a familiar way—the omen of change. I could only assume that whatever was inside was military, which might mean Bill would leave sooner than planned.

*But everyone says the war is almost over. Japan is going to surrender. Everyone says so.*

If that was true, then Bill wouldn't have to leave.

The look on his face said otherwise, and my heart sank hard with Billie Holiday's mournful voice punctuating the sadness welling up inside me.

I had counted on him being there for my first week of school, counted on him staying permanently.

"You're leaving, aren't you?" I wanted to end the silence, the waiting.

"I have orders, Chère."

"But why do you have to leave? You said the war is almost over. Why must you go back?" Fear of all the horrible things that could happen to him tumbled through my mind.

"I'm still in the Army, and the war isn't over. There are things I still must do. Orders I must follow. It won't be for long, and once school starts, you won't even notice I'm gone."

I didn't agree. I was absolutely certain it was going to be awful without him.

Ding-Dong. Ding-Dong. The doorbell rang insistently, tearing through the sad peace that had settled between Bill and me.

*What now?* That bell had rung far too many times that day, each time bringing me another wave of anxiety.

Mr. Jefferies answered the door, then a moment later, he ushered Carson Bentley into the living room.

Carson looked dressed for an evening out; a dark navy suit, white dress shirt with a bold hand-painted tie, two-tone dress shoes and a dark gray hat. His expression revealed a mixture of anger and curiosity, his unexpected visit obviously not a deterrent to his mission. With narrowed eyes, he walked in and scanned the room, taking in the scene.

Bill looked at him, his own expression calm, but brewing something underneath. "Carson. What can I do for you?"

"I'll take a bourbon neat, for starters," Carson said, tossing his hat on the side table.

"I'll get it for him, Jacob. You and Laila go on home now. I'll lock up." Bill went to the bar cart, then turned to me. "Go upstairs, Désirée. Carson and I have things to discuss."

I quickly put the records back into the cabinet as Carson stepped further into the living room, his eyes still looking around, assessing every detail.

"You look like you've settled in here, Désirée," he said, his eyes traveling up the length of my body, coming to a stop at my eyes and holding them for a second, silently questioning.

I didn't know what to say in response. His statement sounded more like an accusation than a compliment. "Goodnight, Mr. Bentley," I said, skirting around him to leave the room.

As I walked up the stairs, I heard the back door open, then close, signaling the Jefferies had left. Instead of doing what I'd been told, I sat down halfway up the stairs, wanting to listen to Bill's conversation with Carson. The tension between the two men made me uncomfortable.

"Charlotte told me what to expect, but I wouldn't believe it until I saw it with my own eyes," Carson sneered.

"What is it you want, Carson? Say what you need to say, and have done with it," was Bill's reply.

"I want to know what happened, Bill."

"I'm sure Charlotte has filled you in on the details. I'm sorry if I upset her, but I didn't want her to count on something that will never happen."

"I don't give a damn about Charlotte," Carson snapped back. "I want to know what happened to my friend. The Bill Marchand I know would never go back on his word. He wouldn't have left a friend out in the cold, when all it would have taken was one phone call to help him out. What happened to you?" Carson's tone held venom in it.

"You're the one who sold that stock, Carson, not me, and for the record, I knew nothing about the PanAm deal until after it happened."

"That's hard to believe, Bill. You and that son-of-a-bitch cousin of yours have been tighter than thieves ever since you got home. What surprises me is that you're letting Charlie and that old man turn you against everything you and I planned. Hell, I'd venture to say they've turned you into a carbon copy of that old bastard."

"That's enough, Carson. I won't sit here in my own home listening to you defame my family. I'm sorry if I've disappointed you."

"Disappointed doesn't even come close to how I feel right now, Bill. I just lost a quarter of a million dollars, and it appears I've lost my best friend in the bargain. I'd like to know why."

"Things have changed for me, Carson. I have different priorities."

"Yeah, I can see that," Carson interrupted, his tone dripping with contempt. "Did you get a taste for young tang while you were playing soldier boy overseas? You and that little girl looked pretty cozy."

"I said that's enough," Bill snarled, steel in his voice. "You and I have been friends for a long time, and I'd hate to throw you out of my house, but if you say one more word about my family, any member of my family, I will do it."

"Did I hit a nerve, Bill?"

"Try me, Carson."

A tense silence followed. It felt like it lasted forever.

"Well, pardon me," Carson finally replied, wisely taking heed of Bill's warning. "I seem to have tread too harshly on Marchand toes. I'll see myself out."

Carson came out of the living room, stopping briefly at the foot of the stairs to put on his hat. He turned to look over his shoulder and saw me sitting on the stairs with my hands cupped over my mouth. He narrowed his eyes, staring at me for a few seconds, then tipped his hat and walked out the front door without closing it.

A moment later, Bill went to the door and just stood there, looking out toward the street. His sighs sounded full of frustration, blowing them out with heavy breaths. Finally, he shook his head and stepped back inside, closing the door with a firm click.

When he turned, he saw me watching him. “I thought you’d gone to bed, Chère.” Tightly held emotions marked his face; anger (hopefully not with me), frustration, sadness, and concern.

“I worry about you. Mr. Bentley was angry. I am sorry for za trouble I make for you.” I searched Bill’s eyes for reassurance.

“Ah, Chère. This had nothing to do with you. It would have happened even if we had never met.” He sounded sad, like he had to make a choice he knew was right, but it left an emptiness in his heart.

I couldn’t help but feel responsible, at least partially. If I had never come to America, Bill's life would have been different, probably a lot simpler. That was the harsh truth I couldn’t escape.

“Go to bed now, Chère. We’ll talk in the morning.” He came up the stairs, reaching for my hand, then lifted me to my feet. “Sweet dreams, *ma petite*,” he said, planting a tender kiss on my forehead.

# Chapter 27

## *Sunday Blues*

That night, my dreams were anything but sweet...

*I was running, hiding, searching desperately for something. Nothing was clear, everything around me was dark and fuzzy. Vague voices called to me from a distance I could never reach. "Désirée. Désirée. Where are you?" Sometimes it sounded like Alex, sometimes Papa. "Papa," I called out. "Papa, I'm here. I can't find you. Help me, Papa, please help me."*

I woke with tears streaming down my face, soaking my pillow.

"*Merde!*" I hated those dreams. They left me feeling so helpless and lonely.

When I went outside to clear my head of the lingering ghosts, I heard Bill and Mama Bea's voices drifting up from the patio outside the living room.

"Good. I'm glad that chapter is finally over, Beau. Let's put it behind us," Mama Bea said. "Désirée is another matter."

"What do you mean?"

Mama Bea sighed. "I've been watching the two of you since you got home. She clings to your every word, son, relies on you far too much for a girl her age. And, much as you think you're sheltering your feelings about her, Julianna and Charles have both commented on it. Others might see it too. Tongues will wag, Beau, and that's not a good thing for her, or for you."

He blew out a breath before responding. "I know, but it's not what they think. When I met her—this fragile, remarkable girl—what struck me most about her was that she had been doing what the Army sent me there to do... and she'd done it alone for four years. I knew if I could save her, then maybe I could save myself; maybe I could finally become the man Pops thought I could be. I wish I could ask him what he'd do."

"I'll tell you what he'd do. He'd leave her to me. He'd move on and let her live her life. That's what he'd do."

"I know you're right, but this is so damn hard. I hate putting this all on you. You have your own life, Mama. It doesn't feel fair to burden you with this, after everything you've gone through. This was my choice, not yours."

"Well, darling, I understand the situation, probably better than most. I should be the one to handle it."

Silence followed for several minutes, then Mama Bea spoke again.

"I never thought I'd hear myself say this, but when you come back, Beau, you can't live here with us. It's not good for her or for you. If you really mean what you say about giving her a chance, then you must leave her. You need to go make your own life, son. This situation isn't good for either of you."

Bill's heavy sigh drifted up, stabbing my heart. "You're right, Mama, I know you're right."

Bill was leaving, and she was making him stay away. The feeling of complete abandonment consumed me, and there was no relief from the pain of it. I stewed about it the entire next day until the pain turned to anger. Nothing I could do or say would change it. Right then, I hated everything, hated that nearly everyone I ever cared about had disappeared from my life, or was about to. Bill was leaving me, and my heart was breaking.

Late that night, the gallery beckoned me, as it often did when my mind was troubled. A storm had blown through earlier, leaving the night sky crystal clear and alive with thousands of twinkling lights. The warm, humid air was still thick with the lingering scent of the thunderstorm, then a brief flash of light in the distance, somewhere to the south, momentarily obscured the stars. Another storm was coming. With the old woman's shawl draped around my shoulders, I curled up on the chaise to watch its arrival.

I lit a cigarette from the cigarette case I'd taken from Bill's desk—stolen is probably closer to the truth—and lit it with his lighter. An angry impulse made me take them to punish him for leaving me, but also because smoking helped focus my thoughts during times of heightened emotion, like right then.

The heavy tread of Bill's footsteps coming around the corner of the gallery signaled I wouldn't be alone with my misery for long. I took another drag from the cigarette to steady myself for the confrontation I'd been expecting all day.

Bill walked over and stood at the end of the chaise, looking down at me, his thoughts unreadable. He reached down, slipped the cigarette from my hand, put it to his lips and took a drag, then handed it back.

"Aren't you a little young to be smoking, Chère?"

He asked me that same question on the first night we met, more than a year before. My answer was the same.

"Probably."

"Did you take my lighter, too?" He didn't look angry. Mildly curious is a better description.

I pulled his cigarette case and Zippo lighter from my pocket, tossing them onto the end of the chaise. He didn't pick them up.

"Mama catches you smoking, she'll have a few things to say about it," he warned.

"Probably." Right then, I didn't really care what either of them thought.

Bill took a deep breath, blowing it out with a frustrated sound, then he moved the cigarettes to the table next to me and sat down.

"Is this how it's going to be between us now? You not talking to me or to Mama? This isn't how I want it, Chère. Talk to me." His eyes were gentle but pleading. He wouldn't push hard for my response—he never did—but I had to resolve my feelings before he left.

I put out the cigarette in the ashtray and tried to control the flood of emotions vying for release. When I spoke, it was in French, because I needed him to understand how I felt before he left for good.

"I know you broke the rules to bring me here. You could get into a lot of trouble for it. I don't understand why you would risk so much if you were just going to leave me. You could have left me in France and saved yourself a lot of trouble." I held his gaze, seeking an honest response.

"Yes, I broke the rules, and I'd do it again. I'd break every damn rule they laid down if it meant keeping you safe." He never looked away, his eyes darkening as he spoke.

"But why bother, if you were going to leave me, anyway?"

"I am not leaving you, Désirée. I'm giving you a chance to become the girl you're meant to be." His eyes softened as his mouth relaxed into a crooked smile. He clasped his hands together, resting them on his crossed legs, opening and closing them as if consciously stifling a need to reach over and touch me.

"But I need you, Bill. I came here because I thought you would be with me, but that was just a foolish girl's fantasy, wasn't it?" It was all I could do to hold back the tears burning my eyes. I hated crying about this.

"No, Chère, not so foolish. I've known since we met that we have a connection." He reached over and touched my cheek, then pulled away.

"Mama Bea doesn't want you to like me. She thinks I'm bad for you, or you're bad for me. I don't know which, but she's making you leave me." My breath kept catching in my throat as I tried to hold back my tears.

"That's not what she's doing, Désirée. She knows, better than anyone, how things are between us." He raised his clasped hands to his mouth, looked at me for a long time, then lowered them with a sigh. "There are fourteen years separating us, Chère, and what Lucia said about me is just as true here as it was in France. I'm too old for a young girl like you to think of as anything other than..." He looked away, not completing his thought. With another sigh and a shake of his head, he turned back to me. "Society has its rules, and this is one I will not break."

"I don't care, Bill. I need you here... with me."

"I do care. Listen to me, Chère. I am not leaving you. I'll be around, but not all the time. For your sake, I need to stand back and cover the bases, give you room to grow up and figure things out."

"I already know what I want, Bill. There's nothing to figure out."

"You think you know, Chère, but that may change. The next few years will bring a lot of new experiences your way, and you may change your mind about what you want."

*Time changes everything. That's what I'm afraid of.*

"What does 'cover the bases' mean, Bill? Will someone find out about me? That you broke the rules and brought me here with the other Germans? Is that what you mean?"

He gave me a long, hard look, clearly concerned by my question.

"How do you know they were German? I asked you not to speak with anyone."

"I didn't, except in the ladies' room at that place in England. A woman from the plane whispered to me in German. She asked me who my father was."

"What did you tell her?"

"Nothing. I just put my finger to my lips and shook my head at her."

"Had you ever seen her before?" Bill asked.

"No. I don't remember her from before. Why did you bring Germans here, Bill? They were the mission cargo, weren't they? You made me part of that."

"I can't talk about any of that, and I want you to forget all about it. Alright? No one will ever find out about that. I've buried that base completely."

"How do you know for sure?"

"It's what I do, Chère. I cover the bases and keep my eyes on the bad guys."

"Who are the bad guys, Bill?"

"They're anyone who threatens my family or my country. It's my job to make sure they never come too close. It's late now, Chère. You should be in bed. You have school in the morning."

"I don't want you to leave, Bill. I'm afraid you'll never come back, and I'll be alone again." Tears were dripping down my cheeks, falling onto the folds of the old woman's shawl.

"Don't be afraid, Désirée. I'll come back. I promise," he said, gently cupping my cheek in his hand.

He pulled me to my feet, led me into my room, and tucked me into bed. Before he could leave, I grabbed his hand.

"Stay with me, Bill, at least until I fall asleep. Please stay."

He sat down on the bed next to me, leaned his back against the headboard, and stretched his legs out. I curled up next to him and rested my head on his chest, feeling the steady beat of his heart thump, thumping against my cheek. He pulled me closer, gently stroking my hair.

"Put all your thoughts and worries away now, Chère. Cover up all the boxes. Close all the doors. Sleep now, *ma petite*. We'll see each other soon." He held me as close as he dared, allowing me to cuddle next to him as our hearts beat as one.

A while later, I heard Mama Bea's voice. "Beau?"

"Shh," he whispered, easing himself off the bed, gently resting my head on the pillow. Before he left, he leaned down to place a kiss on my forehead.

"*Je t'aime*, Désirée. *Attends-moi.*"

End Part Two of Désirée's Story

# *Character List*

Désirée Gautier (13 years old)

Former names: Rondeau, Pérot, Steigler, Lang

**Marchand Family:**

William (Bill) Marchand - US Army Major, CIA, Marchand Ind. Exec.

Beatrice Marchand (Mama Bea) - Bill's mother, Professor at Loyola U

Henri Marchand - Bill's uncle (father's brother)

Charles (Charlie) Marchand - Bill's cousin, Henri's son

Julianna Beaulaurier Marchand - Charlie's wife

Madalyn & Henri Marchand - Charlie's children, twins 6 years old

Bertram Beaulaurier - Bill's uncle (mother's brother)

Adele Beaulaurier - Bertram's wife (Julianna's mother)

**Jefferies/Beauly Family:**

Eulaila (Laila) Jefferies - Mama Bea's help

Jacob Jefferies - Mama Bea's help

Millie & Bennie Prince - Jefferies' daughter & husband

Marcus Jefferies - Jefferies' son

Jolie Jefferies (14 years old) - Marcus' daughter

Granny Jo (Joliesse) - Eulaila's grandmother

**Others:**

Carson Bentley - Bill's oldest friend

Charlotte Bentley - Carson's sister

Sister Mary Agnes - Headmistress, Sacred Heart Academy

Evelyn Duret - Student at Sacred Heart

Elenor Duret - Evelyn's mother

Dr. Robert Easton - Neighbor & family doctor

Bobby Easton (15 years old) - Neighbor, Freshman at Newman

Jimmy Wilcox - Freshman at Newman

Eddie Berg - Freshman at Newman

Sam Jenson - Freshman at Newman

Sarah Edelstein - Freshman at Newman

Kaitlyn Delaney - Freshman at Newman

Mr. Henson* - Principal at Newman

Roy Alciatore* - Owner, Antoine's

Leonard – Waiter at Antoine's

Emily Fontenot - Friend of Charlotte Bentley

Parker & Felicia Landry - Owner's, Gaston's Bistro

* denotes an actual person at the time.

# *Acknowledgments*

As anyone who has ever attempted to write a novel will tell you, despite the long, lonely hours it takes to put the words on the page, it doesn't happen in a vacuum. There are many people to thank for their wisdom and support in getting *Désirée's Story* out into the world.

Thank you, Shari Evans, who led the Kingston Writers Group for years. Your steadfast support has been invaluable. And thanks to all the members I've connected with over the years, for your insight and critiques. Many thanks also go to the Kitsap Writers Critique Group who generously contributed their expertise and support to this project and helped me become a better writer.

Sincere gratitude goes to Trent and Annalise Shadburne for the original art and graphic design created for the covers. They captured my vision with their artistry. Thank you for your talent and dedication.

My deepest thanks to my family and friends for sticking with me on this journey—I know it has been a long slog. To my wonderful, brave, beta readers who offered their keen insight to help me improve this story; Sharon Jackson, Susan Sanders, Deb Smith, Gale Smart, Janice Cespedes, Jessica Kirchhofer, Lindy Bryson, and Vicki Schiller, who encouraged me to pursue this quest. I couldn't have done it without your support, dear friends.

My gratitude goes to my sister, Waaknee Lerner, who brings joy to my life every day and who never gave up on me. And to my children, Bliss

Ogilvie and her family, and my son, Diego Moreno, your support means the world to me. And to my husband, Robert, who continues to give me all I could ever need or hope for after forty-plus years of marriage. Thank you, my love.

Finally, I owe so much to Desi, the woman who gave me the inspiration for this story. Her willingness to share a glimpse of her long-held secret prompted my unquenchable thirst to find the answers. Desi never shared more than a few remarks about her early life, but what she shared prompted me to dig deeper into the realm of possibilities; how a young child could survive WW2 and make it to America, only to live her life hiding a secret. I like to think the story I've written would please her. Thanks, Desi. You will live forever in my heart, *ma Belle-mère*.

Denise

## *About the author*

I'm an avid reader and have kept a daily journal my whole life. When I retired in 2015, a dear friend encouraged me to lean into my passion for words. It was the best advice I've ever received. Thus began my writing journey in earnest.

A story had been burning in my mind for nearly twenty years, and I now had the time to write it. After dedicating months researching the historical context of this story, learning more about WWII than I ever expected, I spent years honing my skill to tell it.

*Desiree's Story* is inspired by a secret my stepmother revealed one Sunday afternoon in 1997.

On a more personal note, I live with my husband and sister in our humble forever home, nestled in the woods along a quiet little bay in the Pacific Northwest. I'm still a reader, still a student of something (science, French, cooking, among other pursuits), and I channel my passions by writing stories of resilience, courage, and hope.

Connect with me on:
Facebook: @DeniseMoreno
Instagram: @driesaumoreno
Threads: @driesaumoreno
Bluesky: @denzstuf.bsky.social